Author D. S. Grier really understands what makes boys tick. The emotions and needs of the four brothers in ***Victory on the Home Front*** *are vividly revealed as they struggle with alcoholic parents, making friends, and the realities of World War II. This is a story of hardship, but also of hope as each boy finds his way in the world with the help of key people in their lives.*

—Susan Heim
Co-Author, ***Chicken Soup for the Soul*** and mother of four boys

* * *

Grier's novel offers a compelling view into the minds of boys who are coping with severe parental dysfunction. Their actions to save themselves offer powerful lessons for teachers, families, and others who work with young men.

—Michael Gurian
Author of ***The Wonder of Boys*** and ***A Fine Young Man***

* * *

Be prepared to stay up later than usual, as you won't want to put this book down till you finish it. It isn't the excitement that carries one forward; it's the authenticity. Like the old-time Hollywood serials, when you come to the end of each chapter, you are eager to know what happens next.

—Javan Kienzle
Author of ***Judged By Love,***
The biography of mystery novelist William X. Kienzle

Victory on the Home Front

Copyright © 2012 by D. S. Grier

All rights reserved. No part of this publication may be reproduced or transmitted in any form or by any means, electronic or mechanical, including photocopy, recording, or any information storage and retrieval system, without permission in writing from the publisher.

Please contact publisher for permission to make copies of any part of this work.

Windy City Publishers
2118 Plum Grove Rd., #349
Rolling Meadows, IL 60008
www.windycitypublishers.com

Published in the United States of America
10 9 8 7 6 5 4 3 2 1

First Edition: January 2012

Library of Congress Control Number: 2011925488

ISBN: 978-1-935766-14-8

Front Cover image by Donell Hagen
Cover Production by Amanda Inkiden

Windy City Publishers
Chicago

Victory on the Home Front

by D. S. Grier

For Alex, with my love,
and for the Grier and Hoag families,
whose real-life wartime experiences
inspired this novel

"There is one front and one battle where everyone
in the United States—every man, woman, and child—
is in action, and will be privileged to remain in action
throughout this war.
That front is right here at home,
in our daily lives, and in our daily tasks."

President Franklin D. Roosevelt
28 April 1942

Part One:

St. James Place

chapter one

★

Lester was glad he didn't have to go to the police station this time. His usual attempts to run away from home ended at the Sixth Precinct, where the cops were tired of seeing him. They grumbled about driving Les back to the house and told his mother she should keep him tied to the front porch. Sometimes it hardly seemed worthwhile to make the effort. But Les never stopped trying; he wanted nothing more than to run away.

It was not the town that bothered him, or even the house. Kenmore was a pretty community in upstate New York, and the MacGregor home at 144 St. James Place was one of the nicer homes Les's family had occupied. It was a narrow two-story structure with a finished attic bedroom, hardwood floors, and a spacious front room.

They'd been in this house longer than any other; the MacGregors moved at least once a year, and sometimes twice. Les never knew when the moves were going to happen, or why. Sometimes they would leave without even taking their belongings with them.

No, it was not the town or the house that Les wanted to escape. It was his family.

But today, February 22, 1943—Les's eleventh birthday—was his luckiest day ever. Instead of warming a patrolman's chair this afternoon, he'd been hit by a big blue Buick crossing

Delavan Avenue. His leg was broken and he had some cuts and scrapes, so they took him to the hospital to look at real medical equipment and see what the doctors knew. Les was so excited about the trip that he barely felt his injuries. The white plaster cast was impressive and using the crutches would be a new adventure. Best of all, one of the nurses had slipped him a paper bag containing some swabs, tongue depressors, and cotton balls for his secret laboratory at home.

All around him the hospital ward was bustling with hushed activity. Metal beds stood in straight lines separated by stacks of equipment and chairs. Les waited for his mother on a bed near the window and watched the nurses rushing to and fro, their skirts *snick-snick*ing with starch and purpose. He tried to pretend that he was in a military hospital overseas, having been shot up during a terrific air battle with the Nazi *Luftwaffe*, but it was too clean and quiet here to be anything other than a suburban hospital in upstate New York. Oh well.

In the next bed, a little girl (who was waiting for a doctor to come fish out the button she'd crammed up her nose) turned to look at Les. "You're dirty," she said, and Les knew it was true. His red hair, which needed cutting, fell across his forehead in a sweep that was matted with sweat and blood from the accident. His glasses were perpetually bent and scratched and his handed-down clothing was ripped in a few spots and blackened by grease from the road. His lumpy old rucksack lay on the floor in an oily, bedraggled heap.

His mother was sure to be embarrassed when she got there, which was, for the MacGregor boys, the kiss of death. Mother would rather be infected with rabies or eaten alive by a pack of roving alligators than be embarrassed, and she'd take a pretty dim view of any one of her boys that put her in that position. Les knew when she got to the hospital the first thing she'd do was apologize to everyone so they'd believe she didn't let him go around looking so raggedy on a regular basis. It wasn't true, but she liked to say it was.

Hmmm. Come to think of it, Mother was probably going to be pretty furious with him. She would let him have it for running away again; there would be lectures about the money they would owe the hospital and about having to pay for a yellow taxi to pick him up. He'd catch it from her all the way home and probably through most of the following week. Maybe next time he ran away Les should aim directly for the police station; the cops were easier to get along with and nobody ever charged him a fare for his ride home.

But just as Les got to thinking his birthday might not be so lucky after all, his brother James came into view at the end of the corridor. Wow. Mother must be really steamed if she was going to send her prize boy to pick Les up.

James was something special, and—unfortunately—he knew it. He was tall and polished, with thick, dark, movie-star hair, laughing blue eyes, and a big swelled head to match.

Already James was sweet-talking one of the nurses, asking about the leg and what should be done to care for it. The nurse, a real old battle-ax if ever there was one, was actually dropping her eyelashes and smiling at James; how could that be? If he lived to be one hundred, Les would never know how James pulled it off. What a guy.

After a few minutes James came circling around to Les's bed, sitting gingerly on one corner and tugging the blanket down. "How're you doing, Squirt?" he asked, winking.

"Is Mother going to kill me when I get home?" Les whispered, getting right to the point.

James chuckled. "I wouldn't say death is imminent, but if I were you I'd keep an eye on my good leg," he said softly. "She sent me because she was worried the police would be here. They're getting awfully tired of you over at the Sixth, you know."

Les nodded as James said more loudly, for the benefit of the nurses, "Sheez, kid, you really got banged up. Lucky you weren't wearing your good clothes." As if Les *had* better clothes. Most of what he wore had belonged to James at one point and had been rendered threadbare by Charlie on its way through to Les's closet. But Les was not prepared to argue now; he would follow James's lead and keep up family appearances. Nobody here needed to know the truth. Les nodded his agreement and eased his leg off the bed. Together the boys gathered his crutches and rucksack and made their way out of the hospital and toward the waiting cab.

It was strange to be alone with James, Les thought. It was a little like being alone with President Roosevelt; James was someone who was revered in his own home. James was everything a boy was supposed to aspire to be: student body president, head of every major school organization, football player, and everybody's best friend. He always dated the prettiest, most popular girls and left the others pining for him. What's more, James worked at a store downtown after school and brought home money for the family. As far as Mother and Dad were concerned, their firstborn child might just as well walk on water.

And, coincidentally enough, James thought so too.

It was hard for any of James's three brothers, who were made to feel poky and worthless by comparison, to know what to say to him. And right now Les hadn't a clue. So he stared out the window at the passing storefronts and cars and imagined how bad it would be for him when he got home.

When James directed the taxi driver to stop at the little diner a few blocks from the house, Les was flabbergasted. What was this about? James helped him from the car and walked him inside to sit at a little table by the window. "It's your birthday, Squirt," James said. "I figure you ought to have a little ice cream, since you're probably not getting any at home."

Les shrugged, trying not to seem eager or curious. James never wanted to spend time with him; what made today different? Les watched his brother from behind hooded eyes as James ordered black coffee for himself and a little slice of cake and ice cream for Les.

James carefully regarded his brother, taking in the rumpled hair and dirt-smeared face. They were a study in contrasts: the older brother, so handsome and filled with confidence, and the younger, so ragged, care-worn, and suspicious.

"So if I had one question to ask," James said, leaning forward slightly, "I guess I would like to know why it is you keep running away from home."

Les struggled for a moment with his answer. James lived in the same house; if he couldn't figure out why home wasn't the world's best place to be, it was not Les's place to enlighten him. His mind scrabbled sideways, searching for an innocuous answer.

"Um," Les began, his voice cracking as he hesitated. "I guess I am just interested in adventure. I'm too young to join up, but I've got to do something different with myself. Fifth grade is boring."

James nodded thoughtfully. "I know that feeling," he said. "I have that feeling a lot."

Emboldened, Les continued. "I just want to be someone," he said. "I want to go someplace where nobody knows me and I can *be* something."

"What do you want to be?"

"I don't know," Les admitted. "But it's got to be better than doing anything in Kenmore, New York."

"You work the scrap metal and rubber drives, right? With the Scouts?" James asked. "It's not like you're not contributing."

Les sniffed. "That's kids' work," he said. "All over the whole world men are fighting and being heroes, and I'm stuck here rounding up old tires? That's not the same at all. In fact, it's a little insulting."

"I'm not doing anything either," James pointed out. "Just going to school and selling suits."

"Doesn't matter," Les insisted. "You're in high school, and you'll get to go. By the time I'm old enough, it will probably all be over. I'll never get to do anything!"

"So what do you think running away is going to accomplish?" James asked. "It's not going to make you older."

"It's not," Les admitted. "But I would be away from here. And maybe I can be a messenger or a spy or something. You know, even Uncle Bob's dog got to go to the war. If a German shepherd can go, can't a healthy kid? I can sneak in places nobody else can fit."

"Yeah, but that poor dog was so traumatized it had to be put down," James said. "That should tell you something about the war, Squirt."

The waitress returned with their cake and coffee then, and

gave Les a funny look, eyeing his dirty red hair and flushed cheeks. James put some sugar in his coffee and leaned back, listening.

"And besides all that, what about Aunt Amy? She's a lady, and she's serving," Les said. "Right after Pearl Harbor, it seemed like all the relatives were gone. All except our little part of the family. We're not doing anything good."

"We're about to," James cleared his throat and hesitated, as if unsure whether to speak. "I'm going over just after graduation in June."

Les was stunned. "Do Mother and Dad know?" he asked quietly.

"Dad does," James said. "He and I have been talking about it. We're going to tell Mother tonight. It'll put the absolute capper on your birthday, I'm afraid. Sorry, Squirt; hope you like the cake."

It seemed like the whole room went dim. *Great,* Les thought. *It's* my *birthday, but somehow James manages to make even that seem like it's all about him.*

★

Les sure is a funny kid, James thought later. Lazing over his homework, he listened to his parents arguing in the kitchen below. Mother had not taken the news of his enlistment as well as he and Dad had hoped. The good news was that she'd completely forgotten about Les, his trip to the hospital, and his broken leg. The younger boy had disappeared immediately after dinner, as he often did, and James doubted anybody could find him even if they did try.

James could hear Mother sobbing downstairs. "You've always wanted to hurt me," she was saying to Dad. "You have taken away everything I've ever had. And now my son! What kind of a person *are* you?" A glass smashed and the front door slammed as Dad left.

It had been kind of nice to talk to Les today. James was always so busy he didn't get to spend much time with his brothers; what began as a gesture of sympathy toward Les had led to the stunning realization that they had more in common than James thought: a fierce determination to amount to something, a quick wit, and a desire to run away from home.

James stretched and rolled over on his bed. Surviving in the MacGregor house was not easy to do; a fellow had to figure out his own way. James's way was to be part of everything, to shine like a new penny. Every new activity at school, every hour at the men's clothing shop where he worked, was an hour spent in peace and freedom, being admired instead of criticized.

Sometimes James felt like he was a trapped behind a mask. He showed the world his "good" face, being friendly, capable, and hardworking. Behind the mask lay a different person, however; the inner boy was tired sometimes, had mean thoughts, and was frightened of failing at something. James worried that a single mistake would spell disaster for the little house of cards he'd constructed out of his life; goof-ups would let everyone would know he was a fake and they wouldn't look up to him anymore. Life at home would be dismal; his parents would be disappointed in him and their feelings would be impossible to take.

So James went on living life at a hundred and ten percent on the outside but fearful and strange on the inside. It worked for him. But golly he was tired of it sometimes; it wasn't until he sat talking with Les today that he realized how much.

And now the Army was entering the picture. James had to go; *everyone* had to go if they were healthy and able. In fact, not to go was a little bit shameful; folks would wonder what was wrong with you. Dad had told James it was okay; Mother would understand and ultimately she'd be proud of him for doing his duty. They worked it out that James should try for the Army Air Corps. Dad had done something called balloon reconnaissance during the First World War years ago and it had saved him. He rode up in a tethered balloon over the battlefields and watched and recorded all the action on the ground below. James longed for a similar job to do this time, and flying an airplane seemed good. All the girls liked flyboys, and he wouldn't be on the ground staring helplessly over the edge of a foxhole while bullets whizzed past his ears.

But clearly his mother did not yet see the benefits of this arrangement. He heard the liquor cabinet open, then slam shut downstairs, signaling the continuation of a very long night.

Just then the door to James's room came banging open with a thud.

"What did you do?" James's brother Charlie was suddenly at the end of James's bed, his expression shaded with curiosity and anger. "Mother's crying."

"How do you know it was me?" James rejoined. He loved to needle Charlie.

Charlie was a gangly boy with freckles and resentful blue eyes. He had not yet grown into his arms and legs, which always seemed to be everywhere at once, and his posture was generally defensive. Charlie had suffered from poor health when he was younger—asthma, bad vision, and a slight spinal issue for which he'd had to wear an ugly leather back brace—and both he and Mother had given up on him ever measuring up to his marvelous older brother.

Now Charlie's face was curled into a sneer. "D'you think she'd cry over any of the rest of us?" he asked sarcastically. "Besides, I heard your name. What was it?"

James sat up on the bed. "Well, I guess you should know. Dad and I told her I'm joining up after graduation. She wasn't thrilled about it, but I imagine she'll come around."

For once Charlie had nothing to say. "That's really something," he finally managed, his voice hollow. "Are you scared?"

"Not a bit," James said, grinning. "I can't wait to get over there and show them what's what. The whole blasted war will be over a half hour after they hand me a gun; I'm going to take care of those Nazis once and for all."

Charlie rolled his eyes. "Sure, James," he said scornfully. "Of course you will. Don't you always do everything just right?"

James nodded. "Generally I do," he said.

"You are such an arrogant jerk," Charlie said. "I wonder if the Army makes a helmet big enough to fit over that swelled head of yours."

Charlie slammed the door hard as he left the room. The wall vibrated, shaking loose one of the few pictures that hung there. It fell to the floor, its glass shattering into tiny, sharp fragments.

★

In his secret laboratory behind the wall, Les couldn't hear any of the sobbing or arguing downstairs. In fact, he couldn't hear much of anything and he was glad that nobody knew where he was. His leg was beginning to ache and it was a real bear of a job to get around on those crutches. He really just wanted to be alone and check out his belongings.

He carefully placed the new cotton balls, swabs, and tongue depressors from the hospital into little jars he'd pilfered from the garage. His dad would never miss them, and they would be perfect for his treasures. He wished he had the ability to sterilize the jars, but he guessed that would have to wait.

Lester's secret laboratory was the pride of his life. It had been meticulously constructed behind the wall of the attic bedroom he shared with his eight-year-old brother, Johnny. The room was large and had a dormer in the front, where their beds and bureaus were. The ceiling was steeply pitched where the roof came down and thin walls had been erected where the slope was too great for even a child to stand. Les had quickly realized there was a triangular gap behind those walls and decided to use it to his advantage.

Les had come by a large map from the National Geographic Society, one that stretched nearly the height of that low wall. He hung it carefully and waited nearly a whole week before he could fake an illness and stay home from school. Then he carefully and quietly used a sharp saw to cut the drywall just inside the shape of the poster, crafting a little private entrance to what would become his secret world. His mother, two floors down, heard nothing. She had no idea what he was doing and never would.

Two rusted nails pressed into the backside of the wall formed crude handles that Les could use to pull the map-covered entrance shut behind him. A few flashlights served to illuminate a low hideaway that stretched the entire length of one side of the house. The map protected Les from discovery and made his secret laboratory the very best place in the world to be. It was, Les thought, the most wonderful hideaway he'd ever had in any of the houses where the MacGregors had lived.

Over time Les had perfected his lair. Old boards and bricks made shelves for his treasures, of which there were many. Les collected everything from interesting rocks and old toys to broken tools. He had models and gadgets everywhere. His current treasure was an old busted radio he'd found in his travels around town; he was taking that apart very carefully to see if he could figure out how it worked.

That had been his project for tonight until his thoughts intruded. How could it be that an eleven-year-old boy should go unacknowledged on his birthday? Les blamed James, but only a little. There were no presents anyway, no cake waiting, even before James had shared his news.

Some years were like this, especially when Mother and Dad were drinking. Les didn't know much about why they drank like they did; he guessed it was an old habit.

Mother had grown up in Springport, Michigan, the beautiful eldest daughter of a wealthy lumberyard owner. She carried herself like a princess (or so she told Les) and every boy in town wanted to have her on his arm. "When my sisters and I dressed up and went out walking," she'd sigh, "why, every head would turn in our direction. What a sight!"

Dad's head had turned in Mother's direction during a time called Prohibition, when alcohol was illegal and people had secret parties for drinking. Mother looked at Dad from beneath her long, thick eyelashes and he was hooked. They were both highly intelligent, witty, and charming—a perfect match. They boozed and danced together all during the last days of the Roaring Twenties and, despite the Great Depression, war, and other troubles that would face them later, they never stopped.

Now, nearly twenty years later, the challenges of ordinary life—work, poverty, children, illness, and trouble—had distorted their fun-loving ways. Their wit was used to contrive the most terrible insults and hurtful words; their intelligence and curiosity were dulled by whiskey and wine. Dad went away and gambled at night and Mother seemed to long for the better days of her youth. Neither of them seemed able to find any hope in their surroundings.

They were both so blinded by their separate troubles that they sometimes seemed to forget they had children. They certainly did forget one of their boys today. Les lowered his head over the scrap of blue paper on which he'd been writing with his penny pencil and breathed a deep, heavy sigh.

Just then a sound from the bedroom beyond caught Les's attention. It was his brother Johnny, evidently looking for something to do. "Les?" Johnny said once, twice, then clambered back down the stairs.

Les shook his head. That boy was the most irritating creature known to man. Always following, always asking questions, never leaving anything alone.

Johnny was eight, but sometimes he seemed even younger. He was small for his age and seemed always to be standing on his toes, looking up. Of all four boys he was the most isolated and confused; nobody ever talked with him or told him what was going on. Les often wondered what went on in that blond head of Johnny's and how he managed to piece together the various problems that faced the MacGregor household.

At least this is what Les wondered when he was being charitable. The rest of the time he just found Johnny to be a major pain in the neck. Like now. Honest to Pete, Les would never get anything done if Johnny had his way. The kid needed a hobby of his own.

Well, enough was probably enough anyway. Les didn't want Johnny to catch him in here. He placed the blue piece of paper on top of a small stack at the end of one shelf, slipped out the laboratory entrance, and replaced the map.

Just in time to hear a voice from the doorway.

"What are you doing?" Johnny stood at the top of the stairs, his mouth open in astonishment. "Were you behind that wall? How did you get back there? Why didn't you tell me you could go in? Can I look?"

It was all over now. Whenever his little brother showed up, disaster was sure to follow. Johnny was not interested in doing anything in the usual way, and it was impossible to tell what kind of extraordinary trouble he would make inside that lab. Les curled his hands into fists and tried not to scream. "No, you cannot go in there," he managed. "That's my spot. Only for me."

But Johnny would not be put off. "Please, Les, can't I see? I promise I won't touch anything. Just one little look."

Les knew it was no good. Someday they would put Johnny's picture in the dictionary next to the word *pest*. Les would never have a minute's peace until he let Johnny look into his secret room. But still he held out. "Nope," he said simply. "Case closed."

Johnny's face worked furiously. He sputtered. "But, but…" he began, then stopped. A curious light came into his face. "It would be a shame if Mother and Dad found out there was a hole in the wall of the house," he said. "And it would be really bad for you if they found out you put it there. Especially when Mother is so upset already."

Les stopped just short of a snarl. He was going to kill Johnny someday, truly he was. "Fine," he snapped. "One look and that's it. You are *never* to go in there when I'm not around. If I ever find out you did, Adam gets it."

Johnny flinched at the mention of his beloved cat, then paled. "You wouldn't," he breathed.

"I wouldn't push it if I were you," Les replied. "I have never liked that cat. He's stupid. It would give me pleasure to release him from his ignorance."

"You're cruel," Johnny said. "That cat never did anything to you! Anyway, maybe I'll just cut to the chase and go tell Mother right now. I think she'd like a distraction; she's all upset over something or other."

"I said *fine,*" Les said. "I'm just telling you what will happen if you ever dare to go in there without me or, worse yet, touch something without my explicit permission."

"Fine," Johnny agreed. "Let's go."

As he tugged on the National Geographic map, Les tried to look on the bright side. At least now he could solve the problem of having power behind the wall. Now that Johnny knew about the room, Les could run a cord along the rug and get better lighting for his experiments. It was not a worthwhile trade-off for the unwelcome presence of his younger brother, but it was something.

Maybe it was his lucky day after all.

chapter two

★

The next few days were stiff and tense in the MacGregor home. Mother had gone to bed with her whiskey bottle and cigarettes, and Dad was gone working or gambling or whatever he did when he wasn't home.

"Mother?" Johnny went to her early on the first day, hoping to find out what was going on. He pushed open her bedroom door, just a crack. "Mother, are you sick?"

There was no reply.

"Will you be getting up soon, Mother?" Johnny asked, his voice thin. "I need some lunch money. Mother?"

All at once the dark, silent room seemed to explode. "No!" Mother shouted, sitting bolt upright in bed. "I will not be getting up today; you can find your own damn lunch money, and stop saying 'Mother!' Now get out of here and let me have just a moment of peace and quiet." Her voice trailed off in a sob.

Johnny heard a bottle clink against glass as he closed the bedroom door.

After that, nobody spoke to Mother; the boys fed and cleaned up after themselves and the laundry grew in piles near the corners of their bedrooms. Eventually Mother would decide to get up and deal with all this—for all her foibles, she was very concerned about keeping up appearances—but for now she was simply gone.

Johnny faded into his bedroom until the worst was over. He knew it wouldn't go on for too much longer; then Mother would find him and kiss him and try to make it better.

In the meantime, what to do?

The third day Mother was in bed Les went to a scrap drive with the Boy Scouts. He would be gone for at least two hours. Johnny seized his opportunity to explore, lifting aside the National Geographic map and entering the magical hideaway behind the wall. Les would never really do anything bad to Adam, Johnny knew; Les was a sucker for cats and anyway, Adam was so big and fat that it would be hard to really hurt him. But Johnny looked over his shoulder just the same.

Les had arranged for a lamp in the room, and Johnny turned it on with a soft *click*. It was like turning on the stars in the night sky; magic filled the small space and Johnny drew in his breath. Les had found all kinds of objects and carefully arranged them on shelves made of wood scraps and old bricks; treasures from everywhere gleamed tantalizingly in the dim light. Johnny's rapt gaze swept the shelves, soaking in the magnitude of all there was to see.

Turning, Johnny saw Les's makeshift desk and the old, disassembled radio that waited there. What was Les doing with a radio? How did he know which way to take it apart without wrecking it? Johnny saw manuals and books from the library nearby; had Les really read all of those, and could he follow along? Golly, Les was smart. Johnny had heard Les teach himself to speak some German using a vinyl record from the library; he knew his big brother could do anything.

Johnny crossed to the rows of shelving that held all of Les's collected treasures. He saw neatly lined rows of jars filled with bits of string and nails and—what was that? A jar of cotton swabs? *Wow.* Stacks of paper rested near one end; Johnny felt himself drawn closer to see what they said.

One stack of paper included pages and pages of meticulously drawn designs and plans. The radio set had already been mapped out on paper for later reference, complete with notes about what each of the parts appeared to do. There were also designs of airplanes, tanks, and vessels like they saw on newsreels at the movie theater.

Atop another stack of paper, a small blue note in Les's handwriting caught Johnny's eye. The ink had splotched in a few places, as if drops of water had fallen on it. At the top of the slip of paper were some words, which Johnny slowly sounded out, his lips moving as he read to himself. The words said, "How I Know I Am Adopted."

Johnny frowned. Les, adopted? Why would Les think he was adopted? He read on slowly and carefully.

HOW I KNOW I AM ADOPTED

1. Red hair (!!!)
2. Don't fit in
3. Forgot birthday
4. Ration stamps

There was more, Johnny saw—something about love and support or some such—but Johnny stopped reading at "ration stamps." He slowly sounded out, reread, and tested the words. Something about ration stamps… what was it?

Adults didn't talk to Johnny, but he liked to listen when they talked to one another. He'd once heard Mother say something to Dad about ration stamps. Johnny knew they were something the government gave out to tell people how much food or gas they could buy. Because of the war all that stuff was needed overseas and so everyone at home had to make do with less.

Why would Les think ration stamps had anything to do with being adopted? Johnny wondered. He tried to remember what it was he heard Mother say before. Something about going to the butcher…of course! That was it! Mother had been angry with Dad for losing money at the racetrack. She'd said, "Thank goodness we have all these kids, so we at least have the ration stamps to feed ourselves. At the rate you're going I'll have to pick up one or two more kids so we don't starve altogether."

Les was there; he heard her say that too, Johnny thought. *Could it be? Is it possible that they adopted some of us kids just so they could get the extra ration stamps?*

Johnny began to reconstruct the facts as he knew them. Mother and Dad really only cared about James; the rest of the boys had to get by on their own. Johnny realized other kids weren't treated like that. His friend Kenny always had lots of hugs and kisses at home, along with regular meals and rules and the kinds of things most other boys and girls had. The MacGregor family was different; perhaps it was because they weren't really all MacGregors. Maybe some of them were adopted after all. Maybe Les was right.

It could be that this was all part of an elaborate scheme on the part of his parents. The more kids you have, the more ration stamps the government would give you. Three extra kids meant extra sugar, coffee, and fuel oil for his parents.

Johnny allowed his imagination to run free. It made him feel strangely good to think that this wasn't his real home, forever and ever, and that there might actually be someplace better for him out there in the big, wide world.

He began to think that, if he was adopted, he must have real parents out there somewhere. Maybe Johnny's real father was Spencer Tracy, star of stage and screen. His favorite grandmother, Nanny, always said he bore more than a passing resemblance to the actor. Everyone knew about Spencer Tracy's nice family out there in Hollywood. *Johnny Tracy*—that would be his name. Heck, he'd probably be starring in movies himself pretty soon with a name like that.

He'd have a whole franchise, Johnny thought. *Johnny Tracy, Boy Scout*. He'd travel the world having marvelous adventures and maybe even have his own radio program and set of adventure equipment. *"Boys, you'll never be lost again once you have the special limited edition* Johnny Tracy, Boy Scout *compass, engraved with the boy adventurer's personal seal!"*

Oh, yes, he'd be worth far more than a few measly ration stamps someday, if he played his cards right. He'd show them all, if he could get away.

Carefully restacking Les's papers and closing up the secret laboratory, Johnny retreated to the attic bedroom. He lay down on his bed and stared at the ceiling, thinking. He would need to play it cool, he knew; no sense letting Mother and Dad know he was on to them. He also needed to let Les believe he'd figured all this out without rummaging through the secret laboratory.

He needed to make a plan.

★

Mother got out of bed two days later: a new record. Charlie was in the kitchen fixing himself a sandwich when she came down.

"What on earth?" Mother said, setting her glass down on the counter. "What kind of mess have you been making?"

Charlie looked around. The kitchen was actually not that bad, considering the boys had been cooking for themselves for several days. There was no food on the counter, save that which Charlie had been using to make his sandwich, and the dirty dishes were neatly contained in the sink rather than strewn everywhere. *James must have cleaned,* Charlie thought.

"Just trying to keep ourselves fed," Charlie said.

Mother glared at him. "What's that supposed to mean?" she demanded. "Are you trying to imply that I have been remiss in my duties?"

Charlie was astonished. "Are you trying to imply you've been doing them?"

"Get to your room, now! I will not be spoken to in such a surly tone," Mother shouted. "Don't come out until I send for you."

Charlie trudged upstairs. It was not the first time, nor probably the last, that he had to sit in his room as punishment for being "surly." What a funny word that was. Charlie had heard it so often applied to himself that he had given it lots of thought. "Surly," to Charlie, sounded like a twisting, tangled knot of fraying twine. You saw it lying there and thought it should be straightened up and wound back into a ball. But as soon as you tried, the twine would refuse to be neat again. You would get all frustrated and hurt your hands handling the rough string, and eventually you'd decide it was better just to let it be.

Surly.

Well, Charlie felt like a knotted-up ball of twine. He had nothing to do in his room except homework (nothing doing) or that stupid Joe Ott airplane model that was so upsetting. He had gotten the model for Christmas—a lovely 22-inch Corsair—but his clumsy hands kept gluing the parts wrong and it was infuriating. He hadn't had it out in a while, but just the thought of it gave him a headache.

Why did everything have to be wrong all the time? Sometimes Charlie felt that whatever he touched turned sour; it was as if the mere fact of his interest made things tangle up in messy—no, *surly*—knots. He could feel anger in his stomach constantly, a seething buildup of rage that ran down his arms and legs and threatened to cause him harm. He wanted to scream, to pound, to hurl things at the wall until stuff lay smashed and in chaos around him.

The violence of his anger sometimes worried Charlie. None of his brothers or his father seemed so upset all the time; what made Charlie so different? There must be something wrong with him. It was so unfair; being deficient in any way made Charlie even angrier. When he thought about it—*really* thought about it—he could get himself stirred into a white-hot fury.

It wouldn't be so bad if he didn't have his wonderful, perfect brother James walking around and lording it over him all the time. James would have built the Corsair model in a half an hour, and then added extra touches and probably had it put into a museum. He would then give Charlie one of those pity-filled glances, as if to say, "I'm so sorry I got all the good genes and you got the bad ones."

Just the thought added to Charlie's growing resentment. Charlie knew himself, and believed he was never going to be anything different from the asthmatic boy with a leather back brace who had nothing unique to offer but poor grades, a surly attitude, and thousands of mistakes. He wanted to be handsome, smart, and talented—someone that everyone liked—but instead he was nothing more than a disappointment.

So he channeled all his pent-up anger, his bad feelings about himself, into a terrible hatred of his brother James. James, who put on a show of being so friendly and talented and beloved by everyone, but who was really no better than most. Some days Charlie wanted to punch him, hard. What made him think he was so special? Why, he was no better than anybody else when it came right down to it. He was just a better faker.

But Charlie wouldn't fake for anyone. No, sir. Nobody would ever call him a phony. He might not be Mr. Popular, or do well in school, or be captain of the football team, but by golly he would be a real person. And if people didn't like who he was, well, then that was their problem and not his.

Charlie began to chew on his thumbnail. Drat that James, going into the Army. Mother would be a basket case for months, and they would all have to pay the price as she cried and pined for James. But on the other hand, maybe things would be better when he was gone. Maybe someone would notice there were three more MacGregor brothers who deserved some attention and respect too. There were possibilities somewhere in that, if Charlie could just figure them out.

Looking down, Charlie realized he'd bitten his thumbnail to the point where it stung and bled. Rats. He needed to get busy with something or he'd drive himself crazy. He went to the bureau and picked up the Corsair model. One of the struts was glued all askew, and it made him mad just to look at it.

But suddenly he had an idea.

He set the Corsair on the corner of his desk and went down to the kitchen, where he searched through the empty whiskey bottles and glasses on the counter. He finally found what he was looking for and took one of his father's ashtrays and a box of matches. Returning to his room, he cracked open the window and made a little fire, right there in the ashtray. He used a crumpled test he'd gotten a D on the previous week, which seemed good to burn anyway.

As the little fire started to glow, Charlie began to talk to himself. "Boys! I've got Japs all over my tail! There's heavy flak and I can hardly see. Do you read me?"

Charlie picked up the Corsair and wiggled it through the air. "I say, I'm hit! I'm hit! Where's my wingman? Where's my cover?"

The balsa-wood tail of the Corsair touched the flames in the ashtray, then ignited. Charlie's narrative grew louder; in his head he could hear the buzz and whirr of the airplane and its desperate pilot. "This is it! Who has my coordinates?" Charlie called. The tiny flames grew, came closer to his hand.

Charlie flung open the window and threw out the sad little plane, a pathetic ball of orange fire. "I'm going down!" he shouted to the street outside. "I'm going down!"

And that, Charlie thought, was a wonderful use of a badly assembled model airplane. For the first time in weeks, he smiled.

★

Les and his friend Pete watched Charlie's plane crash in all its fiery glory. "Another good man down," Les said sympathetically. "What a waste of a perfectly good model."

Pete nodded. "Isn't that the fourth one this year?"

"I think so. That was the Corsair from Christmas, I think."

"Tragic," Pete said. "Hey, do you want to make a trade with me?"

Pete was always trying to get Les to trade his stuff. Les always seemed to have something of interest and, because he was so offhand about everything, Pete felt there must be a trove of riches somewhere.

It was an impression Les didn't mind cultivating. After dozens of moves—different schools, different friends, few attachments—Les had learned that it was better to stay quiet and let people wonder about you. Wondering always led to a better impression than knowing, as far as people were concerned. As Nanny always said, "'If you never say anything, people will think you are stupid. If you do, they will *know* you are stupid." Les kept quiet and watched carefully.

Pete was a perfect foil for someone like Les. Gregarious and gullible, Pete unabashedly looked up to Les, introduced him to other kids, and bought in to all Les's experiments and schemes. Les needed Pete, although he would never say it, because on his own Les would still be—well, on his own. Les didn't make friends well, and it helped him to associate with someone who did. Everyone liked Pete and his puppy-like ways, and for Les he was just what the doctor ordered.

"I don't know about trading," Les answered. "What have you got?"

"My dad gave me a medical kit for Christmas, but it's boring," Pete answered. "There are little scalpels and syringes and tools in it, which were great for a while—don't get me wrong—but I've pretty much done everything I can do with them. I'm interested in having something else for a while. What do you have?'

Les shook his head.

"You know, Pete," he began, pushing up the sleeves of his plaid flannel shirt. "I'm going to tell you something that will help you a lot when you undertake these transactions down the road. You leave yourself wide open for me to take advantage of you, which, fortunately, I am too good a friend to do."

Pete frowned. "What are you talking about?"

"You just kicked your own legs out from under you," Les said. "You told me you don't care much about what you have to trade, which would mean that I should only give you stuff I don't care about too. So, okay, you can have my collection of lead soldiers."

"But why would anybody want those? Anybody can make their own lead soldiers all day long."

"What if I told you that those lead soldiers are special? That they came from my Uncle Fritz when he was stationed in England and they are my most valued possessions?" Les continued. "What if I said the museum was interested in my collection but I would never part with it?"

Pete considered this. "I guess it would be more interesting, then. Is all that stuff true? Can I see them?"

Les snorted. "Of course not," he said. "But in trading, my friend, you have to remember that it is not the item that matters, it is how much the owner *values* the item that is important. I know you don't value that medical kit very much, because you just told me, so if I were a bad friend I would not give you anything good for it. Fortunately, I am not a bad friend *and* I am interested in fair commerce."

"What are you going to give me for it, then?"

"My dad gave me a chemistry set for Christmas," Les said. "I'm pretty tired of that, too. Of course, it was a really nice gift, just like your medical kit, but I'm kind of done with it. Does that seem like a fair trade?"

"You bet!" Pete exclaimed. "Can I come inside and get it now?"

"In a minute," Les said. "You go home and get your stuff and I'll go inside to get mine. But don't forget what I told you, okay? It's no fun to trade with someone who doesn't get the rules."

Pete agreed and took off at a dead run. Les hobbled over on his crutches, picked up the remains of the mangled Corsair, and went into the house. He found Johnny up in his room, staring fixedly into space and moving his lips. Shrugging, Les reached under his bed. He had three chemistry sets under there, from the last three Christmases when his father, who was a chemist, perpetually forgot what he had given him the year before. He pulled one out and got ready to walk back outside.

Before he left, he turned to Johnny. "You okay?" Les asked.

Johnny sat up slowly. "I have been thinking," he said, weighing his words.

"Yeah?"

"I've been thinking about *ration stamps,*" Johnny said, his eyes narrowing. "Do you understand?"

"Nope," Les replied, and made his way back downstairs.

★

The afternoon stretched out longer and longer for James; he had a pile of homework to do, but his shift at the H.N. Kraus Men's Store didn't end for another half hour.

There was a tinny jingle as the shop door opened, and James looked up. It was Mrs. Soderquist, who lived a few streets over from the MacGregor home and who had recently lost her only son, Oliver, in the Pacific. Oliver had been just a year ahead of James in school; both boys had worked on the school newspaper and been friends. The news of Oliver's death came as a shock and James was still not sure how he felt about it. It was hard for him to think that Oliver was still not out in the world somewhere, telling corny jokes and grinning at girls.

Mrs. Soderquist carried a suit bag over one arm. Her eyes met James's, but she didn't come over. James imagined it might be hard for her to see him, standing here alive in Kenmore, when her own son was dead somewhere in the ocean. James smiled gently at her but didn't come over to say hello as he usually would. Instead, Mr. Kraus came around the counter and took one of her hands in his own.

"Ruthie," he said simply. "It is good to see you out and about again."

"Hal." She smiled tentatively.

"What can we do for you today?" Mr. Kraus asked. "It's not often we see a lady in our store. Were you looking for a gift for Joe? Some handkerchiefs, perhaps, or a tie?"

"Nothing so enjoyable," Mrs. Soderquist said, gesturing to the bag she carried. "I'm here to find out what to do with Oliver's graduation suit. I bought it a year ago in December, but he left for basic training before he had a chance to wear it. It's brand-new, and I don't know if it's still possible for me to return it, or if it can be sold on consignment… " Her voice wobbled and trailed off before she could finish.

"Now, don't you worry about a thing, Ruthie," Mr. Kraus

said, his voice rough. "We'll take it off your hands and give you forty dollars for it; either store credit or cash, whatever you prefer."

"Thank you," Mrs. Soderquist mumbled, her voice thick. "It would be a such a help."

Mr. Kraus took the bag and handed it to James, who hung it on a hook next to the counter. They never took anything in on consignment or otherwise, so James wasn't sure what they would do with the garment. He felt tense and awkward and uncertain; he walked across the store and busied himself refolding handkerchiefs while he pretended not to listen.

Turning back to Mrs. Soderquist, Mr. Kraus again took her hands in his own. "What else can we do for you, Ruthie? How is Joe?" he said so softly that James had to strain to hear.

"We're fine," Mrs. Soderquist said. "People have been wonderful, and so kind. I'm sure we'll be all right in time."

"You know I am praying for you every day," Mr. Kraus said gently. "Now, let me fetch your forty dollars and let you get on your way."

Mr. Kraus went back to the register. As he did, Mrs. Soderquist seemed to find the courage to approach James. "I hear you're joining up after graduation," she said, her voice flat.

"Yes, Mrs. Soderquist," James replied. He didn't know what to say in the face of her staggering loss, but he tried anyway. "I'm really sorry about Oliver. He was one of the good ones."

Mrs. Soderquist nodded, paused, then stepped a little closer to James. "Are you afraid?" she asked, as if the entire world depended on his answer.

James thought for a moment. "I don't know enough about what it's going to be like to have any honest feelings one way or the other," he said. "I guess I have to wait and get there to see. The idea of it isn't really great, I admit, but we all have to do things we don't want to on occasion and sometimes our imaginations are worse than the reality. I'm trying not to get too worked up until I know something for sure."

Mrs. Soderquist nodded. "My imagination tortures me," she said, her eyes welling with tears. "I can take almost anything except the idea of Oliver being frightened or suffering. The whole concept of going into battle is terrifying to me. How do you think you will make yourself do it? How did Oliver make himself do it?" she breathed, half to herself.

James felt icy tendrils of fear curl around his spine. "I don't know, Mrs. Soderquist," he said. "I don't know how I'm going to make myself do it, but I have to try. Oliver tried, and he did it. Lots of boys are doing it every single day. I have to do it too, somehow."

"Well," Mrs. Soderquist said, straightening her spine. She was trying to pull herself together, with effort. "I wish you the best. I hope you come home safe and sound to your mother."

"Thank you," James said. "I will do my best. For my family, and for you, and for Oliver."

Mrs. Soderquist turned quickly and went back over to the counter, where Mr. Kraus had her money waiting. She rushed out of the store rapidly, her head down. James met Mr. Kraus's gaze and was reassured by his answering nod.

chapter three

★

February was unseasonably warm that year in Kenmore, so it came as something of a shock when March roared in like a lion, bringing with it eight inches of lake-effect snow. The entire city looked and felt like a shaken snow globe; the streets were thick with fluffy falling flakes and the blanketed silence of thick drifts.

The sounds of life were muted within the MacGregor house as well. Mother was still upset about James's decision to join the Army, even though he wouldn't be leaving for months. She was keeping house again, but she began to drink earlier and earlier in the day, chain-smoking all the while, and by the time Dad got home in the evening she was coiled and waiting with nasty words on her tongue. The boys all tiptoed around the corners of the house when they were in it, hoping to avoid notice.

James was gone all the time these days; between school and work and his many activities he hadn't a moment to spare. The family saw him only as he ran in and out to change clothes, grab some food, or drop off his books. This angered Charlie no end. "Oh, sure; stir everybody all up with your news and then leave," he told Les bitterly. "What a pal." Charlie was spending most of his time shut up in his room; nobody was sure what he was doing in there, now that his model plane was both literally and figuratively finished, but Les believed it was safe to assume he was just sulking.

The thick snowfall was good news for the youngest MacGregor boys. School was closed one morning, and the wet lake-effect snow was excellent for packing. Les's broken leg was a concern that was easily remedied by drawing a burlap bag over his cast like a sock and tying it at the top with a length of twine. It wasn't perfect, but it would do. Les and Johnny wasted no time in getting themselves to the vacant lot behind the house, where a crowd of kids from around the neighborhood was certain to form before long.

Sure enough, there were a half-dozen boys waiting in the lot at first light. Les's friend Pete was there, along with Red Bartlett, Tom and Teddy Cohen, Davey Parker, and Bernie Klein. The boys were already working to construct thick forts in the snow.

"You'll lead the Axis, right?" Pete shouted to Les. Because Les knew a little German, he always ended up commander of the Nazi forces. He didn't like it, but somebody had to be the bad guy, and snowballs were going to be thrown all the same. "*Ja*," he hollered back. "*Deutschland über alles*!"

"Hey, how're you going to play on that leg?" Davey called. "Can you run?"

Les couldn't run, so the boys agreed to play a modified version of the war, in which the Axis powers would get an extra man and the Allies couldn't win until Les—the *Führer*—had been captured in his bunker, transported by sled, and imprisoned behind the Allied fortress.

Building the forts and amassing the necessary arsenal took most of the morning. When they finished, both bases were at least eight feet wide and four feet tall. The Axis forces included a low window in their bunker, so Les could see and direct his forces to action.

By the time fighting started, just before noon, eleven kids were on the lot. Six of them would serve under Les on the Axis side with the remaining boys acting as American GIs. Red Bartlett had proclaimed himself President Roosevelt that morning; so far his decision was unchallenged, as always.

Red was the undisputed leader in their neighborhood. He was a thick, sandy-haired boy Les's age with a loud, husky voice and tremendous athletic ability. He could outrun, outwit, and outfight anyone, so all the kids left him alone and did what he said. The only person who ever dared to go his own way in the face of Red's pressure was Les MacGregor. Les never openly challenged Red, but he frequently would walk away from the other boy with little more than a wave and a mutter about it being "time to get on home."

Les's offhand demeanor raised Red's suspicions along with those of the other kids. Red viewed Les with the mixture of respect and suspicion one gives a possible foe, as if Les might be concealing some diabolical plan to overthrow Red's leadership of the neighborhood kids. Les was the only one of the crowd, therefore, that Red treated with deference.

The first volleys in that day's battle were uneventful. The boys shouted and ran and threw their snowballs as hard as they could. Les was sorry he couldn't run and duck with the others, but he busied himself making snowballs and calling directions to his men. The Allied team was having a terrible time getting across the lot to him; he had no reason to fear he would be captured any time soon.

As he watched, Les observed different strategies. Most of the boys lobbed regular, round-packed snowballs from a safe distance; however, some boys snuck up close behind their opponents and dashed big loose handfuls of snow directly in their faces, temporarily blinding them. Others used their close proximity to drop snowballs down an unsuspecting collar, or shove snow into a chilly red ear. This was dirty pool.

Les used these strategies to direct the Axis forces. He saw that by watching the action he could position his men with specific orders and make a great deal of progress. His side was doing extremely well, but with a sudden flash of insight Les realized how he could make them do better.

He had seen one of Red's GIs use an ice ball with considerable impact, and it gave him an idea. He sent Johnny to get some rocks from the side of the driveway, and he used the rocks to fill the centers of snowballs. This added a lot of punch to the snowballs and would definitely help Les's team win the battle.

Les made a handful of the rock balls and gave one to each of his men. Each boy developed his own rock-ball strategy, with varying degrees of success. Tom and Teddy threw theirs from a distance, which drew attention but didn't cause anyone injury. Pete threw his and missed, which had no consequences one way or the other.

It was Johnny's throw that brought the game to a standstill. He snuck up behind Red (aka President Roosevelt) and threw hard, at close range. The rock ball struck Red in the head, knocking him down. Red was very still as he lay on the ground.

Everything came to a crashing halt.

The boys all stood staring at Red. He was the biggest of all the boys, strong as an ox, and now he'd been felled like a mighty oak tree. He lay on the ground, groaning, his eyes screwed shut in pain. Johnny knelt over him, calling his name. After a long moment Red seemed to return to himself and he was not happy. He looked up at Johnny with fury in his eyes. "What did you DO?" he growled. "Did you throw a ROCK at me?"

Johnny blanched. "I didn't mean to; I forgot," he stammered. As Red began to stand, reminding Johnny of his superior height, age, and strength, Johnny began to feel desperate. His puny eight-year-old brain worked feverishly, and in desperation he burst out, "Les made that snowball! It was him!"

Red's injured head turned slowly, his eyes meeting Les's through the Axis snow fort window. "You," he snarled, and took a step. Red had never liked Les. "I'm going to break your other leg, just like you nearly broke my head. I've just about had it with you."

Les tried to stand up. "Look here, Red, it was an accident…" he began. "I never intended those snowballs to be thrown so close up. You know Johnny never does anything the usual way."

Red was unmoved. "I don't care," he said. He stomped over to Les and hauled him fully to his feet, then threw him back to the ground. Les, with his broken leg, was helpless to stop it. "This is the last straw! You have caused trouble in this neighborhood since the day you moved in here. Your crazy ideas of what's fun always end up with somebody getting hurt or losing something—those rubber-band guns that really hurt, or the crazy grenades you made—and then just last week, you tried to show me how to make a dollar disappear in a flash of light and it ended up costing me a whole dollar! I've had enough of you, Les MacGregor. We all have. Get lost, and don't come back here!"

Les started to speak, but Red wouldn't let him. "I mean it!" he shouted. "You and your stupid little brother can't play here anymore. Nobody in this neighborhood is ever going to talk to you again, not if I have anything to say about it. You go on home and don't come back."

Les remained on the ground, his eyes downcast.

"You hear me?" Red turned to the other kids on the vacant lot. "Nobody plays with the MacGregor boys. If they do, they answer to me."

One by one, the kids trickled away from the vacant lot. Even Pete, Les's good friend, left without looking back. Les didn't say anything, and Johnny felt a lump rising in his throat. *Please, God,* he thought. *Don't let me cry in front of everybody.*

Red turned back to the MacGregor boys. "You see? Nobody wants you around anymore," he said. "Go home."

★

An hour later, Johnny was still crying. "Knock it off," Les said for the hundredth time. "Red'll get over it."

But secretly Les wasn't sure Red would. The other boy had seemed to dislike Les from the beginning.

Johnny and Les were in a pickle. Neither of them wanted to go back into the house, where Charlie and Mother were both probably sulking, but there was nothing to do now that Red had kicked them off the vacant lot. So the two boys sat on the front porch, Johnny sniffling from time to time and Les staring moodily at the street.

Finally Les leaned forward and began to get awkwardly to his feet. "What are you doing?" Johnny asked. "You going in?"

"Nope," Les answered. "I'm going to throw some snowballs."

And that's just what Les did. He made snowballs and threw them at the trees, the stop sign, the side of the shed. The angrier he felt, the harder he threw. He started making more snowballs with rocks in the center, too; they made a satisfying *thunk* when they hit their targets.

Johnny got up and started throwing some snowballs of his own. The two boys made a funny picture, snowballs flying in every direction, and Les with a burlap bag tied around one leg.

Just then, a taxicab turned onto the street where the boys were throwing. Les saw the car coming and turned to Johnny. "Let's get him," Les said.

The car came closer, and just as it was about to pass both boys released their snowballs. *Pow, pow*; both snowballs hit their mark. Les's snowball, which had a rock in it, struck the passenger window. The car swerved briefly, then pulled to a stop.

Uh-oh.

Les reached down for his crutches and took off at a fast hobble across the yard. He could hear the driver of the taxicab shouting behind him as he slipped behind the neighbors' house and disappeared into the Wilkinsons' shed. He was amazed that he was able to move so quickly.

Johnny was not as clever or as fast. When he saw the driver coming, he panicked. He turned around, ran up the porch steps, and went right in the front door of the house. He ran through the foyer, wondering where Les was, and dashed into the kitchen. He didn't see Mother, but he knew he was in for it just the same.

There was a knock at the door a moment later. *Uh-oh.* Johnny heard Mother come down the stairs; he crept forward so he could hear.

"Lady, you need to know that your kids just hit my cab with snowballs or ice balls or something," the driver was saying. "I darned near lost control and had an accident. My driving record has been spotless for nine years, and your kids almost ruined everything. They are a menace, and you should do something about it before someone gets into trouble."

Johnny's eyes widened. He and Les were doomed. Where was Les, anyway?

"I'm sorry, sir," Mother was saying. "I think you must be mistaken. My husband and I don't have any kids."

Johnny felt his throat close with what felt like half-laughter, half-shock. Mother was quick on her feet, to be sure, but this was something else… something deeper. *She doesn't have any kids,* he thought. *Who am I? Who is she?*

The driver apologized and left, Mother went back upstairs, and Johnny snuck out the back door to look for Les.

Fifteen minutes later, Johnny found his brother in the Wilkinsons' shed. "Johnny," Les advised, "you've got to wise up. When you're in trouble, you should never, ever run to the house."

★

The snow blew sideways, stinging James's face as he crossed Manchester Place to the Soderquist home. Oliver's graduation suit had sold for more than the forty dollars Mr. Kraus had paid, and James had been asked to deliver the additional money to Oliver's mother. It was a terrible day to be out, and James frankly dreaded seeing Mrs. Soderquist almost as much as he disliked being out in the harsh winter elements. Her sadness was palpable and made him uncomfortable and afraid.

James found the house—a pretty white structure with a wide porch complete with a swing—and walked up the front steps. He rang the bell and waited, trying to put on a happy face and thinking about what he would say when the door opened. He waited for a moment, shivering in the bitter cold, then rang again.

Finally he heard movement inside the house. A quick, light step approached the door, and James stood straighter. The door swung open and a girl was looking back at him through the snow. She had dull blond hair that she wore in a victory roll. Her bangs were swept up into giant curls that framed her face; the style always looked overly complicated to James. Her skin was fair, and she wore wire-rimmed glasses, which she pushed up her nose with the knuckle of one finger. "Hello?" she said.

"Hi," James said, reaching into his pocket. "I have a delivery from Mr. Kraus at the men's store downtown. Is your mother here?"

"No, no," the girl said. "But please come on in. It's freezing, and you're letting the snow in!"

She pushed against the door and, gratefully, James came inside. He shook the snow from his coat and huddled into the warmth for a minute before looking again at the girl. "I'm James," he said.

"I know who you are," she said. "Everyone in school does."

James looked again at the girl. She was plain-looking and serious, with light hair and skin that made her seem like she could fade away at any minute. "I'm Mary Jane," she offered. "I'm in your history class. I sit next to you, on the right."

"Really?" James said, stunned. "Right next to me?"

"Yeah, I can be hard to spot," Mary Jane said, a smile in her voice. "You're always so busy, I'm not surprised you haven't noticed."

"I'm sorry," James said. He stopped and looked at Mary Jane—*really* looked at her—and saw that her eyes were violet blue. Behind her silver-rimmed glasses, she had something exquisite in her face that required only a moment's study to be noticed. Right here in Kenmore—sitting beside him every day in history class, in fact—was the most startling pair of eyes James had ever seen.

"It's all right," Mary Jane said. "Would you like to come in? Mother will be here any minute. She just had to run to the market."

James nodded, took off his gray wool coat, and followed his diminutive hostess through a wide door into the sitting room. Mary Jane perched on the edge of a small settee and motioned to a chair across from her. James sat down, setting the small parcel on his lap. Mary Jane looked, but didn't ask what it was.

"Do you enjoy the history class?" she inquired politely.

"Sure," James said. He looked around the warm sitting room, trying to seem casual. But his gaze kept flicking back to Mary Jane. She sat sedately, as all girls did, with her ankles tucked together and feet to the side. She was looking down at her hands, which were supposed to be folded in her lap. They were fidgeting instead.

James realized why he'd never noticed her before. She was not like other girls, giggling and chattering and hoping for his attention. If he'd walked up to any other door in Kenmore and found a girl behind it, she would be batting her eyelashes at him and flirting madly by now. But not Mary Jane; it was almost as if she didn't care to know James better or even want him to stay.

Mary Jane suddenly looked up and caught James looking at her. Her face seemed momentarily startled under his scrutiny, and then quickly rearranged itself into a placid smile. "Can I get you something to drink?" she asked politely.

James declined, and they sat in silence for a long moment. At length, he said, "I'm sorry about Oliver. He was a good friend."

"Thank you," Mary Jane said simply. Her hands stilled in her lap, and she glanced automatically at the gold star in the window. Every family that sent a boy overseas got a flag with a blue star on it to display. When a boy didn't come home, the blue star was replaced with a gold one. "It's been hard."

The *tick-tick* of the clock on the mantel was the only sound in the room. James became aware of a strange sensation in himself, one that increased his discomfort tenfold. He—who was ordinarily so confident and charming, who always had a way with people (and especially with girls)—was tongue-tied. He actually felt *nervous* around this ordinary slip of a thing who looked at him so seriously from behind her glasses. Why?

Before he could explore the idea further, the front door opened and Mrs. Soderquist came bustling in with bags and snow flying. James stood and rushed to the door to help her with Mary Jane on his heels. Together they collected the groceries she'd brought back from the market and carried them to the kitchen. James shared Mr. Kraus's small parcel with a grateful Mrs. Soderquist, and they chatted awkwardly in the kitchen for a moment before James's nervousness again propelled him to the front door.

Mary Jane followed him, and smiled courteously as he put on his coat. "I'll see you in class tomorrow, then," she said, opening the door and sweeping him outside. James had the feeling that he'd been dismissed, as if the girl with the serious purple eyes had considered and declined his company. It was unbelievable.

Her face remained in James's mind all the way back to the store.

chapter four

★

Two weeks later, Red Bartlett was still angry. He had completely frozen out the MacGregor boys; none of the neighborhood kids would have anything to do with them. Even Les's loyal friend Pete had faded away. Red had seen Pete walking back from school with Les one day and had blackened Pete's eye for it. Now when Pete saw Les there was always a sympathetic look and a fifty-foot distance between them.

Les might have been able to conceal his friendship with Pete if he could bring him indoors. But Les had long ago learned that it was embarrassing to have friends inside the MacGregor house. If Mother or Dad was drinking, the home got mean fast.

No, sneaking around was not an option. Neither was apologizing to Red. So the MacGregor boys found themselves on their own before, after, and even during the school day.

Les went around feeling as if a grenade had gone off in his stomach, leaving a hole where his insides were supposed to be. He was hollow and sad and anxious. He had nobody to eat with at lunchtime, nobody to hang around with at recess, and even the kids who sat near him in class were looking at him strangely. It was as if he didn't exist anymore.

All this over a stupid snowball. Les wished he could go back in time. He regretted that rocky snowball more than anything he had done before in his whole life, and he wished with all his might that what was done could somehow be undone. But would he apologize for it? Absolutely not—not to someone as petty and low as Red Bartlett.

Of course, Les didn't share his feelings of regret, anger, and shame with anybody, even Johnny. No matter how bad he might feel, a boy was not supposed to whine and mope about circumstances that couldn't be helped. Instead, the two boys walked to and from school together each day, keeping a healthy distance between themselves and the rest of the neighborhood kids. They spent their after-school time in the house, Les usually hiding out in his secret laboratory and Johnny reading his comic books. They still participated in Scouts and did their scrap drives like always, but they worked as a pair now.

Now that Les had electricity in his private room, he was able to do much more in there. He had a lamp and was working on making the discarded radio function again. His progress was slow but, as Les figured it, what else did he have to do?

★

James was having a hard time keeping up with everything. As editor of the yearbook, he had deadlines looming, plus there was extra springtime work to be done for nearly every club and organization to which he belonged. The end of his senior year was approaching, and he wasn't sure how he was going to fit everything in.

Making matters worse, Mr. Kraus told James he was about to start the spring inventory and needed him to work both Saturday and Sunday. James wasn't sure when he'd be able to get his homework done with everything he had happening outside of school.

But he never complained. He just smiled and said, "Sure, Mr. Kraus," and added the work to his unending list of obligations. He would get it done somehow.

He just couldn't let anybody down.

It was also better for him to be away from home at the moment, at least until Mother had settled into the idea that he would be going overseas after graduation. She and Dad had stopped openly fighting about it, he knew, but she was still so unhappy and she took every opportunity she could to make nasty comments. She had been drunk again last night, he could tell, and he felt sorry for that.

The only bright spot for James these days was his brand-new friendship with Mary Jane. He had taken her dismissal as a challenge, and he'd begun passing her little notes in history class. At first she just read them and tucked them into the back of her book, giving him a little indulgent smile as she did. After a while, though, she began to write back. She had small, careful penmanship and a terrific sense of humor.

From James:

For the last three months, Mr. Norton has worn the EXACT same bow tie every single day. But today it's different. What's going on?

Mary Jane:

Maybe he's an imposter. The lecture is better today too.

James:

Evil twin? Could be...I see his hair is different too.

Mary Jane:

Oh, I figured it was spiking out due to the shock.

James:

???? The shock of what?

Mary Jane:

The shock of the radical tie change. It can't have been easy.

James loved to watch Mary Jane's face as she wrote. She would chew her lip, pause and think (or pretend to listen, if the teacher was watching), and smile to herself. Her striking eyes would sometimes glance at James with mischief in their depths, and he couldn't help but grin.

From James:

Will you go out with me sometime?

Mary Jane:

Not on your life.

James:

Why not?

Mary Jane:

1. I don't date heartbreakers.
2. You don't have time. You're completely booked up with work, school, etc.
3. Finally (and most importantly), your swelled-up head is so huge I'm not sure we'd be able to take the same bus.

James:

You don't know me at all! I don't have a big ego. Quite the opposite, in fact. It's all a big show, you know.

Mary Jane:

Yes. Well, I do not need to be part of your show. You stick to your cheerleader types and all will be well.

James:

But I don't want to go out with them. I want to go out with you. Please?

Mary Jane tucked the note in the back of her book and pretended to be completely absorbed in Mr. Norton's discussion of the Roman Empire. She didn't look at James again.

★

If it isn't one thing, it's another, Charlie thought as he heard his parents start arguing in the next room. He was lying on the floor, listening to the radio, but their voices were beginning to drown out the program.

"I don't know why she feels she needs to do this," Mother was saying. "She's never been anything but a thorn in my side. I won't be able to take it if she comes to stay. Besides, where will we put her?"

Charlie's ears perked up. Who was coming?

"I guess Charlie can move into James's room," Dad said. "That'll free up some space."

What? Charlie's attention caught, and held. He flicked off the radio and lay back on the rug.

"You almost sound like you're trying to be helpful," Mother was saying. The liquor cabinet slammed shut, and Charlie could hear the sound of a glass being filled. "I'm not sure, because I have never before heard anything resembling helpfulness from you, but that's what it sounds like. So you're on her side?"

Dad was quick with a rejoinder. "I've long since learned that it doesn't pay to take sides where you're concerned," he said. "You're a losing situation all by yourself."

Mother and Dad seemed to have an endless contest going, Charlie thought. It was like they had to deliver the best zinger, the wittiest insult, the cleverest retort. It never stopped.

Mother harrumphed, then began again. "Your mother absolutely must be kept away at all costs," she said. "There will be no peace for any of us if she comes. I know she's lonely since her husband died last year, but it's not up to me to provide company for her. Especially when she threatens the well-being of me and my children."

"Oh, did you suddenly remember you have children?" Dad said. "I'm astonished."

One point to Dad, Charlie thought absently, then cued in on what Mother had been saying. Grandma Barney was coming? This was news.

Of course Mother was furious; she was always upset with Grandma Barney, who was Dad's mother and quite opinionated. Grandma Barney had been married twice, first to Dad's father, and then to Will Barney, who died last year. According to Mother, Grandma Barney believed her wider experiences as a wife gave her the right to interfere wherever she wanted to.

Making matters worse, Grandma Barney was also a Methodist and a teetotaler. It had taken years for Charlie to figure out what this meant, but he knew that—at least as far as Mother was concerned—a Methodist teetotaler was the worst possible kind of person to be. Even now she was starting on her long-practiced litany of reasons.

"You know she will get here and look down the end of her nose at me for enjoying a glass of wine every now and then," Mother was saying. "She will sit in judgment of us all, watching everything we do."

"You mean watching everything *you* do," Dad replied quickly.

Mother continued as if she hadn't heard. "She'll criticize my cooking, my housekeeping, and the way I'm bringing up our boys."

"*Are* you bringing up the boys?" Dad said. "It sure doesn't look like it from here. Besides, she said she just wants to come to help out around here. She is at loose ends since my stepfather died last year."

Game, set, and match to Dad, Charlie thought. Mother was off her game tonight; the Grandma Barney news must really have upset her.

Charlie went into the kitchen. Mother's litany of complaints continued; she was now discussing all the reasons she hated Grandma Barney. Dad was half-listening as he poured himself a drink and reached for the newspaper. Dad probably wouldn't be home long; when Mother got herself worked up, he usually left to play cards at the bar.

"You have to stop this from happening," Mother said finally, lighting a fresh cigarette. "Can't you do that?"

Dad was just opening his mouth to speak when Charlie interrupted. "What's going on?"

"Your Grandmother Barney sent a telegram today saying she's going to be moving in with us for a while," Dad said. "Your mother is just trying to contain her overwhelming joy at the prospect."

"When is she coming?" Charlie asked.

"She's making arrangements now; it will probably be another week or so," Dad said. "Speaking of which, she is going to stay in your room. James's room is larger and will accommodate you both, so you will have to move in there."

"No I won't," Charlie said. "Mom's right. You have to stop this from happening. Can't you do something?"

"THERE! See?" Mother leaped in. "Nobody wants this to happen! If she comes, it will hurt us all. You have got to do something. It's YOUR mother—tell her... tell her we don't have room—whatever you have to say, say it."

Dad's jaw tightened. He pushed his drink forward and

stood. "This is happening whether you like it or not," he announced to Mother. "I'm tired of having the boys run wild and of living with someone who is only half a wife. You need my mother to try—yet again—to teach you how to be an adult. Charlie, you get your room ready during the next week." Then, glaring at Mother, Dad stalked to the back door and walked out.

Mother stifled a sob and walked over to the counter for her glass. She filled it, lit another cigarette, then weaved slowly out into the front room. The radio clicked on and a chair creaked.

Charlie trudged up the stairs in a temper. In the hallway he met Johnny coming out of the bathroom. "What do you want, twerp?" Charlie asked sourly.

"Nothing," Johnny said, surprised.

"Good, 'cause that is just what we're all likely to get from now on," Charlie said.

"What's going on?" Johnny asked.

"Grandma Barney's moving in here," Charlie said. "She's taking my room."

"How long is she going to stay?" Johnny asked.

"Nobody knows," Charlie answered, stepping into his bedroom and whipping the door shut behind him with a thud.

Of course, Johnny thought, his mind spinning. *They're after her ration stamps now too.*

★

Mother had a headache the next morning, so Les and Johnny had to get themselves fed and ready for school. They had a little trouble; Les burned the eggs and somebody knocked over the milk (there was a dispute over whose fault it was), so the boys got off to a late start.

It had snowed again the night before. The sidewalk was slippery, so Johnny walked with a funny, stiff-legged gait to keep himself from taking a tumble and being embarrassed. Les struggled along as best he could on his crutches.

The snow squeaked and crunched beneath their feet. It was almost as if the ground were crying out in pain from being stepped on, Johnny thought. Only the very coldest snow makes a sound like that.

Les and Johnny went to P.S. 56, as their school was called, by crossing between the houses over to Delevan Street and then walking down. Just as they approached the south side of Delevan, Les stopped next to the side door of one of the houses.

Johnny nearly crashed into Les; he had stopped so suddenly. Following his brother's gaze, he saw a little loose bit of fur blowing in the icy breeze. A little mound of snow was resting there peacefully.

Les walked over and brushed some of the snow away. There on the ground was a little half-grown cat that had fallen asleep and frozen to death. The cat was gray and white and cute, even if it was deader than dead.

Johnny looked over at Les and realized he was stretching open one of his coat pockets as if he had a mind to put the cat into it. Johnny opened his mouth to speak, but as he did Les seemed to discard the idea. Les covered the cat again with snow and both boys walked silently to school.

All day Johnny thought about that poor kitty. *What is it like to die*? he wondered. Then he thought, *Being dead must be like being invisible. And I know what it's like to be invisible.*

Johnny was invisible at home, where nobody talked to him. He never knew what was going on or why, and nobody seemed to see fit to help him understand. Sometimes he'd catch bits and pieces by accident, like when Charlie told him about Grandma Barney last night, but disclosures like that almost never happened.

And now Johnny was invisible at school too. The neighborhood kids didn't talk to the MacGregor boys anymore and school had become a lonely place. Class was fine, but lunchtime and recess were isolated affairs. Johnny ate by himself, played by himself, and wished his life could be different. He didn't want to be invisible any more.

Johnny was always relieved at the end of each day when he would meet up with Les at the edge of the playground and they'd begin their walk home. Johnny knew he wasn't invisible to Les and was reassured.

As they walked home that day, they couldn't help but stop at the side door of the house where the dead cat lay. It was still there. Without saying a word, Les picked it up and tucked it under his arm. They walked the rest of the way home in silence. Johnny was dying to ask Les what he would do with the cat, but he knew if he made a nuisance of himself Les wouldn't let him be part of whatever plan he had in mind.

So Johnny held his tongue, even when Les hid the dead cat beneath the mulberry bush in the side yard without another word. He supposed the answers would come soon enough if he played it cool.

chapter five

★

Snow delayed the train the morning Grandma Barney came, which started everything off on the wrong foot. Mother had gotten herself worked up into a state waiting for Dad to bring Grandma Barney from the station. James was sitting with Mother in the front room, listening as she allowed her imagination to roll.

"The first thing she'll do when she gets here is look around and say, 'My, do we have our work cut out for us,'" Mother said. "You just watch. And then when I pour myself a drink to settle my nerves—and you know I will need and deserve a drink by then—she will make this clicking sound with her tongue and say, 'One should cling to the Lord in times of trial, not to a liquor bottle.'"

Mother lit another cigarette and James made a soothing sound in his throat. He was only half-listening to Mother. Mary Jane had finally agreed to go to the movies with him that afternoon. ("If we go when it's light outside, then it's not a date," she'd said. "And I really do want to see *Casablanca* anyway. So I'll ride there with you, and sit with you, and ride back with you, but it is not a date.") James had gotten Mr. Kraus to give him the afternoon off; it was the only time James had ever asked for a day off, and Mr. Kraus was particularly pleased to hear that James would be with the Soderquist girl.

Outside the house, a car door slammed. Mother stood and James noticed that her chin lifted a little, as if she were bracing herself against something. He patted Mother's back and walked with her to the front door.

Grandma Barney came into the house like an old hen, clucking and fussing. It had been years since James last saw her, and she was shorter than he remembered. He took her coat, watched as Mother gave her a defiant half-hug, half-shove, and walked with her into the front room. Grandma Barney asked Mother for a cup of tea, looked around, and immediately said, "Oh my, but we do have our work cut out for us."

James stifled a laugh and Mother stomped off to the kitchen, ostensibly for the tea. James knew she was really going in there for a few nips from the liquor cabinet and probably a cigarette.

Charlie, Les, and Johnny thundered down the stairs and came into the room to say hello. Charlie had finished moving the last of his belongings into James's room a half hour before and was still steamed about having to give up his privacy. Even so, he greeted his grandmother with a soft kiss on the cheek and offered something that was supposed to be a smile but came out more like a grimace.

Mother returned a few minutes later—without any tea for Grandma Barney, but with the smell of whiskey on her breath—and said, "So, what brings you to our doorstep? Nobody else would have you?"

"Well, I like that," Grandma Barney said, with characteristic bluntness. "Nothing like a warm welcome to make a body feel right at home. Hope you keep a lock on your shotgun or I may have to sleep in the shed for safety."

"Maybe you should *stay* in the shed," Charlie muttered.

Grandma Barney was a very small lady with thin hair the color of steel. She stood very straight and always dressed in long, plain calico dresses with stiff black oxford shoes. Everything she did was firm and proper, and despite her diminutive stature nobody ever dared to cross her. She lived far away and the boys had seen her only a few times. They knew Grandma Barney was very stern and that she made Mother upset, and so they tried to keep their distance.

"Young man," Grandma Barney said, looking at Charlie. "It appears my tea is not forthcoming. Would you please show me to my room?"

Charlie took Grandma Barney's two ancient leather bags and led her up the staircase. She moved slowly and puffed out her breath as she walked; Charlie noticed she smelled vaguely of peppermint and tobacco. "You keeping up with me, boy?" she asked, her raspy voice chuckling.

"Yes, Grandma," Charlie answered politely, not wanting to make the situation any more uncomfortable than it already was.

"Which one are you again?" she asked. "Are you the friendly one or the angry one?"

Charlie cleared his throat. "I think I must be the angry one, Grandma Barney," he said.

"Good to know," she said. "You and I have a lot in common. We'll have to have a contest to see which of us can be angry the longest. Who do you think will win?"

"Ummm..." Charlie began. He didn't have the foggiest idea how to respond to that question.

"It's all right, boy," Grandma Barney said. "I'll give you the answer: We're both going to have our moments. I am here to help put life back in order around here, and it's probably going to be hard on everyone for a while. But it's long overdue and much-needed, wouldn't you say?"

Charlie gaped at her.

"Oh, I don't expect any other response from you," Grandma Barney waved her hand at him. "You don't know any different yet. But you will. Oh, yes… you most certainly will!"

Charlie heard her cackle even after the door to her bedroom was closed.

★

The house was quiet now. Grandma Barney was taking a nap, Mother was sulking in the front room listening to the radio, and James had left for his movie.

Upstairs in his secret laboratory, Les was preparing to begin surgery. The dead cat was lying on the table, thawed now beneath the pool of warm lamplight. Next to its furry body, Les had laid out all the tools from the medical kit he'd gotten from his trade with Pete.

On the floor was a pile of towels and old rags, which Les planned to use to sop up any blood that might drain out during the procedure. He was going to open up the cat and look at its insides, so he could learn more about how animals were put together. He had a book from the library about anatomy, and he figured he could tell which organs were which if he spent enough time with it.

All he had to do was make the first incision.

Les picked up the scalpel, weighed it in his hand. It was sharp and silver-shiny. He held it down over the cat, trying to decide where to make the cut. Then he remembered the fur; he would have to shave the kitty before he made the incision.

He ran down and fetched his father's razor then came back up and gently shaved a wide swath across the animal's belly.

He picked up the scalpel again and prepared to operate. This was going to be harder than he thought. He rubbed his forehead and looked at the cat's face. Poor little kitty. It was not very old; not much more than a baby, really. If it had survived Les would have liked to play with it. His own cat, Jinx, was too old and too sedate to play much anymore. She was mostly good for cuddling. And Johnny's cat, Adam, was really not very bright. You couldn't get it to do much of anything that made sense. Les would like a young kitty to play with, one that would leap at balls of yarn and maybe learn a trick or two.

But back to the task at hand. Les again lifted the scalpel and touched it to the cat's shaved tummy. He hovered there for a long minute. He looked again at the poor kitty's face and couldn't push in to make the cut.

He tried again a few more times but something inside just wouldn't let him do it. He sighed and pushed back from the table and tried to think.

★

Outside the secret laboratory, another cat-related drama was about to unfold. Johnny's enormous cat, Adam, was stretched out on the bed. He was tolerating Johnny as the boy tossed string and tried to tickle the cat's tummy. The cat's sheer size and age made it difficult for him to get away, so he rarely made the effort.

Adam had been a great disappointment to Johnny, as cats went. The family generally had pets around; in addition to Adam and Jinx there was also a cat named Sniffer that belonged to Charlie. Sniffer's tail had gotten caught in the kitchen door and broken, so Sniffer's tail was always 90 degrees horizontal.

When Johnny and Les had gone to the Department of Public Works to pick out their pets, Johnny had high hopes that his cat would be clever and highly trainable. Not the kind of cat that would let its tail get caught in a door, in other words. Johnny wanted to teach Adam to do tricks and count and find treasure; it was not long, however, before Johnny realized the cat was not cut out for this type of accomplishment.

The cat was just not that bright.

So, instead of making Adam the smartest cat ever known, Johnny set out to make him the biggest. Adam ate two large meals of cat food each day, plus Johnny gave him eggs in milk and table scraps whenever he could. The black-and-white cat grew enormous and unwieldy; he dwarfed any object he lay upon (and that was pretty much any object in the house—he was not energetic). Adam's size, combined with his remarkable slowness of thought, made him at once a source of fascination and irritation to Johnny.

Johnny began to make games out of ways he could provoke and irritate the cat, but so far Adam was unmoved. Johnny could never decide if it was Adam's loyalty, good nature, or stupidity that kept him calmly purring while Johnny devised new methods of torture, but the cat never even moved itself to growl or hiss. Not once. Even now, as Johnny teased the cat with a piece of string, Adam only gazed fondly at Johnny as if to say, "Is that the best you can do?"

Johnny finally gave up, sighed, and looked out the window. New snow continued to fall on the three and a half feet or so that were already on the ground. The flakes were large, soft, and fluffy and the ground looked like rich cotton or clouds. Soft and deep.

Johnny paused, wondered for a minute, then opened the window. He returned to the bed, picked up the cat, and dropped him outside. The cat never made a sound as he fell down into the snow and disappeared inside the fluffy whiteness. It took Adam a minute to shrug himself from the snow, and Johnny could see that his impact had made a perfect silhouette of a cat with all four feet straight out.

Fascinating.

Adam lumbered up over the snow to the sidewalk and came back to the house. Johnny went downstairs to let him back in through the kitchen door and was surprised when Adam ambled directly up to the bedroom again.

So Johnny dropped him out the window again, this time in a slightly different location to make sure there was plenty of padding to cushion the cat's landing. When Johnny went downstairs to let the cat back in, he was also careful to leave the milk chute open so he wouldn't have to go all the way back down to let the cat in the house; Adam could get into the kitchen on his own.

All in all, Adam repeated the process of dropping, returning, and walking back upstairs about six times before Les emerged from the secret laboratory to save him.

Johnny began to suspect that Adam was secretly a great thrill-seeker.

★

James really enjoyed *Casablanca,* though he pretended not to for Mary Jane's sake. He told her it would only be a real date if he had a good time, and since he hadn't liked the movie he hadn't had a good time, he reasoned. She seemed satisfied with this explanation and agreed to let James take her to a nearby malt shop.

They walked together, laughing and talking and arguing about the film, and James felt like it was the first time he'd ever really enjoyed another person's company so well. Mary Jane was not like any other girl he'd ever known. She never simpered or giggled or sought compliments. She was just herself: a serious, thoughtful girl who kept a daring sense of humor and extraordinary violet eyes partially hidden from view.

James told her this now, and she frowned. "Is that supposed to be a compliment?" she asked. "Somehow it doesn't sound like one."

"Yes, of course it's a compliment," James said. "I really like you."

"No you don't," Mary Jane said. "You only think you do because you think I'm a challenge. If I ever actually went out with you, you would lose interest and go chase some other, pretty girl."

"That's not true," James said. "I admit, you're not my usual type. But I like you much better than my usual type."

Mary Jane laughed. "You're a great one with the compliments today," she said.

They entered the malt shop and found a seat. After they ordered, James regarded Mary Jane intently. "You know," he said. "Nobody else talks to me the way you do. And so I'm going to talk to you like I don't talk to anybody else."

And he did.

He poured out all of his thoughts, telling her of his home and family, and how he had to be perfect to balance them all out. He told her how he felt like he could never really be himself, because he might make a mistake and then everyone would know him for the fraud and the sham he really was. He confessed how tired he was all the time from having to deal with so many expectations. He even told her how afraid he was to join the Army and go overseas, despite the fact that he'd chosen the path with the least danger in it.

"I'm not a hero, like your brother was," James confessed. "I worked hard to find a way to save my own neck. You see? I'm not real—I am a made-up version of myself. And only you know the truth."

Mary Jane's face was white and still. She had regarded James carefully during his speech and she still showed no clear reaction. "Why are you trusting me with your truth?" she asked quietly.

"Because you are so different from everyone else," James said. "You see right through the false version of me, and you are able to tease me about it. It's pretty clear that I can't hide the phony stuff from you so I might as well try to explain why it's there. I know you well enough to believe you won't be frivolous about this; you'll take me seriously and do your best to understand. You are the only person on earth I could ever tell."

"You have been lonely," she said, her voice low.

He couldn't speak. He just nodded.

"I certainly understand that," she said. She reached her hand across the table and covered his fingers with it. They sat like that, together in the malt shop, for a long while.

★

Over the next few days, it became clear how Grandma Barney would fit into the MacGregor household.

She wouldn't.

She said whatever came into her mind the minute it arrived there, and frequently her thoughts were more direct than kind. "You, there," she would say to whomever happened to be unlucky enough to pass by her chair. "Get out into that mess of a kitchen and clean something."

Grandma Barney was not interested in sewing, but she kept a great quilted sewing basket next to her chair. Nobody knew what was in it, but they all knew about the thimble she took from it every now and then. She wore it often, despite the fact that she had nothing to stitch, and used it when necessary. Johnny in particular frequently felt the sting of her thimble hitting his ear as he passed her in the front room. He was pretty sure he hadn't done anything and guessed she just felt like thwacking him.

Grandma Barney wholeheartedly disapproved of most of what occurred in the MacGregor household. On Tuesday Les heard her giving Mother a stern lecture in the kitchen.

"Those boys are running wild," Grandma Barney said. "You don't pay any attention to their comings and goings during the day, and it is only by the grace of God that one of them hasn't killed somebody."

"But—"

"No buts! I am telling you right here and now that you are temporarily relieved of your parenting responsibilities, not that you ever really assumed them in the first place," Grandma Barney continued. "I am ashamed of your behavior. You are an overage adolescent, and it's time you grew up.

Your children need parents, not drunks, and it's high time you woke up and realized it. Until you do, I'm in charge."

Grandma Barney swept out of the kitchen, her black oxford shoes clumping on the wood floor. She walked right past Les without seeing him and went to sit in the front room. Her face was red and her breathing was heavy, as though she had been running for a very long time. Les saw her turn her face to the window and slump her shoulders slightly before reaching into her sewing box. She pulled out a Bible and began to read softly to herself.

In the kitchen, the liquor cabinet opened quietly, surreptitiously, and then closed again.

It was going to be a very long afternoon. Les went back upstairs to his secret laboratory to hide out for a while. Johnny was curled up on the bed with his cat; he had fallen asleep reading a comic book and was snoring softly. The room seemed very still.

Behind the map, Les still had the problem of this dead cat. What was he going to do with it? He knew he couldn't operate on it now; it was too soon after its untimely demise and he just couldn't make himself do the incision.

He leaned back and thought. Over time, he knew, the cat's corpse would rot and decompose. Like the hearse song everyone sang:

Did you ever think when the hearse drives by
That someday soon you too will die?
They'll wrap you up in a bloody sheet
And toss you down a thousand feet.
The worms crawl in, the worms crawl out
The ants play pinochle in your snout.

The big black bug with big red eyes
Crawls in your innards and out your sides.
You squish him up and spread him on bread
And that is what you eat when you are dead.
The worms crawl in, the worms crawl out
In your stomach and out your mouth…

It wasn't pretty, but it was real. Les knew that eventually this would happen to the kitty; its skin would be eaten away by bugs and worms and its bones would be laid bare. Hm. There was an idea there.

Les decided to take the cat out and rebury it in the yard until it had decomposed. He would let nature take care of the hard stuff, and then Les would dig up the bones and reassemble them in his laboratory like a dinosaur in a museum. That was it!

But this would be a problem. How was he going to get the cat out of the bedroom without being spotted and questioned? Grandma Barney was in the front room, in full view of the front door, and Mother was in the kitchen, with a good look out the back. He'd never get out without one of them (heaven forbid it should be Grandma Barney!) asking about the cat.

Thinking quickly, Les went over to his shelves and pulled off a long coil of thick twine. He tied the cat's feet together and anchored them to the end, then went out into the room and quietly, carefully—so as not to wake Johnny—he opened the front window. The old wood groaned once as the pane lifted and Les looked quickly at his brother, but Johnny just shifted in his sleep and resumed his snoring.

Les picked up the cat and prepared to let the twine out

until the kitty reached the ground. Unlike his brother, he was too kind too simply drop the cat outside; he would gently lower it down out of respect for the dead.

Slowly, carefully, the cat's little body slipped toward the earth below. Any second, Les expected to hear a voice calling upstairs, but nobody seemed to notice the corpse hanging outside the window. Once the cat had safely landed on the snow below, Les slipped on his boots and coat and casually went out to conceal it beneath the snowy mulberry bush. He worked quickly and the deed was easily done. Nobody said a word to him until after the cat was safely hidden.

That's when Les returned to the house to see Grandma Barney looking at him with her flinty gaze.

"To mourn a mischief that is past and gone is the next way to draw new mischief on," she said. "Shakespeare wrote that. Do you know what it means?"

Les shook his head.

"It means that one trouble usually follows another when some young boys have enough unsupervised time on their hands," Grandma Barney cackled. "I've got my eye on you, young man. If your mother won't keep track of you, I will!"

chapter six

★

Eventually the snow in Kenmore began to melt and spring came. The windows were left open to let the breezes in, and the grass and gardens seemed to begin thawing all over. Les got his cast off and began to feel right again.

Springtime even seemed to warm the relations between Mother and Grandma Barney. They still argued, but Mother seemed to snipe at her less often. Dad was still gone most evenings, playing cards and betting on sports, but when he was there Mother didn't try to torment him either.

True to her word, Grandma Barney did keep an eye on the MacGregor boys. She kept track of every single coming and going and helped make sure they didn't have, as she said, "more mischief than is necessary around here, for heaven's sake."

That spring marked the first that Les didn't try to run away. Though he thought about it plenty, he had lots of distractions to occupy his mind.

First and foremost was the submission Les was preparing for *True Story* magazine. He had written a great long tale—not entirely true, of course, but very riveting—that imagined an eleven-year-old London boy who was trapped with a broken leg. Because of his injury, the boy couldn't get to the air-raid shelter with the rest of his family and had to wait on the roof during a particularly bad *Luftwaffe* attack. He could see the

German guns blazing in the night sky over London; their red and orange and amber glows illuminated the unending flight of the German bombers and British fighters. Les was working hard to capture the entire vista in tremendous detail and so far it was going fairly well.

Once his True Story was chosen (as Les was certain it would be), he planned to use the twenty-five-dollar prize to outfit his laboratory with some new equipment. He was already working on a device that would allow him to listen in on the telephone lines from inside the lab; just a few more parts now and it would be completed.

Les was also distracted by the movie serial that was playing every Saturday at the Circle Theatre in nearby Buffalo. *Adventures of the Flying Cadets* had started playing when there was snow on the ground that year, and the episodes continued to hold his interest now that the flowers were beginning to bloom. Four soldiers accused of murder had to travel to darkest Africa to fight the Black Hangman and clear their names. James was talking about being a pilot when he entered the Army, and Les's attention was held by thoughts about how his brother, too, would "blaze a trail around the globe… smashing the spies of the skies!"

Movies were an important part of the week for Les and Johnny. For 25 cents they received an entire afternoon's entertainment: cartoons, a newsreel, and at least one serial in addition to the movie matinee itself. The Circle Theatre also gave away free comic books at their matinee shows, so it was worth the three extra cents to take the bus into the city. When Mother remembered, she gave the boys a small allowance, which they supplemented by collecting old soda bottles all week long. This usually was enough to pay for their Saturday excursions, with some money left over to buy candy and grab a handful of the war stamps that were always on sale in the theater lobby.

Les loved the Saturday matinees, especially when the serial was good. He had suffered through some awful ones; for every good series, like *James Tracy* or *Flash Gordon*, there was usually something to be endured, like *Jungle Girl* or anything with cowboys in it. Westerns were Les's least favorite. The kids all knew the good cartoons and serials from the bad; when Woody Woodpecker came on there was a general groaning across the theater, but everyone clapped when the Looney Tunes music began.

Yes, the movies were great fun for Les with one powerful exception: his brother.

Johnny was an incessant talker who refused to behave like a normal person; he drove Les crazy with his chatter before, during, and after the movie. All Les wanted to do was listen to the show he was watching, and instead he had to feel his brother's hot whispery breath in his ear and listen to his endless questions and commentary during the film.

Les decided to talk to Johnny before going to the theater one warm Saturday in April. Les didn't want to miss a moment of the serial; the four aviators were in Africa and had just discovered the professor and his daughter being held captive following the Black Hangman's assassination of an entire expedition. It was terrible and thrilling, and Johnny was going to ruin the whole experience with his constant talking.

Of course Johnny didn't understand when Les tried to bring up the subject. "What do you mean, I'm jabbering too much during the movies?" he asked, his expression hurt.

"I'm just having a good time. You hardly pay any attention to me anyway. I thought you liked going to the matinee with me!"

"I mean it, Johnny," Les insisted. "Please try to be quiet during the show. It is really hard for me to concentrate on the movie when you're jabbering in my ear the whole time. I'm paying money to see the movie, not to listen to you. Why can't you just behave like everyone else?"

Les thought this conversation would take care of the matter. He looked forward to the movie all week; they were going to see *Edge of Darkness* with Errol Flynn. He even collected extra soda bottles to buy some candy for himself and Johnny during the show.

Unfortunately, Les had miscalculated in his approach to Johnny.

Johnny was crushed by Les's request that he stay quiet. In the whole world, Les was the only person who paid attention to Johnny at all. If Les didn't want Johnny talking to him anymore, who was left? It didn't take very long for Johnny's hurt to turn into anger, and for anger to turn into a plan for getting even.

Johnny knew *exactly* which buttons to push.

It began on the bus. Les and Johnny boarded and moved to one of the rear seats, where they could look out the window and study the other passengers unnoticed. With a sly look at his brother, Johnny started in. "Am I allowed to talk to you on the bus, Les, or should I stop now?" he asked, the picture of innocence.

"Knock it off, Johnny," Les said, irritated. "You know I'm only talking about during the show."

"Okay," Johnny said. "I just wanted to be clear about the

new rules. I have a lot to say, you know. Maybe I'll try to get it all out of my system right now."

"There *are* limits," Les said, giving his brother a warning look.

"Oh, sure," Johnny said. "But maybe I should find them out before we get to the theater. How about if I sing? I was thinking the other day about that movie *Yankee Doodle Dandy* and remembering some of those tunes Cagney sang. I might like to practice."

Les shuddered, which was all the incentive Johnny needed. He opened his mouth and began to sing "You're a Grand Old Flag" with vigor. People turned and looked, but nobody asked Johnny to be quiet. So he sang louder.

Embarrassed, Les did the only thing he could. He got up and moved. He marched all the way up to the front of the bus, where he sat down and tried to pretend he didn't know Johnny.

But no sooner had Lester reached his new seat than Johnny stopped singing and began to shout. "HEY, LES," Johnny called, his voice shrill over the engine. "WHY ARE YOU SITTING ALL THE WAY UP THERE? DON'T YOU WANT TO SIT BY ME ANYMORE? LES?"

The bus driver eyed Johnny in the mirror, but said nothing. In fact, Les could have sworn he saw the driver smile.

Les closed his eyes and wished he could vanish into thin air. He rode just like that all the way to the Circle Theatre, trying but failing not to hear his brother as he talked, sang, and exclaimed loudly the entire time. It was humiliating.

When they arrived at the theater, Les got off the bus quickly and went into the building by himself. He quickly paid for his ticket and his candy and hustled into a seat at one side of the theater, where he hunched down and tried to hide.

Sadly, these efforts were in vain. Within just minutes of taking his seat, he heard Johnny's voice calling through the theater. "LES? LES! WHERE ARE YOU? I CAN'T SEE YOU," Johnny said in a penetrating tone that Les was certain could have woken the dead. "HAS ANYONE HERE SEEN MY BROTHER, LESTER MACGREGOR? LES!!!"

Les hunched down farther, but it was too late. Johnny had spotted him from the back of the theater and came over to sit down. "HERE YOU ARE, LES," Johnny said loudly. "I ALMOST DIDN'T SEE YOU. I'LL JUST SIT DOWN RIGHT HERE."

Les groaned as his brother made himself comfortable in the next seat. Shooting Johnny a dark glance, Les said, "You have made your point. Can you please stop? I have been looking forward to this show all week."

"STOP WHAT?" Johnny said.

"Stop all your yelling and singing and being embarrassing," Les hissed back. "I want to listen to the movie, not to you. You're irritating me and everyone else around you. Please, just behave like everybody else."

"OH, SURE, LES," Johnny said. "I'LL STOP EMBARRASSING YOU RIGHT NOW. SO SORRY!"

For the next few minutes, the theater was again quiet except for the low hum of whispered conversation and people taking their seats. Les began to relax into his seat and look forward to the show once more. The theater lights dimmed and the show started. Johnny behaved himself well until the newsreel began; then he suddenly seemed to remember that he had candy. He started fiddling loudly with the cellophane wrappers, which squeaked and crinkled abundantly under the best of circumstances. And Johnny was deliberately making the noise worse. He rubbed the cellophane between his fingers with glee, making an annoying racket for everyone who sat around him. Les shushed him and two of the kids sitting in front of Johnny turned around to glare.

But Johnny didn't stop. He smiled cheerfully at the kids in front of him and continued rattling his wrappers as if there were no problem at all in the world. So Les got up and moved. He left his seat and went clear across the aisle to another place.

"WHERE ARE YOU GOING, LES?" Johnny asked, somehow loud and plaintive at the same time. An usher came down the aisle and told Johnny that if he wasn't quiet he would be asked to leave the theater, and the show was quiet after that. Les stayed in his new seat and for the first time in his memory was able to watch a movie in peace.

★

"I'd like you to meet my family," James said to Mary Jane one sunny afternoon after school. He was walking her home after a yearbook staff meeting, and the bright sky was just beginning to think about settling into an evening calm.

"Are you sure?" she asked.

"Absolutely," he said. "I was thinking about dinner this Friday. I know you won't go to the dance with me, but it would be a friendly thing to do, right? As an alternative?"

Mary Jane considered it. "All right," she said. "If it's all right with your mother."

James reached over and squeezed her hand. "I'm sure she'll be delighted," he said.

He talked to Mother and Grandma Barney that evening, and they agreed that it would be nice to meet James's new friend. They couldn't do the kind of dinner they liked to, with the rationing of good meat, but they could put together something special, Grandma Barney thought. Mother was interested in bringing out her china, and so it was settled.

On Friday James brought Mary Jane up the front steps just before dinner. Mother and Dad stood stiffly in the foyer, greeting them and obviously trying to be the picture of happy, welcoming parents. James was relieved by their obvious efforts to be gracious and gave Mother a pat on the shoulder as they passed through to the front room. Mary Jane had brought a pie for dessert and she carried it back into the kitchen with Mother.

James breathed a sigh of relief. So far, so good. He could see that Mother had been drinking, but so far she was behaving well.

But it was not to last.

Once in the kitchen, Mother introduced Mary Jane to Grandma Barney and then poured herself a glass of wine. "Would you like one too?" she asked Mary Jane.

"Oh, no; I don't drink," Mary Jane said. Grandma Barney handed Mary Jane a spoon and asked her to stir the potatoes. Mother sat down on a high stool and lit a cigarette. She seemed to study Mary Jane for a long minute, and then she spoke.

"Well, I must say, you're not what I expected," Mother said. "All the other girls James brings home with him are much prettier."

Grandma Barney exclaimed, "My word!" and shot a warning glare at her daughter-in-law.

Mary Jane's face flamed, but her voice was steady.

"I don't mind," she said. "I know the kinds of girls James usually takes around. James and I are just friends."

"I see," said Mother. Her cigarette had burned down some, and there was a long ash hanging off the end of it. Mary Jane observed the ash and waited for Mother to flick it off into a nearby ashtray before it fell and burned something. But Mother didn't. She drew another puff from the cigarette and watched the ash get even longer. She seemed to enjoy Mary Jane's discomfort.

Mary Jane had to battle the urge to walk over and flick the ash off the cigarette herself. Instead she stood firm and stirred the potatoes.

"I must say, it does make a lady feel her age when she is being introduced to one of her son's … friends," Mother said slowly. "I'm accustomed to being the only female in the house—besides my mother-in-law, of course, who hardly counts—and this is an entirely new experience for me."

"But I thought you just said that James brought lots of pretty girls around," Mary Jane said.

"Oh, yes; well," Mother mumbled and said something in a voice so low that Mary Jane couldn't hear it. The girl decided not to ask Mother to repeat herself. Perhaps it was better not to know.

Grandma Barney came and took up the potatoes, giving Mary Jane a reason to begin carrying dishes into the dining room. Very soon the entire family was sitting around the great dining room table and dinner was served. Mary Jane knew Charlie from school, but this was the first time she'd met Les and Johnny. She answered the family's questions and listened carefully as they retold and laughed over their stories.

The wine flowed heavily during dinner. At one point, Mary Jane thought she felt Dad's hand on her knee, but she couldn't be sure. She carefully crossed her legs in the other direction and turned toward James, just in case. James smiled at her and Mother's eyes narrowed. She took a healthy sip of her wine and spoke. "I was quite the looker in my day, you know," she said. "Beauty really is something to be prized, wouldn't you agree?"

Mary Jane smiled uncomfortably. "Certainly," she said.

"Oh, how I recall those days," Mother said. "Dark hair... dark, perfect eyes... red lips—the kind of looks that make a man stand up and take notice. Not those pale, ghostly looks that make you wonder if a girl is there or not. No, sir."

Mary Jane tried to cover her shock. "Perhaps I'll go into the kitchen and fetch the pie," she said.

"No, that's all right," said Mother. "Nobody here really wants the pie. It was nice of you to bring it, but—truly—we're all just stuffed from that remarkable dinner I just cooked."

Grandma Barney made a choking sound.

Mary Jane was torn. She wanted to be a gracious guest, but she was fairly certain it was all right to bend the rules of etiquette when one's hostess was so awful.

"Do you know, I believe I'm needed at home," Mary Jane said, standing. "I certainly do appreciate the meal *you* cooked, Mrs. Barney. And of course I am grateful for your hospitality, but I really must be going."

"So soon?" Mother said. "Why, the evening's only just beginning. You are an awfully serious girl, aren't you? Don't you ever have fun?"

"I do like to have fun," Mary Jane said. "That's why I am not staying here."

James stood, and put his hand on Mary Jane's elbow. "I'll walk with you," he said. He took Mary Jane to the door, slipped her coat over her shoulders, and went with her into the night air.

"I'm sorry," he said.

"Don't be," Mary Jane answered. "It is not your fault. Your mother seems… well, she seems jealous. I'm sorry for her. And I'm sorry for you, if that's what your home is like."

James was quiet for a long time. Finally he took her hand. "Are we still friends?" he asked.

"Better than ever," Mary Jane said, squeezing his hand with her own. "Before you ask, though… no, I will not go on a date with you. But I do like you."

They walked the rest of the distance in companionable silence. When they reached Mary Jane's front door, she turned suddenly and took hold of James's lapel. He stood in stunned silence as she stood up on tiptoe and gave him a soft, lingering kiss. She turned wordlessly and dashed into the house before he could say a single word.

When James returned home a few minutes later, Grandma Barney was sitting alone at the dining room table. "I sure do like that girl," she said. "You'd better put a ring on her finger before you leave this spring."

James gave Grandma Barney a kiss and went to find his mother. She was sitting on the back stoop with a freshly opened bottle of wine at her side. He sat down next to her and said, "Quite a display you made, I'd say."

Mother was silent.

"In case you were wondering, Mary Jane is fine," James went on. "But I'm not. Not really. I have no idea what that was all about, but I don't ever want to hear that again."

James paused and looked up at the sky. "I know you have a lot of expectations of me," he said. "I have knocked myself out trying to please you, Dad, and everyone else my whole life long. It's been really hard sometimes to carry the weight of those expectations."

Mother turned to look at him, and James saw in the dim porch light that the dark eyes that were once so "perfect" were red-rimmed and tired. She looked old and worn and weak, and he was tempted to let her off the hook. But he didn't.

"It's time I started pleasing myself once in a while," James said. "And Mary Jane pleases me very much. I want to marry her."

He heard Mother draw in a sharp breath.

"I'm *going* to marry her, Mother," he said. "You might as well start getting used to the idea now. And once Mary Jane is my wife I will not allow her to be treated the way she was tonight. Not ever."

Mother put her head into her hands. The cigarette fell to the ground and James stood up. "Good night," he said, and went into the house.

The door swung shut behind him and his footsteps died away. James never heard his mother's soft sob or the "I'm sorry" that drifted away on the evening breeze.

chapter seven

★

Grandma Barney had managed to imprison Charlie next to her in the front room. His hands were trapped within a coil of itchy wool yarn that she was balling up. She was silent, but every now and then she would look at Charlie sharply over the top of her glasses and give a small "Hmph."

Finally he bit. "What?" he asked sullenly. "Why do you keep doing that?"

"You should learn to show respect to your elders," Grandma Barney said. "You have a chip on your shoulder a mile wide and someday someone is going to knock it off for you."

"What does that even mean?" Charlie muttered beneath his breath. "That's dumb."

Grandma Barney swooped in. "What does it even *mean*?" she asked incredulously. "It's a common expression. Don't you know how it started?"

Charlie sneered. "Don't you know how it started?" he mimicked in a high falsetto. "No, I don't know how it started."

"First of all you can end the insolence," Grandma Barney said sternly. "You are not proving anything to me, and I'll have your father take you to the woodshed so fast your head will spin. You will show respect to your elders, young man."

With that she gave a harsh tug on the yarn and Charlie got a little burn on the sides of his fingers. "Ow!" he protested.

"That's the very least of what you have coming to you," she said. "Now, as for the other. In the old days, when a boy wanted to have a fight, he would put a chip of wood on his shoulder and dare another person to knock it off. So nowadays, when someone is angry, they say he has a chip on his shoulder and is daring someone—anyone—to take him on. You, my boy, have the largest chip I've ever seen on anyone besides myself."

"Yourself?" Charlie asked warily.

"You think I got this old without a few bad days?" Grandma Barney said. "Why, I could tell you stories that would curl your hair. I wasn't always the sunny, cheerful person you see before you now."

Charlie laughed without meaning to. Grandma Barney, cheerful?

She peered at him. "You might be wise to take a lesson from me, young man," she said.

"How?" Charlie asked. "By smiling at everybody and giving out hugs?"

"No," Grandma Barney said. "There are ways of being kind without seeming like it. I am often kind, you know, though I do have my fun."

"How are you kind?" Charlie asked.

"Why do you think I am here?" Grandma Barney asked. "I'll tell you a little secret. It's not because I want to be."

Charlie was puzzled.

"Never mind," Grandma Barney said. "You don't need to be burdened with the weight of everything around you, not at your age. Suffice it to say that my presence here has more to do with you than with me."

"You've certainly been running the household," Charlie said.

"Yes, I have," Grandma Barney replied. "And that is not my preference, let me tell you."

She sniffed for good measure, then paused to wind her yarn. "Charlie, my boy, I see more of myself in you than in any one of the other boys around here. You have spunk. You are simply in want of a way to channel it. A brisk temper, used rightly, is not necessarily bad. You just have to figure out how to take your energy and make it work for you rather than against you. Just like that girl James brought home last night. She knows how to channel her spunk."

Charlie was silent.

"Old-lady advice is not necessarily bad advice, you know," Grandma Barney continued. "Sometimes a life thoroughly lived can provide something of value. We'll talk more again later, my boy, when that chip on your shoulder is smaller and you're ready to listen."

Unfortunately for Charlie, his grandmother's words were all too soon forgotten. There were too many problems to be upset about. The unfairness and injustice in his life kept him angry and sullen for days. His teachers were stupid. His parents were awful. His friends—well, all right, the kids he knew but didn't really associate with—were not worth the powder to blow them up.

Charlie went through his school days with a sneer on his face. Perhaps as a result, nobody really reached out to him. Oh, sure, there was the occasional teacher who knew James and would greet Charlie with a hopeful expression. But within minutes of meeting Charlie that hope died and was replaced with wary reticence. Charlie's grades were bad and his days were long stretches of loneliness punctuated by hostility and disappointment.

Then, one day, there was Larry Phelps. Larry had moved to Kenmore from Cleveland in December, and his class schedule was still working itself out. That bright Thursday in April, he was suddenly seated next to Charlie in science class. Charlie greeted him with his customary scowl and was disappointed when Larry smiled back.

Mr. Norman was preparing to demonstrate the principle of electrostatics. He had set up a Bakelite rod and was going to rub a piece of fur against it. Once this was done, the rod would take on an electrical charge. When it was touched to the knob at the top of an electroscope, the tiny metal leaves at the base of the instrument would separate.

Charlie's mind was already wandering when he suddenly noticed the piece of fur Mr. Norman was using. It was gray and had the undeniable markings of… a tabby cat?

Mr. Norman was using cat fur? Where had he gotten it?

Next to Charlie, Larry gasped. "Do you see that?" he asked. "It's a cat!"

The boy in front of them turned. "My brother had Mr. Norman last year," he said. "He says Mr. Norman gets new pieces of fur all the time, and they're all cats! His neighbors can't keep track of their pets."

Larry and Charlie were horrified. Larry giggled awkwardly and elbowed Charlie in the ribs. Mr. Norman cleared his throat noisily and said, "Could we all return our attention to the demonstration in progress, please?"

Charlie sighed and crossed his arms. He spent the rest of the class obstinately refusing to take notes and rolling his eyes at everything Mr. Norman said or did. The teacher was obviously frustrated, but as he was quite accustomed to Charlie's behavior, he said nothing.

Larry caught up with Charlie afterward. "I'm going to the five-and-dime for a soda," Larry said. "Want to come?"

"No, thanks," Charlie said. "I've got to get home."

"I'll walk with you," Larry said. Charlie shrugged. "It's your choice," he replied, and started toward the street.

Larry kept up. "Where do you live?" he asked Charlie.

"Just over on St. James," Charlie answered.

"Oh, okay," Larry said, undaunted. "I'm on Delevan."

Charlie grunted and they walked on. Larry tried a few more times to start conversations, but Charlie was not interested. He didn't care about having friends at school.

Just then they came to the corner of Elmwood and Delevan and Larry gasped. Up ahead, Charlie could see Red Bartlett and Bernie Klein from his neighborhood giving a hard time to a little kid with braces on his legs. The boy was small and seemed to be having some difficulty with the metal-and-leather contraptions; he was crying as the bigger boys called, "Gimp! Gimp! Cry-baby gimp!"

"That's my little brother, Ray," Larry breathed. He seemed unable to believe his eyes. "He's only in kindergarten; what are they doing?"

Charlie, whose memories of his own back brace were still fresh, felt all the force of his temper rising in him. Those boys had no business messing with a little kid like that.

Before he knew what he was doing, Charlie had flung his books down on the grass and was running with a loud yell toward Red and Bernie. He smashed into the pair like a tornado, and the three of them went down onto the pavement hard. "Leave that kid alone!" Charlie shouted. "You rotten, stupid boys!"

The next few moments were a blur of punches, rolls, scuffles and even a few curse words. It might have been two minutes or ten; Charlie was never able to precisely recall what happened. In one instant he was running and yelling, and in the next he was staring at Red and Bernie as they lay on the ground beaten, bloody, and winded. Larry had come over to comfort his younger brother and they both now stared at Charlie, who was panting with exertion and fury.

Charlie had never felt better in all his life. All of his pent-up anger and resentment had exploded out of him at the sight of that single injustice, and for once he was able to do something about it. He had seen a problem and instead of standing by with curled-up fists and mute rage, he had stepped in and solved it. It was incredible.

Ray's lower lip trembled and his eyelashes were spiky with tears. Larry held his arm around the little boy as he spoke to Charlie. "Thanks," he said. "I don't know why you did that for us, but I'm real glad you did."

"Me too," Charlie said with a half smile.

"Well, I ain't," Red said, sitting up. "This is one more reason I don't like anybody named MacGregor. You and your brothers are going to pay for this."

"Nobody's going to pay," Charlie said. "You come near me or my brothers, and you'll be sorry. I mean it. Same goes for Larry and Ray here; you'd better pick on somebody your own size."

And with that Charlie picked up his books and headed for home. For the first time in his life he felt like somebody's hero.

He wondered if that's what Grandma Barney had meant about using your temper in a good way. Even if not, it sure felt good.

★

The evening was quiet in the attic where Johnny and Les slept. Johnny was playing with little metal soldiers on his bed and wondering where his brother was; the room was quiet and there were no telltale sounds emanating from the secret laboratory. The only noises to be heard were Adam's soft purring and the scudding sound effects Johnny made as his Army men battled and fell. The window was open and a gentle breeze blew the soft white curtains with fresh twilight air.

All of a sudden Johnny began to hear low creaking noises from the roof. What on earth—! He dropped his soldiers and flew over to the window to poke out his head. What he saw astonished him. There, balanced precariously on the copper eaves that ran around the whole house, was Les.

"What are you doing out there?" Johnny demanded.

Les seemed startled, then angry. "Don't sneak up on me like that," he said. "Don't you see I might fall?"

"You could fall anyway," Johnny said. "What are you doing?"

Les sighed with exasperation and continued toward the window. "Get out of the way," he said, slipping past Johnny and into the attic bedroom.

Once safely inside, Les said he was just doing an experiment. He had noticed the copper eaves ran around the entire perimeter of the roof and he wondered if he could walk on them. He also had some wires to put out there, for a project he was working on in his laboratory.

Johnny was impressed. "Can I do it too?" he asked.

"Absolutely not," Les said. "It's dangerous and you're not old enough."

"But I'm lighter than you; it's not so bad," Johnny said.

"No," Les said. "And quit asking. Don't bring it up again or I'll pound you."

"Okay," Johnny said, but there was a gleam in his eye that Les failed to notice.

★

Night fell across St. James Place and the house grew quieter. Johnny thought it had been a nice evening for once. Mother and Grandma Barney were in the front room with the radio; Dad was fixing himself a snack in the kitchen, and the boys were either finishing their homework or climbing into bed. The evening was warm and drowsy and comfortable.

Just as Johnny's eyes began to drift shut, the whole town was blasted with the sound of the air-raid siren. The sound was loud and long and punctuated only by Dad's staccato cursing in the kitchen. As air-raid warden for the neighborhood, he would have to abandon his snack and go out to make sure the neighbors were darkening their windows as they should. It was an important job, but Dad always said the air-raid drills were scheduled for the times he least wanted to go out for a walk.

Johnny came down the stairs and could see Mother and Grandma Barney working to hang the blackout curtains in the windows. The boys had already turned out their lights upstairs; Johnny had bumped into Charlie on his way down and noticed he was just as grumpy as Dad about the entire process. "Why do we have to do this?" Charlie was complaining to James. "The Lackawanna steel plant is all lit up for miles around anyway; it's not like our curtains make any difference to a bomber. Jeez."

James's soft chuckle was the only reply Johnny heard as he made his way down the hall.

The front door closed with a click as Dad left. Johnny tried to picture what Dad would do once he was out in the neighborhood; he wore an armband and a whistle, Johnny knew, and his job was to knock on doors and tell people when they needed to do a better job covering their windows. Nobody ever seemed to give Dad any static about it.

Johnny wondered what other families did during air-raid drills. He read sometimes that you were supposed to sit together in the cellar and sing and pray. Maybe some families did that. He imagined his neighbors making popcorn and swapping funny stories and enjoying one another's company during the air raid times. Maybe some families listened to the radio together while they waited for the air raid to be over.

He knew his family would just go to bed. Mother wouldn't like to do her needlework in the dim light of the single lamp they kept burning in the front room, and there were no lights on upstairs to do homework by. He could already hear Mother and Grandma Barney talking softly in the kitchen as they finished tidying up the remnants of Dad's abandoned snack.

It was late; there really was no reason to stay up, but for some reason Johnny wanted to. He wanted to pretend for a while that the MacGregors were just like all other families in America. It was a strange sensation for Johnny; he, who always wanted to be different, was—for the first time—interested in being ordinary.

He wondered what it would be like. He pictured himself in the middle of a Norman Rockwell painting, eating turkey or smiling or getting a haircut.

That's what it would be like when he finally came home to live with the Spencer Tracy family in Hollywood, California. His parents would serve big dinners every day, with turkey and trimmings, and they would cuddle Johnny in the evenings and read him long books that would be made into movies for him to star in. They would help him with his homework and come to his Scout meetings and take him on long vacations to the Grand Canyon.

Wouldn't that be something?

And so the MacGregor family passed the early hours between darkness and sleep. Dad walked the neighborhood, whistling tunelessly and looking for lights in the neighbors' windows. Mother and Grandma Barney were asleep.

James's eyes were open and he pondered in silence the work that would soon be required of him in the Army. Shooting, jumping out of planes, diving into battle—all of these tasks required a bravery he wasn't sure he had. There, in the quiet night of an air-raid drill, James for the first time acknowledged the difference between being dutiful and actually doing a duty. It chilled him, and made him wonder.

In the next bed, Charlie drifted in and out of a doze. It had been a long day but his spirit was easy. He had done something bad, but it had been done for a good reason. He liked good reasons. As he fell asleep, his dreaming mind asked a question about good things done for bad reasons too. Like James. His body jerked once, violently, and then he slept.

Up in the attic Johnny snored gently. But Les was awake, with big ideas on his mind. Today he'd worked hard in his secret laboratory and ran some wires up over the roof. The results would be tremendous. He'd followed the instructions in a library book and linked a receiver to the neighborhood phone line. Starting tomorrow he would be able to listen to all the calls he wanted.

For Les, even in wartime—even in a home that was itself war-torn—life was sometimes peaceful and good.

chapter eight

★

By mid-May, Kenmore was outdoors again. Ladies gossiped on front porches and children ran and played until the streetlights went off at night.

At least, some of the children did.

Les MacGregor was far more in tune with the gossip of the ladies than with the play of children. His telephone experiment was working beautifully; he had used an alligator clip and headphones to tap the household phone line and was now privy to the conversations of the party line that connected to his own home and those of his neighbors. He spent hours sitting in the cellar listening, and he now knew that Mrs. Wilkinson was not sure when to plant her tomatoes given the possibility of a late freeze, that Mr. Cohen's mother was coming to visit and that her daughter-in-law was not the LEAST pleased about it, thank you very much, and that the Kleins were worried about their boy in the Pacific.

Les was most startled and intrigued, however, by the information he learned about his own family on the phone.

It began one afternoon when he heard Grandma Barney pick up the phone after school. Grandma Barney? Who did she have to call? Les's father was an only child, and Grandma Barney had no other family that Les knew of. He was startled when he heard her ask for Springport, Michigan.

In a moment Les heard Nanny Harris pick up the phone.

Nanny was Les's other grandmother, and as far as he knew these two women had never spoken and had no reason to do so now.

"Esther," Grandma Barney began, her voice low. "It's me. Nettie."

Les was shocked. Why were they talking?

"Oh, I've been hoping to hear from you," Nanny said. "How is everything there?"

"Not very well," Grandma Barney—Nettie—said. "The boys are fine and I've got the household managed, but the drinking is no better. And my son is just as bad as your daughter—when he's here, that is. I'm worried about what's going to happen when James leaves in a month. I don't know that I can manage it then."

Les heard Nanny sigh. "I thought this might happen. I'm sorry you have had to cope with so much of this. It can't be easy for you."

"It's all right," Grandma Barney said. "But I'm worried about the younger ones. If the fighting gets any worse, I don't want them to see it. Can you help?"

"Of course," Nanny said instantly. "I'll call tonight and invite them all to spend the summer here with me in Springport. When school lets out make sure to put them on the train before James leaves. There's plenty of family here to help. Do you want me to send anyone to help you?"

There was more, but Les didn't hear any of it. Springport! For a whole summer! It felt like a dream come true.

Then Nanny said something that brought him crashing back to earth. "What if they won't part with the boys? James will be gone, and they'll feel so alone. They may not let the boys come."

Grandma Barney sighed. "You're right," she admitted. "But if they don't, the summer will be horrible. I shudder to think what they'll all go through. I'll have to think about this; it may be very difficult."

Les listened to them talk a few minutes more. When they hung up, he sat back and beamed. There was a light at the end of this long, dark tunnel with his family. His grandmothers were on the case, and even if they couldn't make it happen, he could. He had lots of time to plan and was ready to do whatever it took. He was going to Springport this summer one way or another.

★

While Les was eavesdropping in his secret laboratory, Johnny was preparing a daring experiment of his own.

Ever since Johnny saw Les come in the bedroom window he had been wanting to try walking around the entire roof himself. It seemed like such a great adventure, and if Les could do it then he could too.

Johnny opened the window and hoisted out a leg. He sat for a moment on the window ledge, feeling the cool spring air on his face, and enjoying as if for the first time the dizzying view of the entire neighborhood. Johnny wished he had a camera to photograph all the aerial views around the house.

Slowly, carefully, Johnny lifted his other leg over the sash and stood on the eaves. Now this was different. He suddenly felt very high and a little frightened. The roof was pitched back at such an angle that once he moved past the dormer he wouldn't be able to lean against it. He would have to balance with his arms out as he walked around the entire roof. This was not a promising prospect.

Suddenly the spring air felt cold to Johnny.

He kept moving nevertheless, inching his way sideways across the copper eaves until he was just past the edge of the dormer. Reaching out a hand, he found that if he bent just right, he could just barely touch his fingertips to the shingles of the pitched roof as he walked. It was unnerving, to say the least.

He paused.

He felt all funny, like he wasn't quite sure which way was up and which way was down. His heart began to pound in his chest and he struggled to breathe normally. He tried to right himself and found that he was more frightened than ever. The ground was very far away and it suddenly occurred to Johnny that if he fell he probably wouldn't survive.

At that thought Johnny's breath began to come in quicker gasps. This was definitely not good.

Then suddenly, when Johnny's fear was at its peak, the eaves beneath his feet groaned. His weight, standing there, was too much. And it didn't end there, not with a simple groan, like a creaking door or a bending branch, it was a *grooooaaaannnnn*… a sound that made Johnny listen for the inevitable break. He waited for a long moment, but nothing happened.

Johnny was done; he needed to get back through that window as soon as humanly possible.

He scrambled back and threw himself inside. How on earth had Les done that all the way around the whole house? His brother must have a death wish. Johnny sat trembling for at least fifteen minutes before he was able to calm himself. Never, never again.

★

James and Mary Jane sat together on her front porch swing. Her mother had brought them some lemonade and they were studying together for a history exam.

Mary Jane was reading a passage aloud, trying to justify one of her answers, when James suddenly halted the swing. She looked up and saw him gazing intently at her. "What is it?" she asked.

"Mary Jane," he began. "Will you go on a date with me?"

"Absolutely not," she replied. "You are way too full of yourself and I'm not your type. Forget it."

"Why do you say that?" James said. "Haven't I proven by now that I am a pretty nice fellow? We spend nearly all our free time together, and we have so much fun. Everyone thinks we're dating anyway."

"Sure, you're nice and we have fun," Mary Jane answered, as she shifted to face him. "But you're just a little *too* nice, I think, and a little too much fun. I'm not going to let you make me a member of the James MacGregor Heartbreak Club. You'll go off and find some other girl and I'll be alone with my miserable thoughts. No way! I like you, but I am one hundred percent *not* going to start dating you."

He smiled in the face of her laughter. "Well," he said. "If you won't go on a date with me, can I ask you something else?"

"You can ask," Mary Jane said. "But the answer to your next question will also probably be no."

"What do you think I'm going to ask?"

"You want me to make another pie for your mother, don't you?" she said, laughing. "Well, I won't."

James laughed too and looked at her for a long moment

before he reached into his pocket. "Actually, no," he said. "I haven't given up on getting you to date me yet. You've given me two reasons for your refusal: first, that I have a swelled head. I have a remedy for that."

He handed her a long needle. When she looked at him with a question in her violet eyes, he gestured toward it. "That's so you can prick me when I'm all puffed up and let the hot air out. Now will you date me?"

She shook her head and he put his hand back into his pocket. "The other reason is that you think I'm going to get tired of you and leave you heartbroken," he began. "There's only one way for me to assure you that won't happen."

He handed her a small red matchbox. Opening it, Mary Jane found a small tin ring, the kind that came in a box of Cracker Jack. "It's not much, but I don't have any money," he said. "Someday when we're older and wealthy, I promise to replace it with a real diamond, the kind you deserve."

Mary Jane gasped. "James!" she cried.

"I spoke to your parents last night," he said, sliding off the porch swing and dropping to one knee. "Mary Jane, you must know how much I love you. You are my very best friend. Will you marry me?"

Mary Jane felt tears fill her eyes. How was it possible that someone like James MacGregor should notice her, should want to be with her forever? She loved him so well, not because of his looks and achievements and style, but in spite of them. She loved the boy *inside,* the one who felt all these surface pretenses were necessary to protect his vulnerable heart. And now he was offering his vulnerable heart to her.

"Oh, yes!" she said, tears in her eyes. "Yes, of course I will!"

James stood and caught her in his embrace. "Good," he said. "And then, when we're married, will you *then* let me take you out on a date?"

★

As expected, Grandma Barney was thrilled by the news of James's engagement to Mary Jane. "It's about time someone took my advice," she said, wrapping him in a hug.

The reactions James got from Mother and Dad, however, were more difficult to understand. Upon hearing the news, Mother burst into noisy tears and left the room. Dad gave James a long look, put his arm around him, and led him to the front room.

"Are you sure this is what you want?" Dad asked. "She's not forcing you into it?"

"Why would you think that?" James asked. "Of course not."

"Is she pregnant?"

"What! No," James said, shocked. "Dad, Mary Jane is a nice girl. Why would you think that?"

"I just had to ask," Dad said. "Now let me say this—you can still get out of this if you want to."

"Dad, I'm the one who proposed," James said. "I *want* to marry her."

"Well, that's fine … that's fine," Dad said. "Now, there are a few things you need to know about being married. You can still have your fun; you just need to be a lot more careful."

James's mouth fell open. "What are you talking about?"

"You know," Dad said. "You can still find a girl and take her out on the side; you just need to make sure nobody sees you and that Mary Jane doesn't find out."

"Dad," James said, his voice cracking. "Is this what you do?"

Dad shook his head as if James were a dimwit. “It’s what most men do,” he said. “That’s what I’m trying to point out to you, son. You are so young; you have no idea what’s in front of you. One day you’ll look around and find yourself in a beat-up old house, trapped in a dead-end job, with a drunk, obnoxious wife and too many kids. You’ll want to escape, and I’m telling you there are ways, if you’re careful.”

James tasted bile in his mouth. “Are *you* careful?”

“You bet I am,” Dad said. “I’m no dummy. You get but one shot at life, son, and you’d better get it right. I’ve made mistakes, but I still find ways of making it all worthwhile.”

And with that, the boy who wanted nothing more than to please his parents and meet all the expectations placed upon him—the boy who tried to be perfect and good and worthy—simply vanished. James felt his heart rending in his chest and knew he would never be the same again. He stood without a word and walked away from his father, the man who ran to the bar or racetrack to avoid raising his own sons. He walked away from the blind innocence of his youth and stepped into a future that would be entirely of his own making.

Just a few weeks remained before he left for basic training. In those weeks he would spend every moment he could with Mary Jane. At this point she was his family. She would be the good and worthy hope that would see him through, and he would do whatever he could to deserve her.

A few days later, word came.

Les’s submission to *True Story* magazine had been rejected. According to the letter, the editors enjoyed the narrative but believed there was “some doubt as to the veracity of its content." In other words, they thought it might not be true.

"How should they know whether it was true or not?" Les demanded of Johnny. "It could very well BE true. Shouldn't they send a fact checker or something? They can't just speculate and decide offhand something isn't true before they check it out first."

"But if they did check it out, wouldn't they find out it wasn't true?" Johnny asked.

"That's not the point," Les argued. "The point is they DIDN'T check it out, so they don't know. They have no basis to reject this story. It's a good story and it very well COULD be true."

"But it isn't true," Johnny said again.

"But that's not the point," Les repeated.

Johnny was quiet while Les paced back and forth across the attic. The truth was, he wasn't sure he understood the argument they were having.

"Maybe you could submit the story someplace else," Johnny said. "Is there a *Not-True Story* magazine?"

Les turned in disgust and began to move aside the National Geographic map that covered his laboratory. Sometimes Johnny could be such an idiot.

Inside the narrow, low-ceilinged space, Les contemplated his phone equipment. He didn't feel like eavesdropping today; the fact was he didn't feel much like anything since overhearing his grandmothers' conversation the other day. Now that he had news on his true/not true story, his decision was all but made. He would run away again and this time he would bring Johnny with him. He couldn't leave his young brother here, not after hearing what his grandmothers had said on the phone.

He began to fiddle with his lab equipment. He had some planning to do, but it was easier for him to think while he was working on something.

Les had built a little short-wave radio transmitter and antenna and was experimenting with both. He was having some trouble getting them to work properly, but he felt he was close to a solution. When he was finished—oh boy!—he would be able to communicate with nearly anyone. He might even be a spy, relaying information from Free France or other military or liberation groups. The notion was so exciting. He might not be able to go and fight yet, but he could do his work at home using the tools he had at his disposal.

Les spent the remainder of the afternoon fixing, adjusting, and testing. By the end of the day he had the system up and running.

And best of all, he had a plan for getting himself and Johnny to Springport.

★

There was no time for a wedding before James was to report for duty. He was despondent about leaving Mary Jane, but there was nothing to be done about it. She was willing to wait until he came home safely from the war. They promised to write as often as they could. "It will be just like passing notes in history class," Mary Jane said.

James was feeling better about going into the Army since he realized that about fifteen of his classmates were going too. They would all be leaving together on the train for basic training at Fort Riley the day after graduation. It somehow made it easier to know that he would be with friends he knew; whatever he did or wherever he went, he wouldn't be alone.

That made a big difference.

As for his fears, he managed to tamp them down with the notion that he would not be doing the same duties as all the other boys. James was going to work hard to get into pilot school. He would fly the plane, not jump out of it, and nobody would ever catch him down in a foxhole. He stood a much better chance of surviving this war as a pilot than he would if he were any old Joe stuck in the trenches.

And best of all, he wouldn't be home anymore. His parents were driving him crazy these days. His mother was always either drinking or crying, and his dad seemed to have detached himself entirely from the house, either with work, gambling, or whatever else it was he did. James hardly saw his brothers.

His last day at work was the Saturday before graduation. The men's store was busy, with fathers and sons coming in for last-minute purchases and alterations before the big day. James was constantly changing the stock and ringing up customers while Mr. Kraus did alterations. James didn't have much time to think or be sad about leaving his job, so when his shift finally ended it seemed something of a surprise to him.

Mr. Kraus came over to the counter, where James was standing, and leaned against one elbow. His broad forehead was furrowed into a frown. "My boy," he said. "I'm going to miss you."

James felt an unexpected tightening in his throat. "I'll miss you too, sir," he said. "I've enjoyed working for you."

"You are without a doubt one of the hardest workers I have ever had here at the store," Mr. Kraus continued. "You've done everything I've asked, whether it's cleaning a toilet or selling a suit, and you've never once complained. I admire that you care about this business as much as I do. I know you have been a busy young man, with all your school activities and so forth, but you've never failed to show up here and do your best. You have a bright future ahead of you, son."

Although he tried to smile, James couldn't. To cover his embarrassment, he fumbled in his pocket for the store key he carried. "Here you are, sir," he said, handing it over.

"Thank you," said Mr. Kraus. "And now I have something for you." The older man gave James a small pin, an envelope, and a piece of paper. On the paper, it read "Special Honorary Member, Kenmore Lions Club."

"What's this?" James asked.

"You've done a lot for our town," Mr. Kraus said. "The men of our community thought it was only right to give you a special membership and a gift to go with it. That envelope has fifty dollars inside for you to use. We've never given an award before, but you're a very unusual young person."

"I'm not so different," James said. "We're all doing what we can, with the war on. Are you sure about this?"

Mr. Kraus smiled and put his hand on James's shoulder. "Yes, of course we are," he said. "We know you're going to go far in this life, and we hope you remember us along the way."

★

"Fifty dollars!" Charlie exclaimed in disgust when he heard the news. The ominous specters of jealousy and anger once again reared their ugly heads in his soul, and he felt like smashing something.

"Yes, isn't it great?" James was holding his Lions Club pin and contemplating what to do with his certificate. He lay back on his bed, crossing his legs and beaming. "I can't believe they really did it."

"Me either," Charlie snorted. "You've really got everyone snowed, haven't you?"

"How do you mean?" James asked sharply. "I *have* worked hard. Don't you think I've earned this?"

"You've worked hard, all right, but not for anybody other than yourself," Charlie said. "You're not like all those other people who do what they do to help the war effort or to help improve the community. You just want to make yourself feel like you're something special. Your swelled head is bigger than ever, and I'm sick of it."

"Now, wait a minute," James said. "I won't deny that I get something out of all this too, but I'm still doing the right thing. That's better than getting in fights and earning bad grades all the time."

"Bad things for good reasons, good things for bad reasons," Charlie mumbled to himself. "That's what it's all about, I guess."

James was quiet for a minute, then he sat up. "You know, Charlie," he said, his voice taking on a new tone. "When I'm gone, life around here can be different for you. You have a chance to start fresh too."

Charlie snorted.

James tried again. "I'm serious," he said. "I know I've been a shadow over you all these years. When I'm gone, they'll be looking to you. You need to be ready to show them what you're made of. Assuming, of course, that what you're made of is *not* piss and vinegar."

Sitting down on the edge of the bed, James sought Charlie's gaze. "Look, I have recently realized that you are right to be angry, in lots of ways," he said quietly, in a voice that was close to a whisper. "There are lots of problems in our house that are terrible, and neither you nor I deserve to be part of them. I'm getting out, and I'm moving on with Mary Jane. You need to find something to hang on to, just like I have."

"What is there?" Charlie asked. "You show it to me and I'm on my way. But right now, I see nothing."

I see nothing.

Every kid up and down St. James Place stopped what he was doing and stared as the shiny black automobile stopped in front of the MacGregor house. Two men in dark suits stepped out and looked around for a moment before walking up and ringing the bell.

Lester, who had spent much of the morning hiding in his secret spot beneath the front porch, happened to be in the kitchen getting a drink of water when the men came. Johnny came wheeling in the kitchen door, all flushed face and eager whispers, and both boys peered out across the hall. They watched as the men showed official-looking badges to Mother, who was shaking her head and frowning.

After a moment she invited them in and went to the telephone. The boys heard her ask for Dad in an anxious, whispery voice. When she went back to the front room, where the men were sitting, she told them her husband would be home shortly and offered them a glass of lemonade. Both men accepted, as it was an unusually warm day, and together they waited for Dad to get home.

Johnny and Les were flabbergasted. What was this? They were silent, scarcely daring to breathe, as the men made chitchat with Mother and passed the time.

Nearly a half hour later (the longest half hour in human history, Les thought) Dad strode in the door and sat down. He took off his hat and asked to see the men's identification again.

When he caught sight of the badges, Johnny gasped. The men were from the Federal Bureau of Investigation. The FBI! Honest to gosh G-Men!! *This is it*, he thought. *They're on to the ration stamp scheme! I'm finally going to live with Spencer Tracy!!*

The men began to speak, their voices low. Les and Johnny watched as their parents shook their heads, seemed confused, and made denials. *They're in so much trouble*, Johnny thought. *Look at them plead… I wonder if they'll have to go in to the pokey…*

"But, sir," Dad was saying. "Please be reasonable. You may check with my employer."

But the men kept talking and soon James was called home from school. Les and Johnny could hear little, but they did hear James protesting about his service to the country, how he didn't know anything about the issues they were raising, and so forth. They looked all over James's service papers and asked lots of questions.

Eventually one of the men stood and announced he would be inspecting the house. He left the room and, with Mother hard on his heels, began looking all along the walls and baseboards where the phone lines ran. The pair of them clumped heavily down the basement stairs.

Dad was pacing up and down one side of the room,

muttering to himself. One of the men came over and talked with him in a low voice. They went back to the couch and reviewed some papers that the man had in his briefcase.

There were more footsteps on the basement stairs, and the second man returned to the living room with Mother. He was holding a set of alligator clips and a pair of headphones in his hands. Suddenly Dad stood up and gave a loud shout. "LESTER!!" His voice ricocheted against the plaster, startling both Johnny and Les as they listened in the hallway.

Les calmed himself and tiptoed back into the kitchen. He came out again with a normal gait, looking for all the world like he hadn't just been standing in the hallway eavesdropping. "Yes, Dad?" he said, all innocence.

"Lester, these men are from the FBI," Dad began, his face red. "They have quite a story to tell us. They say that someone in our home has been tapping the neighborhood phone lines. Would you happen to know anything about this?"

"Well," Les began. He really couldn't see any way out of the situation. "Um…" his brain worked frantically.

"Les," Dad said again, sternly. "James is never here, Charlie doesn't have the patience, and Johnny is too young. I know it's not me, or Mother, or Grandma Barney, so this leaves you. I'd suggest you start talking. What do you know about this?"

Les sighed, his shoulders slumping. "Yes, I've been doing some experiments," he finally said. "I'm sorry."

"Young man," one of the agents said. "There is a war on. We have to be very careful about all communications. You might have gotten yourself in very deep trouble. Very deep trouble indeed."

Les looked at his shoes. "What gave me away?" he asked.

"Low-quality carbon headphones," one of the agents said. "They drew power from the line. Every time you tuned in to listen, the power to the phone system fell off several volts. Dead giveaway, son."

"Do I have to go to jail?" Les asked.

"Of course not," the second agent said. "But we need to ensure that you cease and desist all unauthorized—er, that is to say—*extraordinary* communications from this home. Immediately."

Dad spoke up then. "Just because you are not going to prison does not mean you are going to skate free and clear on this, Lester," he said sternly. "You have cost these men and your mother and me a great deal of trouble today. I am going to think about your punishment this afternoon and we'll discuss it over dinner."

Les nodded and looked at the floor. "Yes, sir," he said.

"Go get your equipment," Dad said. Les turned and hurried through the hallway, nearly bumping into Johnny as he went.

"Well?" Johnny demanded in a harsh whisper as he followed Les up the stairs. "Aren't you going to tell them the rest?"

"What rest?" Les asked. "Isn't this enough?"

"About us kids and Grandma Barney and the ration stamps," Johnny said. "They need to know so I can go live with Spencer Tracy in Hollywood and be a major star of stage and screen."

Les stopped on the stairs. "You get stranger every day," he told his brother.

chapter nine

★

Dad decided that Les should be severely punished for his run-in with the law. "Your mother and I were thinking of sending you kids to Springport this summer," Dad said. "But not now. Instead, you'll stay home and help your mother and me with some projects around the house. I might even see about finding you a job at the plant this summer to keep you out of trouble."

Well, Les thought, *that settles it.* It was time for him to make a break for it. He was going to Springport one way or another; Johnny too.

Les was able to organize his escape the weekend of James's graduation. The whole family was in an uproar of activity between the events at school and getting James packed and ready to go on Monday. Les used his time to pack his rucksack with clothes and toothbrushes for both himself and Johnny. He contemplated bringing Grandma Barney in on his plan, since he knew she wanted him in Springport too, but decided against it. Too risky. It would have to wait.

Over and over, all weekend long, Les went over his plan. It seemed fairly foolproof as long as it could be executed well. And, more importantly, if Johnny cooperated. You could never tell what that kid was going to do.

The rest of the family seemed not to notice. Mother was beside herself anyway; she spent most of Saturday crying, drinking, and positioning the blue star that would hang in their window. Every family with a son in the service had a blue star, but to listen to Mother anyone would think that no other boy had ever gone to do his duty in the Army. Her sobs could be heard around the block, Les was sure.

Every now and then Grandma Barney would go into the kitchen and try to reason with Mother; these sessions usually ended in loud arguments. At one point the boys even heard glass breaking as a jelly jar smashed against the wall. Even Dad was helpless in the face of such anguish.

Mother was not even able to pull herself together enough to attend James's graduation ceremony. Dad and Grandma Barney went on their own and reported it to be a very fine service. There were lots of boys getting ready to leave on tomorrow's train with James, so there was a tinge of sadness everywhere, but everyone was very pleased and proud of all that James and his classmates had accomplished.

After the ceremony, James and Mary Jane went out for the evening and Les committed one of the great shameful acts of his life. He stole into James's bedroom and rummaged through his brother's drawers until he located the fifty-dollar gift from the Kenmore Lions Club. The money was in a tin box half-hidden in a dresser drawer. Les felt really sorry about taking it, but he had written a note that he placed in the box and closed into the drawer. It read,

Dear James,

I am borrowing your $50 because it is very important for me and Johnny to get to Nanny and Grandad's in Springport as fast as we can. I promise to repay it soon. If you find this, please don't tell anyone. Good luck in the Army and come home safe.

Love,
Les

Les hated taking his brother's money, but there was no way he could trade in enough soda bottles to buy two train tickets by tomorrow. So there it was. Now all he had to do was make his final preparations.

Dear Grandma Barney,

Johnny and I are going to take the train to Springport. I know you understand why. I will make sure to have Nanny call you when we get there. Please don't let anyone try to follow us. We will be just fine.

You have been very kind to our family and we are glad you have been here. Take good care of everyone and we'll be in touch.

Love,
Les

★

Dear Dad and Mother,

I know you are upset with me over the FBI coming to the house. I am very sorry about that. I am also sorry if I cause you any more upsets because I am running away again, this time with Johnny. We are only going to Springport. We know you have a lot on your mind and think it might be good for everyone if we moved away.

Nanny will call you when we get there to let you know everything is okay.

Love,
Les

★

That evening, as twilight descended over the back yard, Les walked out with a shovel and started to dig under the mulberry bush. He thought to take the bones of the cat with him to Springport so he could reassemble them in peace.

Unfortunately, the cat was just the same. Only mushier.

Les shoveled the dirt back into the hole and considered the entire experiment just another of his failures. One he would soon be leaving behind for a new start, a new life.

★

Black Rock Station was a madhouse when the MacGregor family arrived on Monday. They all came, even Mother, to see James off into the Army.

Les had his rucksack with him; he'd told Mother it was full of stuff to occupy himself and Johnny on the way to the station and back. That idea, surprisingly enough, had come from James himself.

James had come to the attic room early that morning, before Johnny came up from breakfast, with Les's note in his hand. "You're running away?" James asked. "Going back to Springport?"

"Yes," Les had said, embarrassed.

"Good," James answered, surprising Les. "This house is no place for little kids. You get back to Nanny's and find something good again. You can pay me back when I get home."

"Thank you," Les said, his eyes filling with tears. He was surprised by his own feelings. "I'm going to miss you. Please do a good job and stay safe."

James reached over and tousled Les's red hair. "You got it, Squirt."

Now, just a few hours later, they all stood on a station platform filled with a sea of coats and uniforms and handkerchiefs. Lots of people were crying and hugging and shouting. The chaos was perfect for Les to make his getaway. Grabbing Johnny's hand, he darted through the crowd to the ticket counter. "Two tickets to Springport, Michigan," he panted. Johnny stared at him in wonderment.

The stationmaster frowned. "Where are your parents?" he asked.

Les gestured back to where Mother and Dad stood on the platform. James was watching and doing his best to keep them distracted. "Right there," he said. "They're putting my brother on the train for the Army, and they told us to come get these tickets for ourselves while they said good-bye. They're very sad and upset and want a minute alone with James."

The stationmaster looked around and saw Mother crying. "Yes, I can see," he said. "All right, here you are. Your destination is Jackson, Michigan, with one transfer in Toledo. You will have to get to Springport on your own. Now go find your parents."

Les nodded, took the tickets, and grabbed Johnny's hand. He turned and walked back as if he were going to join his parents on the platform, and then turned sharply and boarded another car.

"What are we DOING?" Johnny asked. "Are we running away?"

"You bet," Les said. "Now be quiet and don't bother me again until we're on the way. I want this to go right."

From the train window Les could see his family on the station platform. James looked smaller from here, and very nervous. His parents were reaching, embracing, and weeping, while Grandma Barney and Charlie stood slightly off to one side. Mary Jane waited until Mother and Dad were finished, then touched James's face softly with her hand.

The train whistle blew and James gave one last little hug and wave. He boarded the train on one of the front cars along with some of his buddies. Les could see his Mother crying into her handkerchief, Dad looking pained, and then suddenly the train lurched forward.

They were on their way. They had made it.

Part Two:

Grand Street

chapter ten

★

Les had imagined their arrival in Springport many different ways. Usually Nanny and Grandad and all the aunts and uncles were there with their arms outstretched and welcoming. "Les! Johnny!" they would call. "We're so glad you're here!" There would be too many kisses and pinched cheeks, Les knew, but other than that it would be a delightful return for the children.

Sometimes Les thought it would be quiet. He and Johnny would go to the front door of the house on Grand Street, knock, and be received with surprise and admiration. There would be a hot meal, lots of chatter, and then a warm pillow with a cozy kiss good night.

What Les had not imagined—and what he actually got—was Nanny tapping her foot at the station, her face grim. Les had always wondered about the phrase "madder than a wet hen." He could never before imagine what that might look like. When he saw Nanny at the station in Jackson that day, however, he knew.

Nanny was not a big lady—in fact, she was a little less than average height, and very thin—but that day she seemed enormous and scary. Her delicate face looked spitting mad, and Les and Johnny knew they were about to catch it.

"Do you boys have ANY idea how much trouble you have caused?" Nanny began. "Your poor family, at the station—

with no idea where you were. Your mother nearly died of fright, and with James going away just then too. Oh! How could you be so careless? So thoughtless? So cold?"

"But I thought you wanted us to come," Les began.

"Not like this, I didn't! You nearly worried us all to death. I've half a mind to give you a thrashing and then put you back on the train toward home, so your father can thrash you again," Nanny said. "Unbelievable. You just wait until Grandad gets hold of you. You'll be lucky to escape with your hides."

Nanny seemed to be unable to look at the boys. Where were their hugs? Their kisses?

"Now we are all trying to decide what to do with you," Nanny continued. "Nobody knows what's to be your punishment or how long you'll be here. Your parents are thinking over their mistakes and trying to adapt at home. We'll be talking on the phone tonight to see what they are planning."

"I'm sorry, Nanny," Les said. "We didn't mean to scare anyone, we just wanted to come here."

Nanny snorted. "Next time, use your heads," she said. "Anything could have happened to you on that train, and your folks were certain to miss you and be frightened. If you want to come here, next time why don't you ask first? We are all fit to be tied."

Les and Johnny wore hangdog expressions as they followed Nanny out of the station.

They were in for it.

★

Springport was as different from Kenmore as night was from day.

Springport was home to fewer than a thousand people. Its entire downtown area encompassed less than one square mile; the rest was farmland.

It was a place where everyone knew one another, where secrets were hard to keep, and where life (at least for the MacGregor boys) seemed simple and good.

Nanny and Grandad lived in a big white house near the heart of town. Once it had been very large, with a big second story and an attic, but there had been a fire and when they rebuilt they set the attic right on top of the downstairs and called it good. Nanny kept the home as clean as a whistle and it was always a pleasure for the boys to visit. Even now, when they knew they were in big trouble, being inside the walls of the house was like breathing a sigh of spring air after a very long winter.

They entered through the kitchen door, Nanny bustling with clucks and shuffles and calling for Grandad as the screen door slammed behind them. Les had been named for his grandfather, and he found it disconcerting to hear his own name called in reference to someone else. "Lester!" she called. "The boys are here!"

They could hear the *thunk* of Grandad's footsteps on the stairs, then in the hallway.

Grandad was a nice-looking gentleman when he wasn't angry. He had white hair and a mustache, and his eyes were big and friendly. He didn't smile much, but he had a kindly demeanor that told you he was in a good place most of the time.

Except, of course, right now.

"You boys really did it this time," he said. Grandad was a man of few words. "I don't think I have to tell you that this can never happen again," he said, his voice a low rumble.

"No, sir," each of the boys said.

"I've been giving this some thought," Grandad said. He gestured loosely at a thick brown razor strap that lay on the kitchen table. "Sure would hate to use that punishment, even if it is what your actions call for."

Johnny shuddered. He couldn't imagine his quiet Grandad wielding a razor strap. He started to say something, stopped, and ended up making a sound that was halfway between a groan and a squeal.

Grandad seemed not to notice. "What you boys did was completely irresponsible. It also showed disrespect for your parents," he continued. "So, since you evidently need to learn both responsibility and respect, I've decided you're going to get a heavy dose of both. You're going to work for me at the lumberyard this summer whenever I need you. Is that understood?"

"Yes, sir," both boys acknowledged, secretly relieved. The lumberyard was a great place to be; Grandad's solution hardly felt like punishment. However, they couldn't say so or else he might decide to use that razor strap after all.

Grandad was not finished. "And when Nanny needs something here, whether it's putting up the canning or sweeping the floor, your help will be expected. In fact, I don't even want her to need to ask. Is that clear?"

Both boys agreed willingly, and Grandad seemed satisfied. "I'd suggest you go inside to your room. Stay put until I tell you, and think seriously about what you have done."

Both boys eagerly made their escape. They walked quickly back into the house and up the stairs to the attic room they shared. It had been their mother's room when she was growing up in this same house.

Les kept waiting for Johnny to start in on him. After all, it had not been Johnny's idea to run away, but both boys were being punished for it. Now that they were alone, he figured Johnny would really light into him. But nothing happened.

Finally he broke the silence. "Les?" he said. "I'm really glad we're here."

"Me, too," Les replied with a smile. "It was worth it."

★

Back in Kenmore, Charlie was—for the first time in his life—enjoying the privilege of being an only child. He had his room all to himself, the younger boys weren't endlessly thumping in the attic overhead, and there was a soothing quiet throughout the house.

After the initial trauma of losing Les and Johnny at the station (not to mention James), Mother and Dad had settled into a series of quiet discussions in the kitchen. Grandma Barney was in there too, and Charlie had the impression that as the days passed some important decisions were being reached. He did his best to stay away, wanting to stretch the peace out as long as possible.

This state of affairs lasted for a whole week. Charlie felt as if the entire household were poised on the brink of something. It was like being in the silent eye of a hurricane, when you knew there were more storms on the way but weren't sure when to expect them.

Finally, after many long days of quiet talk and phone calls

to Springport, Grandma Barney came knocking at his door. She looked tired, and seemed to have aged considerably.

Her message to Charlie was short. "You're leaving for Springport tomorrow," she said. "Pack your suitcase."

★

James was not impressed by Kansas in general, or by Fort Riley in particular. It was flat and dull, and there was very little happening to distract him. His early weeks of Army life were a hectic blur of ongoing organization. After the initial business of his uniform, haircut, and paperwork, he and his fellow troops were organized into groups and barracks. The funny thing was that although James was accustomed to being a leader and organizer back in Kenmore, he was now the *organizee*. He didn't have to think too much, since people were always directing him and shouting orders. All he had to do now was respond, quickly and orderly and well.

It was actually pretty easy, when you came right down to it. At least, the mental part was.

The physical part of training was a completely different story.

The Army put James and his buddies through their paces, with push-ups, pull-ups, sit-ups, precision drills, running and shooting and scampering all across the tedious Kansas landscape. There was a crazy cross-country trail with deep trenches and high hurdles, which the boys had to race through daily, and an obstacle course with ropes and tractor tires and the like.

James ended each day with a ravenous appetite, a sincere need for sleep, and a sense of rapid physical change. His muscles were always sore, but they were growing bigger and it felt good to be in shape. He also enjoyed coming to know some of the other troops. His bunkmate was a tall, skinny boy from Alabama who snored loudly and told dirty jokes all day. Despite his off-color sense of humor, Alabama (as he was known by the other men) was funny. James's stomach muscles and face often ached from laughing, just as much as the rest of his body ached from the Army's daily exercise regimen.

Nevertheless, James was eager for basic training to be over. He wanted to get into flight school as soon as he could; he urgently felt that he should be studying the work he'd *really* be doing in the military, instead of running and shooting like any old Joe. He wouldn't be digging trenches or sliding on his belly though muck (no sir!) and he might as well get busy with his serious training as soon as possible.

He was counting the days.

The L.P. Harris Lumber Company was one of the busier places in Springport. There were always dozens of men coming and going with their trucks and wagons, talking business with Grandad, or toting off loads of supplies for various projects around town. Grandad knew everyone, and he was trusted for his no-nonsense, quiet manner; his generosity; and his decency.

When Les and Johnny arrived at the lumberyard for work the first morning, they were welcomed like long-lost family by everyone who stopped by. The boys understood that it wasn't anything to do with them; the mere fact that they were L.P.'s grandsons made them important in the community. Everyone seemed to want to know the things

L.P. knew and assumed they would love the people L.P. loved. It was a special privilege.

Grandad told the boys they would be unloading shingles that day. A full carload had come in on the train the day before, and the boys' job was to lift the heavy packages of shingles, move them over to the long rolling ramp that hooked to the lip of the railcar, and slide them into a waiting wagon bed for stacking. It was long, hard, heavy work for two boys.

Les and Johnny began the day with high spirits, however. They were happy to be at the lumberyard, no matter what they had to do, and there were always folks coming by to say hello and encourage them in their work. They pushed and shoved and heaved the shingles into position at the top of the ramp and were rewarded with a squealing, pitching, rumbling noise as each package slid down on the rollers.

After about an hour, however, the work had begun to grow old. Johnny grew tired first, being smaller, and as hard as he tried he found it impossible not to whine. Just a little. Although Les was bigger and stronger, he too was growing weary of the chore. Still, he kept pushing Johnny to quit bellyaching and keep going. "The more we do, the sooner we can be done," Les kept saying. "Just one more, and one more after that. Come on!"

But Johnny was tired, and becoming distracted by a big group of boys playing on the grassy lawn next to the lumberyard. This was Uncle Fritz and Aunt Mary's house, and their three children had dragged over at least eight other kids from around the neighborhood to play what looked like a game of war. "Look at the fun they are having, Les," he said. "How much longer? I want to go and play too."

Looking over, Les could see the boys shouting and chasing each other with sticks. As usual, the ringleader was his cousin Roger Harris. Looking at the boy, a small nugget of an idea began to form in Les's mind. "Let's take a break," Les told his brother. "I'm going to check something out. Stay here."

Johnny sat thankfully down on a pile of shingles and began to mop his brow. "No problem," he said.

Les walked over to Uncle Fritz and Aunt Mary's to call for Roger. Roger was eleven, just like Les, though his build was larger and sturdier. He had fair hair and tanned skin and a voice that was soft and friendly. When Les called to him, Roger immediately ran over to pound his shoulder and shout a welcome. "Mom told me you and Johnny were here, but that we couldn't see you yet because you are being punished for running away," he said. "When are you going to be done over there?"

"That depends on you," Les said. "You interested in showing this group some fun?"

Fewer than fifteen minutes later, Les and Johnny were ringleaders in a veritable carnival of activity at the lumberyard. With Roger's help, the boys had set up an assembly line of shingles and kids, and were keeping all of them moving as fast as they could. Johnny and Roger stood in the railcar, where they helped each kid heft a big package of shingles onto the rolling ramp's highest point. The kid would then sit on the shingles with one leg over each side of the ramp, and ride bumpety-bump down to the wagon below. Waiting at the bottom, Les helped each child stack the shingles where they belonged.

Within an hour and a half, the job was done. Roger led the crowd of children back home while Les and Johnny went into the lumberyard office to check in with Grandad. "We're all done now," Les said. "Can we go over to Roger's and play?"

Grandad looked at them sternly. "I saw how you boys did that job," he said. "Or rather, how you conned the other kids into doing it for you. That was not the intent of this exercise, you know. The punishment was intended for you, not the rest of the neighborhood."

Les looked at the floor and shuffled his feet. "We know," he admitted.

"I'm just going to have to think of something else, I can see," Grandad continued. "You're still not off the hook. I'll be home tonight with another job for you to do in the morning. Until then you can go and play with Roger. Have fun and stay out of trouble, boys."

Les and Johnny hid their grins until they were outside Grandad's office. Then Johnny whooped loudly and they both took off at a dead run.

By the time Les and Johnny came home that evening, they were both worn out, sore, and hoarse from shouting. Johnny had a hard time holding his head up at dinner, and more than once caught himself as he was about to fall into the mashed potatoes.

Nanny was having none of it. "You boys had better perk up," she said more than once. "Grandad is having poker night here and I'm going to need your help setting up."

Both boys sat a little straighter and tried to focus. "Who's coming?" Les asked.

"Your uncles Fritz and Fred, along with Mr. Allen, Mr. Cortright, and Mr. Wiselogle," Grandad said. "I've been looking forward to this for a while; I'm going to clean Tom out this time. You boys had better behave yourselves. This is serious business."

With that, Nanny got up and began to bustle. She brought out dessert (apple pie!) and began putting peanuts, candy, and snacks into little bowls for the poker game. When the boys finished they got up to help her and with Grandad's help soon had the table cleared and ready to go.

Grandad got a funny twinkle in his eye as he removed the tablecloth and looked at the polished wood surface of the dining room table. "Boys, this table needs some polishing," he said with a slight grin. "Les, run and fetch me the lemon oil and a couple of rags."

When Les came back he saw Grandad standing sideways, with his face down against the surface of the table. "Yup, that'll do," he said as he unscrewed the cap from the bottle and began to work in the lemon oil. He spent a long time polishing, rubbing, looking, and then polishing again.

"Why are you polishing so much, Grandad?" Johnny asked.

"Got guests coming," Grandad said. "Can't very well ask 'em to play poker on an old beat-up table."

This made sense. Mother always cleaned extra when company was coming too.

Finally Grandad was done. Johnny handed him the cards and Nanny brought out all the bowls of snacks from the kitchen. She called to the boys then and they made trips with glasses and bottles of whiskey, which she lined up on the sideboard for the men to drink while they played. "That ought to give your grandfather an advantage right there," she snorted.

"Do you have the ashtrays?" Grandad asked. "The nice ones?"

"Of course I do," Nanny said. As she bustled past him into the kitchen, however, Johnny heard her mumble, "Tobacco is a filthy weed; from the devil it doth proceed." Nanny did not have much use for tobacco.

The uncles arrived first. Fred and Fritz came directly into the dining room and went to the sideboard, where they helped themselves to some whiskey right away. Uncle Fritz came over and clapped the boys on their shoulders. "I see you were out with Roger today," he said. "Did you have fun?"

"I'll say they did," Grandad interjected before either Les or Johnny could answer. "Conned all the neighborhood kids into doing their work for them at the lumberyard. If this keeps up I'm going to have to fire Charlie and start worrying about the child labor laws."

Uncle Fritz chuckled. "I see you have the table polished, Dad," he said knowingly. "Looks nice."

Grandad snorted and went into the kitchen for something. Uncle Fritz knelt down low next to Johnny. "Do you know why he does that?" he asked. Johnny shook his head. "Your Grandad can see the reflection of every card he deals on the surface of that table. What's more, he can remember all of them."

Johnny gasped. "But isn't that cheating?"

"Not precisely," Uncle Fritz said thoughtfully. "I guess some people would think so, but I suppose your Grandad sees it as taking advantage of a good situation. The reflection wouldn't do him any good if he wasn't smart enough to remember everything he saw. So it's almost like he's upping the difficulty level of the game to make it more exciting, wouldn't you say?"

Johnny was thoughtful. "I guess so," he acknowledged. "Also, the table is shiny for everyone if they can use it."

"Exactly," Uncle Fritz chuckled.

Within the hour, the boys were upstairs in bed drifting to sleep. They could hear the comforting rumble of conversation and laughter at the poker table as their grandfather cleaned out everybody else's pockets with his good memory and polished dining room table.

chapter eleven

★

Nanny brought Charlie home from the station the following Tuesday. He was received with more pleasure than his younger brothers had been, since he had arrived by legitimate means. Charlie was just as grateful and happy to be in Springport as his brothers were; the easy summertime smell of Nanny and Grandad's house made him feel like breathing a huge sigh of contentment. It was as if all the anger and surliness that had found a home in his spirit went right out the front window, freeing him to experience something new and fresh.

Charlie immediately went to the lumberyard, where his brothers were already hard at work restocking shelves. They acknowledged each other with a quick glance and greeting, and Charlie went to look for Grandad. He found him taking inventory in a back room, counting and recounting and making notes on a little penny tablet.

Charlie had feared Grandad might put him to work too, so he was very relieved to be sent over to Aunt Myrtelle's house for a surprise. Grandad wouldn't say much about what awaited Charlie, but his mustache twitched a little and he seemed to be suppressing some secret excitement.

Uncle Fred and Aunt Myrtelle lived on Maple Street in an old-fashioned white clapboard house with a low fence in front. Nanny had helped Aunt Myrtelle plant huge rosebushes along the front of the house, and they were already beginning to bloom in the summer sunshine.

Aunt Myrtelle came to the door almost before Charlie could knock and enfolded him in a comforting embrace. She was the quietest and most serene of Nanny and Grandad's daughters; her manner never failed to be gracious and humble and sweet. She was the sort of person who was content to let herself fade into the background from time to time; in this regard she was very unlike her more vibrant, effusive, and temperamental sisters. She and Uncle Fred had no children of their own, and they doted on their nieces and nephews. Charlie loved her because she was more interested in him than he was himself, and unfailingly supportive.

Today she was practically coming out of her skin with the pleasure of a new surprise for her nephew. She brought him around to the back of the house to the garage. Peering through the shimmering dust motes and stacks of old junk, Charlie saw an old car, which Aunt Myrtelle said was for him. "It doesn't run now," she said, nearly breathless in her excitement. "But with your mechanical skill, I'll bet you will have it humming in no time. Won't it be fun?"

Charlie walked up to the vehicle. It was an old Model A Ford from the late 1920s, and it looked like it was in pretty good shape for its age. He thought briefly of his failed models and experiments from home and hesitated, but something about Aunt Myrtelle's enthusiasm was contagious and he thought perhaps getting the car running was something he could actually do. For the first time in a very long time, he felt something very much like hope.

Someone thought he could do this. Someone saw him,

knew who he was, and still believed he was capable of good ideas, of strong work.

"Grandad got it as payment from someone at the lumberyard, and we all thought of you right away," Aunt Myrtelle said. "You're going to have lots of time on your hands this summer, so you might as well spend it here. If you can get it running, you can drive it all you want."

Charlie didn't know what to say. "Thanks, Aunt Myrtelle," he said over the lump in his throat.

She came over and slipped an arm around his shoulders. "I know, Charlie," she said softly. "Very few boys your age get an opportunity like this. But nobody deserves it more than you do. Now, get to work."

Even in Springport, it was impossible to forget there was a war on. People collected scrap rubber and metal for the war effort; Grandad kept a big bin at the lumberyard for people to deposit whatever they had. People used ration stamps here, too, and shared the food they grew in their victory gardens.

Folks talked a lot about the hometown boys who had gone to fight. James was considered a hometown boy too, because of Grandad. Les and Johnny were proud to have a brother in the Army. The boys felt they had lots of family members doing their part in the war. Right after Pearl Harbor, it seemed that any Harris who was eligible and able went off to enlist right away.

Aunt Norma's husband, Uncle Bob, had gone first; in 1941 he'd enlisted in the Army. Uncle Bob also enlisted his pet dog, Ralph, after reading of dogs being trained for bomb-sniffing and delivering messages. Ralph was a smart dog and it was hard for Uncle Bob to leave his pet at home. Ralph did well at first, but after a year or two of military life, the dog became shell-shocked and traumatized by the horrors of war and Uncle Bob was forced to put him down.

Uncle Fritz had also enlisted right after Pearl Harbor. A stray bullet had cut his days in the Army short, however, in early 1942. The bullet had shattered his knee, causing permanent damage, and he would not return to the front.

Aunt Amy Jane, the youngest of the Harris girls, was last to enlist. She went into the Women's Army Corps as soon as she was old enough and was now stationed somewhere in Europe.

The family members who remained behind tried to help one another as much as possible. Aunt Norma was on her own in the house on Duck Lake, so Grandad and Uncle Fred came to help with heavy work like shoveling or mowing. Charlie, Les, and Johnny also helped with some of the gardening and household work when they could.

As the summer wore on, all three MacGregor boys settled into a comfortable routine in Springport. Les and Johnny worked at the lumberyard each morning for a few hours, then went over to Roger's to play. They came back, exhausted, to Nanny and Grandad's house on Grand Street for dinner, then visited with whichever aunts and uncles came by in the evening before dropping off to sleep in their cozy attic loft. The summer breeze and hum of mosquitoes, along with their exertion of the day, put them to sleep almost immediately each night.

Charlie spent each day at Aunt Myrtelle's, alternately soaking up his share of love and affection and working on the car. He made friends with Chauncey Snow, owner of the local garage, who was willing to spend time with Charlie because he was L.P.'s grandson. Chauncey showed Charlie the basics of mechanical work and even had him help with some of his customers' automobiles in exchange for extra parts. It turned out that Charlie was very good at mechanical work, and it pleased him no end to finally have identified something special he could do. Like his brothers, Charlie fell asleep satisfied and happy each night.

On the weekends, the boys all went to Aunt Norma's house on nearby Duck Lake. Much of the family was there; Nanny, Grandad, and various aunts and uncles would come and go throughout the lazy summer days. There was always laughter, conversation, and even an exciting feud or two to liven up the party. Every now and then the boys would happen upon a whispered conversation about Mother and Dad and how they were *really* doing so far away, but these instances were rare and easily forgotten.

Summer in Springport was bliss.

★

Summer at Fort Riley was hot.

Even James's bunkmate, Alabama (who was accustomed to such weather), complained about the arid heat and unrelenting dryness. The land—and the men—were constantly parched. James sometimes felt like he was turning into a worn-out, shriveled-up raisin.

The only bright spot in the daily grind of exercise, work, and sleep was the fact that James had been assigned to primary flight school at the conclusion of his basic training. The other troops were mustering out to locations in Europe and the Pacific, where they would be trapped like mice in the trenches, but lucky James was staying in Kansas for more training.

He gleefully wrote to Mary Jane.

My Darling,

Only another two weeks and they will send me to Garden City, Kansas, for primary flight training. I can't wait to start. If I do well there, then it's on to advanced training.

Folks here seem happy with me so far. I can't imagine otherwise; there are very few troublemakers here and life moves fast. Army life is pretty simple when it comes down to it. It's all routine and regimentation and you don't have to think too hard, if you're a good worker and do as you're told.

I think of you every moment, and hope you are getting along all right. Are you making any pies?

I will write again as soon as I have an address. I miss you!

All my love,
James

★

Grandma Barney sat quietly in the strange waiting room. It was utterly silent, except for her breathing.

It had been a long night, and she was tired.

Mother had begun drinking after Charlie left for Springport and, as long as she was conscious, she did not stop. She had been on this latest bender for the better part of a week. Dad had gone out on a Tuesday and didn't come back until Friday, drunk and nasty and abusive. That night he and Mother had gotten into a huge fight that ended in terrible violence. Mother had a cracked rib and multiple contusions (according to the doctor) and Dad had a cut on his forehead that required thirteen stitches.

Their battling had awakened Grandma Barney and she called the police. It took a while for them to arrive, and by the time they did Mother was unconscious. Mother and Dad had been taken to the hospital for evaluation, and Grandma Barney sat waiting, her purse in her lap and her heart in her throat.

Thank God the boys got away, she thought, over and over and over again. She would never stop believing that it was nothing short of divine intervention that spared them all of this.

A doctor came into the room and knelt before Grandma Barney's chair. "You are the mother?" he said softly.

When Grandma Barney nodded, fearing the worst, he touched her knee and told her it would be all right. "Your daughter-in-law was worse off, obviously, than your son, but they both are stable and receiving excellent care."

Grandma Barney breathed a sigh of relief.

"They were both extremely intoxicated," the doctor said. "You were right to bring them both in when you did."

The room was silent. Grandma Barney waited for what she knew must be next.

"I assume this is habitual behavior for them," the doctor said.

"Yes," Grandma Barney said, her voice low. "They don't usually get this violent, but the rest of it—the drinking, especially—yes, that's all quite common."

"I think you will want to consider strategies for getting them rehabilitated," the doctor said. "We can admit them here or, if you have another idea in mind, I can put them into your care just as soon as they are well enough to leave the hospital."

"They can stay here," Grandma Barney said. "We have some family money—my in-laws and I—and we can use it to help them. How can I make sure they don't get out before they're ready? Am I…committing them, or something?"

"We'll help you speak with them and make sure they stay," the doctor said kindly. He touched her hand and moved away, giving her time to think.

Grandma Barney put her head into her hands and wept.

★

The family gathered at Nanny and Grandad's, as they always did, to celebrate the Fourth of July. Nanny and Grandad had seven children who, together with their spouses and children, made for quite a houseful.

Springport had a small but complete parade, with fire trucks and some tractors and a government official or two. There were fireworks at night, usually, and almost always some good-natured fireworks between the aunts during the day-long barbecue.

The Harris aunts usually had some small, funny argument going during the day. It would start small, perhaps over some childhood recollection, and it would grow during the course of the day until all the aunts were laughing hysterically.

Les was standing near the table, getting a drink and talking to Nanny, when today's discussion began. It had to do with Aunt Mary's victory garden—the vegetable patch she had planted to help provide extra food during the war. Aunt Mary had planted her garden in the shape of a "V", which Aunt Norma said looked silly.

"It does not," Aunt Mary said. "It's patriotic."

"Patriotic?" Aunt Myrtelle said. "It's not patriotic. It's dopey. Your yard looks like it has a giant check mark on it."

Aunt Norma agreed. "It would have been one thing if you'd gotten the 'V' planted evenly," she said. "But you didn't. It's all askew, and it looks ridiculous. Did Fritz let you do that by yourself?"

"He did," Aunt Mary said. "He says it looks nice."

"Fritzie," Aunt Norma called over to her brother. "Do you like that giant check mark in your yard?"

"I'm not going to answer that," Fritz said, humor in his eyes. "She'll make me sleep in the shed!"

Aunt Myrtelle and Aunt Norma looked at each other, and Aunt Myrtelle began to laugh. Her laughter was thin, high, and infectious, and Aunt Norma caught the bug. She added her own rich chuckle to the mix and before too long all three ladies were laughing over the lopsided victory garden, even Aunt Mary.

Uncle Fritz motioned to Les, and they walked away from the ladies' table to join the men outdoors.

"Are you having a good time, Les?" Uncle Fritz asked.

Les glanced up, astonished. It was the first time in his memory that anyone had ever asked him if he was enjoying himself. In fact, he could not remember a time that any adult had spoken to him in a way that was not disciplinary or directive. "Yes," he said.

"Good," Uncle Fritz said. "I am going to take Roger and the girls fishing tomorrow; would you like to come?"

"Yes, please!" Les could hardly contain his excitement.

"Then it's settled," the older man said, tousling Les's hair. "But be ready; I'm going to be coming for you awfully early. I like to get out there before the fish wake up."

Uncle Fritz walked Les around to the back, where the men were standing. The Harris uncles were by Grandad's old barbecue grill, drinking beer and swapping stories.

Les heard Uncle Fred telling the other men about a farm out in Devereaux where a man had been killed in a tractor accident two years before. "He wanted his ashes scattered over his fields from a plane, which his wife and kids gladly did for him," Uncle Fred said. "Problem was, the wife got so worried about where the ashes went that she refused to dust the house ever again."

The men burst into gales of laughter, and so did Les. Grandad made a little motion with his hand to the boy, which meant he wanted to talk about grown-up topics with the men. Les took the hint and walked around to the front lawn, where the smaller kids—Johnny, along with Roger and his sisters Kitty and Dee—were playing. They were playing a loud, tiring game of cowboys and Indians, which left them sunburned by early afternoon. As the long day waned, Roger brought out some firecrackers and they lit them off in the street, making a terrible racket.

After dinner, the regular town fireworks started. The family walked in a massive pack down to the ballpark, where they spread out their blankets. Several people came over to say hello to Grandad as dusk fell. By this time everyone was laughing and warm, even the aunts.

Les lay back with his arms behind his head, waiting for the show to start. It felt good to be part of a family that didn't fight all the time. He enjoyed having a grown-up look him in the eye and speak to him. He liked to be told what was going on, to be part of something.

The first fireworks exploded in the sky above and Les felt the joy of it all the way down to his toes.

★

Two days later the holiday fun was beginning to dissipate a little for Les. His cousin Roger had gone and gotten himself grounded for a week, all because he had locked his younger sisters in an upstairs closet. His mother, Aunt Mary, had refused to understand that Kitty and Dee had released Roger's three pet hamsters into the laundry chute and deserved punishment for their misdeeds. Roger's poor little pets must have been traumatized! It seemed only fitting that the girls be put into a small dark space so they, too, could see how it felt.

But by the time Aunt Mary found the girls, screaming and kicking against the closet door, she was so upset with Roger she wouldn't listen. He was confined to his room for a week and couldn't play with anybody.

Les didn't mind playing with Kitty and Dee for short periods, but he thought girls were pretty silly so he was quickly in search of something else to do. Charlie wouldn't let him help with the car and Grandad didn't need any afternoon help at the lumberyard.

Even Nanny was busy today; Madam was over and they were drinking coffee in the kitchen.

Les didn't know what Madam's real name was. She lived about five houses down from Nanny and Grandad and she had worked for the family for years. Her husband was Grandad's partner at the lumberyard until he died some fifteen years before. At that point Nanny hired her to help around the house. She usually came over about one day a week. It wasn't clear to Les why Nanny paid Madam, because Nanny would never let Madam do any work. Nanny and Madam mostly just sat in the kitchen at a table, talking together.

Madam was a short, stocky lady who had bright copper hair done up in fancy marcel waves. She wore heavy pancake makeup, richly colored velvet clothes and shoes—even in the summertime—and looked like she'd just stepped out of the Ziegfeld Follies. She had a sense of humor that Les had heard Nanny call "ribald," which meant that she sometimes used bad language or shock value for a laugh. Of course, Nanny always laughed.

They made quite a contrast, Nanny and Madam—Madam with her fine velvet clothing and wicked humor, the paid employee; and Nanny Harris, president of the church ladies' guild, dressed in her print cotton housedress and apron, the benevolent employer and friend. On the surface they appeared to have little in common, but Les felt that they must share something very important since they spent so much time together. Madam was one of the few people who could make Nanny laugh—truly laugh, the kind of belly laugh that made tears run down her cheeks. Perhaps, Les thought, the laughter was important enough to keep the friendship going.

Now, two days after the Fourth of July, Madam was sitting in Nanny's warm kitchen, decked out in heavy red velvet. She had a tiny black hat perched on her hair and held one pinky out as she sipped from her teacup. "I heard a *rumor* about you the other day, Esther," she began. "And I must say I was rather *shocked*."

Nanny looked sharply at Madam. "What did you hear?"

"Why, I heard you had been *drinking* in the *tavern* right

during the middle of the *day*," Madam said with flourish.

Les heard Nanny burst into gales of laughter. "Why, Madam," she said. "Of course it's not true. I think you know me better than that."

"I don't know," Madam chortled with glee. "I heard *all* about it. You were seen *stumbling* down the front steps of the *tavern* just last week."

"Yes, I was," Nanny said. "But I was most definitely not drinking. I have never touched a drop of the filthy stuff. If you listen, I'll tell you what happened."

Madam raised her nose in the air. "I won't hear a *word* of it, Esther Harris," she pronounced. "Your *shameful secret* is out, and the *whole town* knows it."

Nanny laughed even harder. "Let me tell you," she began. "I was not drinking at all, I went into the tavern to collect money for the Republican Party. I just tripped on the steps on my way out, that's all."

"Mmm-hmmmm. I'm sure that's *just how* it happened," Madam said, in a tone that made it clear she didn't believe it at all.

"It's true!" Nanny exclaimed. "I fell over those silly semicircular steps outside the tavern, that's all. I didn't even want to go in there in the first place."

"Oh, *sure* you didn't," Madam's guffaw exploded. "You're just *making up* your cover story now that you've already been *caught*. Republican Party, my *eye*."

"Now, Madam," Nanny said, laughing. "You know it's true!"

The two women sailed off into gales of hysterics. Les smiled, watching them, but decided it wasn't how he wanted to spend his day. He went to find Johnny and see what he was up to. Les found his brother flopped on the bed in the attic room, staring at the ceiling. "I'm bored," Johnny complained.

The boys talked it over. Lacking any other great source of inspiration, they decided to go down to the train depot. The depot was a small, hunkered-down building right across from the Springport Elevator. Although trains continued to chug through town, dropping lumber, grain, and supplies, the depot was a quiet place. It smelled funny, of old sulfur and mildew, and was generally empty during the day. The only time anyone came by was just before the train arrived.

When the boys got there, they found the building deserted, hot, and dank. Johnny was content to peer in the windows, but Les was more determined. He circled the building until he found a window that was slightly open.

"Johnny! Come here!" Les hissed. He wanted to whisper just in case some grown-up happened to be standing around. Johnny came over obediently and Les grunted as he hoisted the smaller boy onto his thin shoulders. "Can you lift the sash?" Les whispered.

Johnny opened the window and just seconds later he was through. He came around and opened the door for his brother and they went inside.

The depot was completely silent, and the boys' imaginations ran wild. The passenger benches near the door could be occupied by Civil War soldiers, weeping ladies, or foreign spies. The old passenger train schedule hung on a paneled wall near the ticket window; next to it someone had tacked a handwritten list of the current freight trains' arrival times. Just beyond was the telegraph office, containing a rough wooden table covered with old yellowing papers and dusty equipment.

Les and Johnny took in the sight of the old depot with a feeling that was somewhere between reverence and wild abandonment. Les thought for the first time that Roger had done them a favor by getting himself grounded.

"Hey, Les!" Johnny shouted, leaping up onto a wooden bench. He extended his finger and thumb into the shape of a gun. "Stick 'em up!"

Les lifted his hands into the air. "You won't get away with this," he said slowly. "Why don't you put the gun away and we can talk like reasonable folks."

"Not on your life," Johnny said. "Now, I want you to stop the train that's coming into the station now. Then you'll write a note to the engineer and make him take on some water. Do you understand?"

Les nodded. "Please don't hurt me," he said, pantomiming the scene just as the boys had seen it in *The Great Train Robbery*. He pretended to pull on a long chain, and then sat down to pantomime the writing of a note. "I got me a family at home."

"You'll be fine so long as you do what I say," Johnny said. "Now get me that note."

They reenacted the entire first scene from the movie at least twenty times, adding different variations as they went. Each rendition concluded with Johnny pretending to tie Les up and leave him on the floor. Instead of tying Les up, however, Johnny just tickled him endlessly. Les retaliated in kind, and soon they were both rolling around on the dusty floor, laughing and hollering.

Once they had worn themselves out, the two boys stretched out flat, gasping. "Wouldn't it be neat if we could get this old depot running again?" Les wondered aloud.

"You could be the stationmaster and telegraph operator," Johnny said, "and I'll run the ticket window. We'll polish the whole place right up again and once it's cleaned up and pretty, people will start to come back."

"I wonder if Grandad would give us the money," Les said. "Probably; of everyone in town I'm guessing the lumberyard owner would most like to have a working depot. It would bring people here and get the town booming in a big way. Plus, he already works a lot with the freight side of the railroad; it wouldn't be a big stretch to get him on the passenger stuff too."

"Yeah, all we need to do is ask him," Johnny said. "I know he'll agree."

"He'll want us to run it, probably," Les thought. "We would have to move here. We couldn't go home again."

"That's true," Johnny said. "Would you be sorry?"

"Not one bit," Les said without hesitation. "Would you?"

"Nope," Johnny said. They looked at each other and giggled.

"Springport forever," Les sighed. "How wonderful that would be."

They both lay silently for a moment. "Do you think we ought to look around some more?" Johnny asked.

"Yeah, we should," Les said. "Then we'll be able to tell Grandad exactly what's needed to get this place fixed up again." He got up and walked back to the telegraph room.

"Les?" Johnny asked. He really should have been used to his brother's tendency to wander off deep in thought, but it always grated on him anyway. Johnny continued to rest on the floor for a few minutes while he waited to see what would happen next.

Les went back into the telegraph room and looked over the table. The wiring was still intact, so he checked it all out and tried to determine how the machine would work. What if someone were trying to send a wire right now? Could Les turn everything on and get a message? He knew there was a new, modern Western Union office in Jackson that handled all the telegrams these days, but maybe this could still work.

There was an old telegraph key on the table, and a battery. Les sat down and began exploring the setup to see what he could do with it. Just as he was starting to make progress, however, he began to hear his brother in the next room.

"LESter... oh, LEEEESter," Johnny was calling. "I'm getting awfully BOOOOORRRED out here all by mySEEELLF. What are you doing?"

"Knock it off, Johnny," Les called. "I'm trying to figure out this equipment. Quit hollering at me."

"But I'm BOOOOOOORRRRED out here," Johnny said plaintively. It was so frustrating and disappointing to have Les's attention and then lose it again, just like that. "When are you going to be done? I wanted to keep playing."

"I don't know," Les replied, his annoyance beginning to show. "Go find something else to do if you're bored. I'm busy."

Johnny sighed and stood up. Dusting himself off, he circled the depot one more time before announcing to Les that he would be waiting outside. He went out the front and sat on the step for a few minutes, feeling quite sorry for himself. Les was always ditching him in favor of some stupid project.

Johnny noticed an old water pump nearby. It was rusty and covered with moss, but there was still some water around the base to indicate that it must get used sometimes. Water sounded cool and fresh, and Johnny walked over to see if he could figure out how the pump worked so he could get a drink.

As he neared the ancient contraption, Johnny had to jump back. There were bees humming and alighting all across the surface and base of the pump. Johnny was barefoot, so he had to be careful not to step on any bees while he was trying to get his drink of water.

Or did he?

Johnny knew a bee could sting a bare foot, but he also reasoned that a big bare foot could kill a bee. Their stingers were all pointed down as they crawled on the moist wooden board anyway. Tentatively, Johnny stretched out a leg and brought his foot down on one of the bees that crawled in the water at the base of the pump. He felt the coolness of the water, then a little wiggle, and the bee was still.

Interesting.

Johnny did this once more, and then again. Then, just as he began to think this game might be fun, one of the bees died stinger-up. Johnny's foot seemed to explode. There was an instant of painful disbelief, and then a powerful surge of pain that rammed all the way up Johnny's leg in a white-hot blaze of fire. He had never been stung by a bee before, and he had no idea how very much it hurt. He felt like he was getting his leg amputated with no anesthetic.

Johnny yelled like he had never yelled in his entire life. He screeched and hollered and screamed like a banshee, nearly losing himself in a fit of hysterics and bringing Les running out of the depot.

Les didn't know what had happened, but he acted fast

anyway. He ran over, scooped Johnny up, and ran all the way back to Nanny's with his brother half-slung over his shoulder. Johnny yelled in his ear the whole way home, which helped give Les strength and speed.

Johnny actually started to feel better before they got to Nanny's front porch, but he continued to holler anyway. It felt good to have his big brother's undivided attention and care.

chapter twelve

★

My dearest Mary Jane,

The night here is quiet, and I can't stop thinking of you. I wish you were here to talk with me and make me laugh... right now it seems like there isn't much to laugh about.

The airbase in Garden City is even hotter than the grounds at Fort Riley. The air is stifling, and the temperature frequently dodges up over 100 degrees. When you're out working on flat tarmac airfield or runway, the temperature is unendurable.

Fortunately, I have some classroom time to help give me a break from the heat. It is cooler indoors, and it is nice not to have to climb around or move for a while. Plus, I think of you every time I am in the classroom. A classroom is where I first began to know and love you.

I am getting along fine here, and they're going to let me go through Advanced Training School. Only a few more months to go and I will have my wings. I haven't any idea where I'll be sent for Advanced Training, but it will probably be right here in Kansas.

They say I'm a natural-born pilot. Now—before you laugh at me—it's not my swelled head talking, I'm just repeating what the higher-ups say about me! It's not bragging if someone else said it first.

And I do love to fly. There is something about that moment when the plane's wheels first leave the ground and you feel yourself airborne—you are beginning to soar, and it's wonderful. The rest of the flight is fun too, but it's those moments when you are first up that are the best. It feels like anything is possible.

I think of you every time. I wish you could know how this felt, the soaring. You would love it.

Hey—in your last letter, you wrote something I didn't understand about Mother and Dad. Why did you say they weren't home? I must be missing something; I have not heard from either of them or from Grandma Barney. It has been strange, actually; I know they are busy but I expected at least one letter from home. If you know what is going on there, will you please write and tell me?

I have been getting some very good physical workouts the last few days here. They want to make sure we are in good shape before we leave. First we have 30 minutes of calisthenics, then run the cross-country course and then do the obstacle course. It really makes for a good appetite.

Can't think of anything more to write. I'm dreaming of you every night and keeping you in my heart every moment of the day.

All my love,
James

★

Dear James,

I am glad to hear from you, even if you were bragging a little. I disagree about what constitutes bragging, by the way; if someone else says it and you repeat it, you're still bragging! I hope you're not talking this way to the other men in your unit, as it will lead to one of two outcomes: either someone in your own division will shoot you long before you get to the front, or you will stop needing a plane and be able to float up right to the sky with your head puffed up like a giant balloon.

It is so good to hear how well you are enjoying the flying. I confess I worried about it a little, but if you love it then you'll work hard at it and stay safe. I am reassured!

Now, about your family. I thought that you knew, which is why I didn't say anything sooner. I saw your Grandma Barney in town a month or so ago and she told me she was home alone and invited me to stop by. I went, and she said that your folks are "drying out" in a special hospital downstate. I don't know what happened, but somehow your grandmother got them to a place that is supposed to help them stop drinking so much. I can't imagine what it took to get them there, and I must say I am impressed that such a tiny lady had the ability to work such a big change, all by herself!

Now that I know you haven't heard from anyone at home, I'll tell you that your brothers aren't there, either; Les and Johnny ran away to Springport (I don't know if you knew this or not) and Charlie was sent there too, a few days later. Your Grandma Barney says they are having a wonderful time.

Now that your house is so much more friendly and comfortable, I have been there more often. I really enjoy your grandmother's company and I think she's glad to have a visitor. I brought her a pie the other day and she laughed like nobody's business and ate a piece right there on the spot.

I miss you a lot and wish you were here every minute. Enjoy your soaring, and keep safe!

Love, love, love,
Mary Jane

★

One warm Saturday in late July, Uncle Fritz stopped by during breakfast to pick up some papers for the lumberyard. "Sit down and have some coffee," Grandad said. "We need to chat, since I won't be coming in to work today."

"Why not?" Uncle Fritz asked.

"I've decided that today is the day I'm going to teach Charlie how to drive the Packard," Grandad said.

Charlie's fork stilled in the air. "Really?" he asked.

"If you can drive, you can get yourself out to Duck Lake to help your aunt Norma from time to time," Grandad said. "I've got to get over to Albion today for a new hat, and I figured it would be a good trip for some learning. You'll drive."

Grandad turned to Uncle Fritz and began to talk lumberyard business. Charlie ran upstairs and got himself dressed and ready, then zipped back down to the dining room. Grandad and Uncle Fritz were just finishing their talk. Grandad stood, wiped his hands on his napkin, and told Charlie he would be ready to leave in just a minute. Grandad carried his plate out to the kitchen and went upstairs.

"Hey, Charlie," Uncle Fritz whispered. "I've got a pointer for you. It'll get you in good with your Grandad."

"What is it?" Charlie asked.

"Your Grandad believes it's important to keep up a decent speed in the car," Uncle Fritz said confidentially. "He doesn't like to go any less than seventy miles an hour in his Packard."

"Seventy?" Charlie said. "That's pretty fast."

"Yep," Uncle Fritz said seriously. "You'll have to do your best. Have you driven before?"

"A little bit," Charlie said. "But never that fast."

"You'll be fine," Uncle Fritz said reassuringly. They could already hear Grandad's feet on the stairs; it was time to go.

He and Grandad got into the Packard and Charlie took off. There was no speed limit in Michigan, so he flew at lightning speed over the roads toward Albion. He managed to keep the needle of the speedometer well over seventy most of the way.

Grandad was quiet, watching. He offered no suggestions,

just let Charlie drive at a frantic pace all the way. They arrived at the hat shop, Grandad disappeared for fifteen minutes, and then it was back on the road. They zipped like a blue streak toward Springport, Charlie perspiring and using all his muscles to control the wheel of the car.

Still, Grandad said nothing.

As they neared Springport, there was a left turn by a gas station. Charlie knew he was going too fast to make the turn, so he managed somehow to get the car into the gas station and stopped by one of the pumps. "We could probably use some gas," he said, panting slightly. Grandad agreed and they filled up the tank.

Then it was back on the road. Charlie managed to get back to the house on Grand Street and pulled into the driveway. He stopped the car and drooped slightly against the seat, exhausted from the strain of maneuvering the car at such a fast clip without having an accident.

Grandad made no move to leave the vehicle. He put the new hat on his head and looked at Charlie. "Not too bad," he said. "But you might slow down a little. I don't know where you got the idea that we were in such a hurry. It's just a hat."

The following Tuesday, Les and Roger got up early to go fishing. They were up and out of the house by 5:30, long before Johnny was awake.

Madam and Nanny were in the kitchen, gossiping over their coffee. "… And do you *know*," Madam was saying. "The daughter was *never* heard from *again*." With these words, Madam's stenciled eyebrows raised knowingly, and she wagged her head at Nanny.

Nanny gasped slightly, then caught sight of Johnny. "Well, good morning, sunshine!" she warbled, as if she had been caught doing something wrong. She quickly rose to fetch some breakfast for the boy.

Madam regarded Johnny. He was uncomfortable under her gaze, and stared at his hands on the kitchen table.

"I was *hoping* to see you today," Madam said. "I *have* something for you."

Johnny looked up. "For me?" he asked.

Madam nodded and reached for her satchel. "It's a *mystery,*" she hinted, digging in the bottom of the bag. "I was—oh, my heavens, where did they go?" She began to rummage more forcefully, putting her face right down into the bag. Sighing heavily, she evidently gave up. She turned the entire bag upside down, dumping its contents out over the table. The expected cosmetics, handkerchiefs, keys, and money went flying, as did a number of less-ordinary items. Johnny noticed a teabag, an alarm clock, and three used shotgun shells. It was these last items that Madam swept into her palm and held out to Johnny. "You see?" she said. "A mystery."

"Why is it a mystery?" Johnny asked, perplexed.

"Well, where did they *come* from?" Madam said. "*Who* was shot? And where is the *body*? You must have *some* imagination."

"It was probably just a dumb old animal," Johnny said.

Madam shook her head. "I *shudder* to think of the inability of today's youth to think *creatively,*" she sighed dramatically. Over by the stove, Nanny made a noise that sounded something like a giggle. "Don't you want to know where I *found* them?"

"Okay," Johnny said, waiting.

"They were on the ground *outside your Grandad's office,*" Madam said, after something of a pause.

Johnny's eyes grew round. "What does that mean?"

"*You* tell *me,*" Madam said. "*That* is the mystery."

"Where do I start?" Johnny asked. Nanny set his plate of eggs in front of him and he dug in.

"I have *no idea,*" Madam said, replacing the items in her satchel. "I have heard *nothing* and of course would like nothing better than to know what has happened. Can you find out for me?"

Johnny promised he would. He hurriedly wolfed down his breakfast and ran upstairs. He collected a flashlight, Grandad's magnifying glass, and some rope, all of which he bundled into his small rucksack. Flying downstairs again, he shouted a good-bye to Nanny and Madam as the screen door thwacked shut behind him.

As he walked past the open kitchen window, he thought he heard Madam tell Nanny, "Oh, he'll be busy all day now. Let's get back to the story… "

He decided to start investigating at the railroad depot. Train tracks were always a great place to start looking if you were searching for a body. Plus, there were always hobos on railcars; one of them might be the person who dropped the shotgun shells. Johnny had it all reasoned out—sometimes in the serials the bad guys went to church because they felt sorry.

A few men were around, but nobody took notice of Johnny. They were too busy working with the railcars, loading supplies on and taking them off. Johnny looked at the big cars along the siding and decided that a little exploration was in order.

He saw that there were empty railcars toward the back of the train. *I should check there,* he thought. *Those last cars are exactly the place I'd hide if I were a hobo.*

Johnny walked back to the open cars and peeked through the sides. It was dark, too dark to observe who or what might be inside. Johnny stepped inside and waited for his eyes to adjust. He clicked on his flashlight and walked from one end of the car to the other, looking for evidence… nothing.

The next few railcars were the same way. Johnny approached the platform near the grain elevator and saw that several boxcars had been prepared for loads of wheat. Their side doors were open, and eight-foot to ten-foot plank walls had been constructed inside each one. The temporary walls would hold in the wheat that would be blown into the cars, so the wheat didn't just roll out the open boxcar doors and fall on the ground. Johnny realized that a smart hobo could climb up the planks of a temporary wall, drop down on the other side, and be completely hidden from view.

Looking around, Johnny saw that nobody had noticed him yet. Swinging his rucksack over his shoulder, he approached the first boxcar and climbed the wooden planks. Up, up, up he went; then he swung a leg over and came down the other side. He shone his flashlight around… no hoboes. Just some bits of grain clinging to the inside walls and floor of the car.

Suddenly the train gave a sharp lurch forward. Johnny lost his balance and sat down hard on the floor. The train stopped and Johnny saw the lip of the chute as it came over the plank wall. Johnny didn't even have time to shout for help before the wheat started flying in.

It poured in fast; too fast, in fact, for Johnny to get easily out of the car. He moved toward the plank wall again, but the dust from the wheat was everywhere. It flew into Johnny's eyes and mouth, and made it nearly impossible for him to breathe, let alone call for help. It seemed that all he could do was choke and cough and panic.

Making matters worse, the smooth, slippery grains of wheat acted like quicksand, grasping at his legs and holding him fast. It began to occur to Johnny that he might drown in the wheat. Absolutely nobody knew he was in there, and he couldn't get out. The dust prevented him from shouting, and he was completely trapped.

Frantically, he wiggled and squirmed and tried to get higher, to keep his head above the wheat as it rose. He couldn't breathe; the whole world was a clouded tornado of dust and sucking, grasping wheat. The adrenaline in his body kept him moving up somehow; he was near the plank wall and could almost grab hold… and then he did.

He pulled himself up with all his strength, and soon he was up against the wall, hanging on with every muscle in his body. His eyes squeezed shut, he climbed and gasped and wheezed until he was at the top of the temporary plank wall.

The wheat stopped. Silence echoed in Johnny's ears, and then there were big, strong hands pulling him out of the boxcar and into the sunshine.

★

Mr. Fred Modjeska, owner of the Springport Elevator, brought Johnny home. "We found a little something in our wheat stores," he told Nanny, and then proceeded with the tale of Johnny's exploit. Nanny and Madam were properly horrified and Johnny was sent to his room.

He lay facedown, sobbing into his pillow, when Madam came up the stairs and sat down next to him on the bed. "I have told your grandmother that I am to blame," she said softly. Her usual dramatic way of speaking was gone; it was as if a tiny pin had punctured the balloon of her being. "It was wrong of me to send you out alone; I had no idea you would find yourself in such danger."

Johnny didn't move. His face was still pressed into his pillow and his breath came in soft, shuddering gasps.

"You know, I don't spend any time with children," Madam continued. "All I have to think about is myself."

Silence.

"So for someone like me who doesn't make it a habit to think of the needs of a little fellow like you—well, it can be hard to remember what children need," she said. "This morning I forgot what was important, and it nearly cost you everything."

More silence.

"I made up the story about the shotgun shells so you would have something interesting to do today when you were by yourself."

Johnny rolled over, his tear-streaked face unreadable. "So the shells weren't actually outside Grandad's office?"

"No, my dear," Madam said. "They were my husband's, left over from years ago. I planned to give them to you anyway, but then I had an idea that I thought would keep you occupied for a while."

"You just wanted me to go so you could have fun with Nanny?"

Madam's nodded, her face sad. In the dim attic light, Johnny thought the makeup she wore made her look false, like a clown. Her bright red hair, her painted-on face; why did she do that? Underneath all that she seemed to him to be a very normal-looking lady. He felt sorry to see her so upset; it was easier to think of her the way she was with Nanny, laughing and sharing stories. He had an urge to make her feel better.

"You're not around kids much," Johnny said. "You don't know that kids always get in the way."

"They do?"

"Of course they do," Johnny said. There was not a trace of irony in his eight-year-old voice. "That's what Mother always says. Don't feel bad. At least you were trying to give me something fun to do, instead of letting me hang around upstairs bored all day, like at home."

Madam stared at him for a long moment. "You'll never know how truly sorry I am," she finally said. "You're a good boy." She kissed Johnny on the forehead and went back downstairs, her skirt whispering as she walked.

chapter thirteen

★

By late July, the lumberyard was operating at full tilt. Since Michigan got so cold in the wintertime, most folks tried to do their construction and improvement projects during the summer months. Men were buying concrete, sand, wood, bricks, nails, and so forth just as fast as the railcars could bring these materials into town.

Grandad had hired some extra help to keep up with everything, and of course Les and Johnny continued to do some of the smaller projects that needed finishing around the place. They had to be careful to be a help and not a nuisance; Grandad complained whenever he felt the boys had been "caught underfoot." They were careful to do good work and make Grandad proud of them.

During the summertime, Grandad also operated a giant cucumber sorting machine; this was a legacy from his own father who had started a cider mill in Springport after emigrating from Canada in the 1800s. The cider mill was gone, but the Harrises still had an interest in some area agriculture and worked with local farmers to get produce to market.

With the humming of the cucumber machine came the new sounds of foreign tongues. Springport in the summertime was host to a half-dozen Mexican families that came north from the lower states to work on the farms. They picked celery and cucumbers and fruit, and they were often at the lumberyard speaking rapidly to one another and gesturing broadly.

Les and Johnny were fascinated by these migrant workers. They stayed in town for only a few weeks, as long as it took for the crops to be picked, but when they were there they actually lived at the lumberyard. There was a separate, smaller work building with an open concrete foundation that Grandad used for storage. The exposed foundation was divided by concrete blocks into a series of four rooms, each lacking a front wall. Each room was about ten feet square, the size of a small bedroom, and yet the six migrant families lived in these open, three-sided rooms, children and all.

Although at first this arrangement seemed to Les and Johnny like a grand adventure—who wouldn't want to live like they were camping every day?—the boys soon realized how difficult life was for these families. There was no place for them to wash, no easy way for them to cook, and they had no belongings to speak of.

And yet these families seemed so happy together. There was much laughter, the children were hugged and praised, and nobody fought. Boys the same age as Les and Johnny had to go out and help in the fields, but they were warmly recognized at home for their efforts.

One day, Les saw a little brown girl of about four years old standing near the lumberyard office. She was dressed in a raggedy dress and holding a battered old leather purse. He wondered if she was lost, and went out to her.

"Hello?" Les said. The girl was startled, but she smiled at him.

"No hablo Inglés," the girl said. "Not Eeenglish."

Les nodded. "Okay," he said. "Where is your mother? *Madre?*"

The girl thought, then pointed to the little concrete rooms behind her. "*Tengo bolsa,*" she said excitedly, pointing to her purse. "*Como mi madre.*"

"Your purse?" Les said. "Your purse is like your mother?"

The girl began speaking rapidly and gesturing proudly to her purse. She pantomimed putting it over her shoulder and shopping like a grown-up lady. "*Soy importante,*" she said, "*como mi madre.*"

Importante... important, Les gathered. *The purse makes her feel important, like her mother.*

Les couldn't imagine having only one possession. What would that be like? How would it be to come from nothing, to live outdoors?

The little girl waved and ran off. Les watched as she scurried back to her concrete den and was scooped up by her mother into a warm hug. The girl was laughing; she didn't seem unhappy at all.

Look at that, Les thought. *She and her family are happy, and they have nothing. My family has a lot more than they do; maybe there is a chance for us to find some happiness too, if we look hard enough.*

★

Charlie was spending every day over at Aunt Myrtelle's, working on the Model A. The blasted automobile was making him furious. Sometimes he wasn't sure whether to fix it or beat it with a crowbar.

He had done all kinds of work to it, but the car just wouldn't start. It seemed as if Charlie would fix one problem only to realize there were three others right behind it. He'd earned enough (and learned enough) working at Mr. Snow's garage to be able to put in all new spark plugs and points, along with a new condenser, air filter, and battery. Still nothing.

He took out the carburetor and disassembled it using the manual at Mr. Snow's garage. There were some spots that needed fixing, but overall it was in good shape. Charlie reinstalled the carburetor and was then absolutely certain that fuel was getting into the engine as it should. Still nothing.

Mr. Snow didn't know what to tell him, either.

"Did you double-check everything?" he asked Charlie. "All the parts are installed correctly?"

"Yes, sir," Charlie said.

"Did you check the timing and the points?"

"Yep; everything looks just like it should."

"No wires broken or touching?"

"Not that I can see," Charlie said.

Mr. Snow shrugged. "Why don't you bring the coil in here, and we'll double-check it," he suggested. "Maybe that's the problem."

But it wasn't. Charlie was beyond frustrated. He went back over to Aunt Myrtelle's, reinstalled the coil, and sat down on the garage floor, staring at the car.

It might as well be a sculpture, he thought. *That's the only value it has.*

If he were home, working on one of his model airplanes, he would have lit it on fire and thrown it out the window by now. But the car was too big, and too significant a gift, to destroy. Grandad had given it to him, and Charlie had to make this work, if only for Grandad's sake.

But how? Charlie felt angry and hopeless and utterly stymied.

Charlie heard Aunt Myrtelle's footsteps approaching the door of the garage. She entered carrying a glass of lemonade and found him sitting on the floor. "May I sit by you?" she asked, handing him the glass.

"Sure."

She lowered herself to the ground, tucked her skirt over her knees, and said, "What's wrong with it?"

"I don't know."

"Pretty frustrating, then," she continued thoughtfully. "What are you going to do? Do you have any ideas?"

Charlie grinned lopsidedly at her. "Shoot it? Put us both out of our misery?"

Aunt Myrtelle laughed. "You're a better problem-solver than that, Charlie," she said, patting his knee.

"Am I?"

"Of course," she said. Charlie sipped his lemonade; they were both silent and thoughtful for a minute. Finally Aunt Myrtelle said, "I don't know anything about engines, really, but I have an idea that they are made up of a whole bunch of parts with specific jobs. Each one must do its job properly—play its role—or the engine won't run.

"It looks to me like you've got a stubborn part in there. A part that doesn't know what it's supposed to do or how to do it. You've got to find that part and set it straight, so it can be a functioning part of the fluid whole."

Charlie didn't say anything. He just stared sullenly at the car and sipped his lemonade.

"Now, there are a lot of ways for you to tackle the problem of a stubborn part," Aunt Myrtelle went on. "You can try to force it, or you can coax it, or you can look at it and try to understand ways of improving the conditions in which it is trying to operate. If I know you—and I think I do—you're probably inclined to force it right now. But I doubt that's the right thing to do."

"What do you suggest?" Charlie asked.

"I'd suggest you come into the house with me and have dinner and play with the cat. I think time away from this will help you clear your head and replenish your stores of patience. When you come back—tomorrow, the day after, or even next week—you will feel ready to look at this project with fresh eyes and help each part do what it needs to do. The urge to force it will be gone."

Charlie looked at his aunt. She had a smile for him, and she leaned over to kiss his cheek. "You are so determined," she said admiringly. "But sometimes even determination needs a respite."

She stood and dusted herself off, then held out a hand. Charlie took it, and they walked together back into the house.

James's plane roared down the runway, silver wings slicing. He felt the vibration of the tarmac beneath his wheels, growing faster, noisier, harder, and then—air. He loved the feeling of takeoff, when his stomach seemed to flip over and the earth slipped away. He let his eyes leave the instrument panel for a moment, gazing into the sky, seeing nothing for an instant as the clouds thickened, then dissipated.

Above the clouds the sky was perfectly clear. It was raining on the ground—dismal and gray—but once the nose of James's plane parted the clouds, the sky was bright. *It must always be this way,* James thought. *No matter how bad the weather looks down below, the sky is always sunny.*

James's thoughts turned, as they always did, to Mary Jane. *I must remember to write to her and tell her about the sky and the clouds.*

The air was smooth, no turbulence. The engine thrummed and James verified his position and course. Everything looked good. He was headed west, out over the plains, where on a clear day it seemed like the earth and sky went forever. He scanned the horizon and saw the metallic shimmer of another plane dozens of miles away to his left. It was a beautiful day for flying.

Cruising altitude. James let himself settle into his seat, relaxing into the flight. It was pretty easy, if you didn't think too hard or let yourself fret over every single movement of a needle. He and his plane were a single creation, working together to pierce the blue sky with action and movement. James felt as if he owned the whole world up here.

But then his plane betrayed him. One instant, James and the plane were as one, soaring together as man and machine; the next, James was soaring in silence, his machine dead beneath his hands. The engine was completely silent; all James could hear was the whistle of air and the terrifying thud of his own heart as it pounded in his ears.

James reacted instantaneously; his months of training kicked in. He immediately asserted control of the plane to guide it into a stable descent and began working through a checklist to locate the cause of the engine trouble.

He had done all his preflight checks and knew the fuel mixture was good; everything else had been in order when he left the ground. He checked the fuel supply—good; throttle position—good; what was it? He kept going, checking quickly as the plane continued to descend.

It was the ignition. Checking the magneto switch, James

could see that both the regular and backup magnetos had failed. There was no restarting this plane. It was nothing he could have caught in a preflight check; it was just one of those failures that sometimes happen.

James's heart was pounding and he felt sick. He had trained for this type of situation but he never really thought it would happen. And all that training had not prepared him for the blind, numbing panic he'd be feeling when and if something like this happened.

The terrain below was… well, it was not terrain. It was a major city. James was descending into Denver, Colorado, with its buildings and houses, cars and schools. There was no safe place to land. James would cause damage not only to himself but also to people and property on the ground if he crashed here.

James needed to bank hard and fast to the left so he could come down just to the north of Denver. His odds of finding a flat expanse of farm field to land in were better up there. James's arm and shoulder muscles strained as he lifted the plane's wings and came around in a smooth glide. Sweat beaded up on his forehead.

James radioed and provided his coordinates. In a voice that was deceptively calm and clear, he told the tower where he thought he'd be landing and what the cause of the engine trouble was. The rain began to hit the plane again as he came down through the clouds.

There was only a small expanse of field to work with. The rural area at which James had aimed was not as rural as he'd hoped. He would have to set the plane down quickly and stop her fast to avoid hitting a small compound of farmhouses, silos, and barns.

It's okay, James told himself, his thoughts hammering along with the rhythm of his heart. *It's okay, it's okay, it's okay.*

"I'll put her down gently," he said into his radio as the earth came quickly up to meet him.

The plane's wheels touched down in the field and James braked hard. The plane's wings caught in the field of tall corn and slowed quickly, stopping more than fifty yards away from the farmyard.

James sat back and wiped his brow. He knew he had done well, but his heart didn't seem to want to stop pounding. He gave himself a minute to regain his composure, then lifted himself from the plane and went to the farmhouse to say hello.

★

"Hello," Grandma Barney said. Mother and Dad were coming into the house on St. James Place, home again after more than a month in the hospital. The taxi pulled away from the curb and the front door closed with a soft thud.

"Mama," Dad said, leaning in to kiss Grandma Barney's cheek. "How have you been?"

"Oh, just fine," Grandma Barney said. "Better, now that you are here."

Mother didn't say anything as she brushed past them into the front room. "Things look good," she said. "Although undoubtedly I will have much to do to get the house back in order."

Grandma Barney smiled to herself. "I think you'll find that everything is very clean, my dear," she said. "Please don't feel the need to tax yourself. You've been through a lot."

"No thanks to you," Mother said. "Though I do appreciate your staying here to make sure the house didn't burn down in my absence."

Grandma Barney gritted her teeth, determined to let the comment pass. It was time to turn over a new leaf.

Dad took the bags up to the bedroom, leaving the two women alone.

"I would like very much to see if we can put matters right between us," Grandma Barney said, sitting down. "I think it would be better for the entire family if you and I could bury the hatchet and live together as friends."

Mother regarded Grandma Barney through narrow eyes. "You move in here, take over my home, send my children away, and basically have me and my husband *committed*," she said. "And now you want to bury the hatchet?"

Grandma Barney tried to muster a smile. "I do," she replied. "You must know that all those choices were made for the good of you and your family. I care about you; you have been part of my life and family for nearly twenty years. You are the mother of my grandchildren, and they deserve a happy, well-functioning home."

"I agree," Mother said. "They do. And that is precisely why you are not going to be part of it any longer. You may pack your things and leave today."

Grandma Barney gasped. "But where will I go?" she asked. "I've sold my house, and—"

"You will find something, I'm sure," Mother interrupted coldly. "Go stay with someone else, or get an apartment."

"Did you decide this by yourself, or did—"

"We have discussed it, and your son is in full agreement," Mother continued right over the top of Grandma Barney. "It's either you or me and, for the sake of our family, it has been decided that it shall be you. Get packing."

chapter fourteen

★

In addition to selling lumber and processing cucumbers, Grandad had interests in other products, like coal. On a regular basis the train would come through and bring cars directly into the coal siding. The railcars would open from the bottom and drop a load of coal into a concrete bin that was nearly twenty feet deep.

That's when Charlie Rankin took over.

Charlie Rankin was Grandad's most trusted and devoted employee. He had worked at the lumberyard as long as he or anyone else could remember, and the coal was his specialty. He shoveled, weighed, transported, and delivered coal all day every day; in fact, he usually looked like a lump of coal because the black dust from it perpetually covered his face, hair, and clothing. Les thought he resembled a character in a Dickens novel; he was tall and thin and slightly stooped, with a big nose and large hands and feet.

Charlie lived in a little house at the edge of the lumberyard. It was better than the three-walled boxes in which the migrant families were living, but not by much.

Over the years Charlie got so adept at loading the coal into his delivery truck that he could tell just by looking how much was there. He would often take the truck over to weigh it just to be sure, but he almost never had to go back to make adjustments. He knew immediately whether there was a half ton, one ton, or two.

One day Charlie came over to speak with Johnny. He was usually too busy to say much to the MacGregor boys, but Johnny was clearly bored and beginning to show signs of getting into mischief. "Hi, Nubbin," Charlie said. "Do you want to come with me on a delivery?"

Johnny nodded and followed Charlie to the coal truck. "Where are we going?"

"You'll see," Charlie said. He helped Johnny up the big steps into the truck cab. Johnny slid across the hot, hard red leather seat and leaned forward to look out the windshield. "You'd better sit back," Charlie advised. "Your face will hit the dash when we get up some speed."

Johnny pushed himself back, trying to ignore the heat of the leather against his legs. Charlie started the truck with a rumble and pulled out into the street.

Springport was a small enough town that it didn't take long before the paved streets gave way to dusty dirt roads. Charlie drove Johnny several miles toward Duck Lake, then stopped in front of a big sprawling farmhouse with a big red barn. The house had three blue stars in the window, meaning that they had three sons fighting in the war. There was one gold star too, which meant they had lost a boy.

Charlie backed the truck into the drive and up close to the house. The truck stopped close to a side basement window then threw some gears to lift the truck bed. The back of the truck groaned with effort and Johnny could feel vibrations shaking the entire vehicle. He quickly opened his door and jumped out to watch the action.

Charlie was already out of the truck, unfastening the coal shovel from the back. He hooked a heavy piece of metal—the coal slide—to the lip of the truck bed and put the rest of it through the basement window. He pulled a lever that allowed coal to roll down the slide and into the house, then used the shovel to push the coal down the slide.

When enough coal had gone into the house, Charlie went back up and raised the truck bed some more. He got nearly all the coal out this way but still had to climb up into the truck and use his shovel to empty some coal from the corners.

Johnny watched this entire process without speaking a single word. Charlie didn't talk either. When the truck bed was empty and the basement window again closed, both of them climbed back into the truck. Charlie got busy writing on a little yellow notepad, then put the truck in gear and drove away.

Johnny was startled. "Um, Charlie?" he said.

"Hm," Charlie said.

"Didn't you forget something?"

"What?"

"You didn't get any money from the house," Johnny said.

"Your Grandad doesn't charge for this house," Charlie said.

Johnny thought about that all the way back to town. It occurred to Johnny that there was an awful lot of hardship in this world, especially during wartime. Between the Mexican migrants who lived outdoors, Charlie Rankin who worked so faithfully and had so little, and the family that had given four of its boys to the war effort, there was a good deal of poverty and sacrifice going on in Springport. Even Grandad made his sacrifice, giving free materials to people who needed them.

It's just like what President Roosevelt always says, Johnny thought. *Everyone must do their part and not complain. We're all in this together.*

That night, as Johnny lay in the darkness of the attic bedroom, he told Les what he had seen that day. "That must be what it means to be on the home front," Johnny said. "Everyone has to work together to make sure the right things happen."

Les was quiet, pondering. What Johnny said made sense. Everyone did their part even if they couldn't see how it precisely fit into the larger war effort. Each contribution mattered even if it was impossible to see quite how or why. And sometimes the how and why of it might not be clear right away. Even so, everyone had to try to stick it out and fight for what was just and good and right.

They just had to try their best and hope for better days to come.

Thinking of that made Les remember the Mexican family in Grandad's lumberyard. They were not unhappy, even though they were the people Les saw having the greatest hardship. They were finding a way to make their lives together happy; taking pleasure in their few possessions and their love for one another.

Les thought of his own family. If they could start pulling together and loving one another like that, just imagine how happy they would be.

★

The next day at the lumberyard was a slow one. It was raining, so the men who came in were lingering longer and talking more. It was the kind of day when local news was shared, complaints were traded, and ideas were born.

A small group of farmers had clustered in Grandad's office. They were griping about their corn crops and the birds that were quite literally eating into their profits. Vester Mock was complaining to George Lininger about the crows that were picking their corn plants clean. With a war on, the corn was worth more than ever, but the birds weren't going away. "I don't know what it is," Mr. Lininger said. "The weather, the seed we used... it's never been this bad with the birds before."

"Our harvest is going to be next to nothing," Mr. Mock worried. "If this keeps up, there won't be a clean ear to pick. We'll have to sell it all for feed and take a loss."

Grandad suggested scarecrows and got a huge laugh. "I could stand out there myself with a shotgun and those birds would just sneer at me and keep eating," Mr. Sanford said.

"We ought to put up a bounty on the blasted things," said Mr. Mock.

"I'm in!" shouted Mr. Lininger. "Wouldn't that be something? Each of us puts in some money, and we pay the kids to shoot 'em with their BB guns."

Grandad sat a little straighter. "You know, you could do that," he said thoughtfully. "If each of you put in ten dollars, that would pay for six hundred dead crows at a nickel apiece. I'd be happy to run it for you; we could pay kids for the corpses and I'd burn 'em here."

And so it was decided. There would be a bounty on birds that summer. All across Springport boys were dragging out their BB guns and taking aim at anything that flew. It was excellent target practice and great fun (and profit) for everybody.

Les, Johnny, and Roger had to share a BB gun. Roger had one, but Les and Johnny had left theirs in Kenmore and had to borrow a gun when they wanted to go shooting. Roger was willing to share, but he took a percentage of the bounty. Les had argued this at first but succumbed to Roger's logic that any time someone else was using his gun he was missing out on profits of his own.

It seemed like everyone was shooting birds. Charlie had gone out with Uncle Fritz's .22 and done fairly well, and Roger was at one point even compelled to lend his rifle to his younger sister Kitty, who wanted to try. For a girl she was not a bad shot; she came home with two dead crows and earned herself the price of a movie ticket.

The downside to all the shooting was that it was getting harder to find kids to play with in the afternoon. They were all out in the cornfields.

Les and Johnny were sitting home one Sunday afternoon, openly bored and whining to Nanny and Grandad as they all sat on the front porch. It was a hot, muggy day in late July, the kind of day that makes it difficult to get up and do anything but even harder for a growing boy to sit still.

Nanny fanned herself with a great big straw hat. "Boys, there is plenty around here to do," she said. "Your moaning and wailing isn't going to get very far with me. Why, if you're having trouble I can think of sixteen jobs that need doing, all right there in the house."

"Where's Charlie?" Grandad asked. "Over at Myrtelle's?"

"Anyplace else?" Nanny said with a smile. "I think he's finally ready to go back and tackle that engine."

"I wish I had a car," Les said. "I could drive around all afternoon."

Grandad leaned his head against the back of his big wooden rocker. "Sure, you could," he said. Absently he smacked his hand against his arm. "Darned flies," he said.

The flies were indeed a problem. They swarmed in the kitchen and near the garage and on the front porch, creating a nuisance for anyone who wanted to take just a minute to sit. Their fat, buzzing bodies were nasty and annoying.

"You know," Grandad said out of the blue. "I think I should take a lesson from the farmers. I am going to put a bounty on dead flies."

Les perked up. "How much?"

"I'll give you boys a penny for every five flies you bring me," Grandad said, sounding kind of inspired. "How does that sound?"

Johnny considered both the proposal and the number of flies buzzing around the porch. "I think that could work."

"I'm in!" Les exclaimed. He had a brilliant idea, one that had been waiting for just such an opportunity as this. He ran into the house, the screen door slapping shut behind him as he flew up the stairs. He came down a few minutes later with a little wooden box, some wires, and a six-volt battery in his hand.

Johnny had long since learned to look nonchalant and ask no questions, but Grandad was not familiar with Les's way of thinking. "What's that?" Grandad asked.

"It's a miniature electric chair," Les answered. "I'm going to use it to execute the flies."

"You just happened to have this device made?" Grandad said, incredulous. "What on earth prompted you to do it?"

"I was actually building something else," Les said. "But this seems like a good way to use these parts for the time being."

"Well, now I've seen everything," Grandad said. "How does it work?"

Les showed him that the box had two metal posts on one side to bring power in and two more on the top for power out. The upper posts each had needles mounted on them at ninety degrees, so they almost touched. Off to the side were the battery and an old-fashioned-looking throw switch.

Les used his hands to capture a live housefly. Pinning it between the two needles, he threw the switch and the power zapped through the fly, killing it almost instantly.

"Yep," Grandad said. "Now I sure have seen everything." He left the boys to their grisly work and went upstairs to take a nap.

Throughout the rest of the afternoon Les and Johnny trapped and electrocuted flies. It was not easy work, but they had a good time; each time they captured a fly between the needles on the death machine, Les would imitate the fly, squealing and sputtering in a high-pitched voice, "Stop! I'm innocent, I tell you! You got the wrong fly!"

At the end of the afternoon, the boys had earned five cents and the satisfying knowledge that, for two dozen irritating flies, justice had at last been served.

★

That night, for the first time, Charlie's Model A project showed signs of real promise.

Charlie took Aunt Myrtelle's advice and went through the entire engine trying to understand what was blocking the effective action of each of its parts. He realized that there was a wire on the lower plate assembly of the distributor that seemed just a little too short. Looking at it, Charlie reasoned that when the assembly tried to turn, it wouldn't be able to rotate far enough for the engine to run. That one single wire was holding it back and preventing the entire distributor—and thus the entire engine—from being able to function as it was supposed to.

Charlie removed the assembly and, using some manuals Mr. Snow had lent him, carefully replaced the short wire with a longer one. The new wire made a loop before it went up to the points, and was easily replaced.

Charlie slipped into the driver's seat and tried again to start the car. At last, the engine turned over, filling Charlie's heart with joy.

It didn't keep running for more than an instant, which was too bad, but it represented a real breakthrough for Charlie. It was the first time in his life that he knew he'd finish a project—really finish it, beginning to end, and it would work like it was supposed to.

Aunt Myrtelle came from the house first, a dish towel in her hands. "Does it work?" she exclaimed, beaming. Uncle Fred, Uncle Fritz, and Aunt Mary came flying out behind her, exclaiming and slapping Charlie on the back.

"Not entirely," Charlie said. "It didn't keep going, but at least it started."

"Oh, you'll be scooting all over town before you know it!" Uncle Fred exclaimed.

Uncle Fritz winked. "Just make sure it goes seventy miles an hour," he said, clapping Charlie's shoulder again.

They stood and talked for a long moment before the adults filed back into the house with enthusiasm. Only Aunt Myrtelle remained behind.

"I'm so proud of you, Charlie," she said, taking his hand in hers. "But I'll also be sorry when the car works again."

"Why is that?" Charlie asked, astonished.

"Because you won't be in my garage anymore," she replied, wistfulness in her tone. "I've loved having you here."

"I'll still keep the car here, and I'll come by all the time."

"It's not the same. I feel that with you here, I've had a chance to see you grow and blossom. I'm going to miss watching the transformation. You know, I've seen a real change in you this summer."

"How's that?" Charlie asked.

"You seem less… angry," she said softly. "Do you feel less angry? More hopeful?"

Charlie gave it some thought. The truth was, he'd been so focused on getting the Model A up and running that he hadn't given much thought to himself one way or the other. "I guess I do, now that you mention it."

"Why do you suppose that is?" Aunt Myrtelle asked.

"I don't know," Charlie admitted. "Been busy, I guess."

But Charlie knew it was more than the act of forgetting himself in a project that had caused the change. It was also being here, in Springport, with Nanny and Grandad and aunts and uncles and friends and respect and love. It was having the liberty to do what he wanted to do, whether it was fix a car or get up late or wander a cornfield looking for birds. It was a warm summertime feeling: special, magical, happy, free.

"There is a point where a boy starts to become a man," Aunt Myrtelle was saying. "I've always wondered what that looks like. And in you, this summer, I got to see it. Thank you for sharing it with me."

★

A few blocks over, across the rooftops, Les and Johnny were trying to fall asleep. The evening breeze was drifting in through the window, billowing Nanny's white curtains and caressing their cheeks.

Les was reciting a poem to his brother:

One fine day
About midnight
Two dead soldiers
Got in a fight
Back to back
They faced each other
Drew their swords
And shot each other
A deaf policeman
Heard the noise
Came out and
Killed the two dead boys.
If you don't believe
This lie, it's true
Ask the blind man
He saw it too.

Johnny was giggling like anything, which made Les smile too. What a good night. What a beautiful summer.

chapter fifteen

★

My dearest Mary Jane,

I am writing to brag. I'm just going to say that now!

My superiors say I am the best pilot in my unit. They have told me to put in for whatever assignment I would like; they say my skills are second to none, I have aced every single written test, and I have even (they say) demonstrated a strong aptitude for strategy.

I like the flying, I enjoy the drills, and I am succeeding. My only problem is I would so much rather be home with you. I am trying to figure out how to get there as quickly as I can (short of getting wounded, of course). I do know a fellow who shot himself deliberately in his foot in order to get back home from the Army; unfortunately, he only hit his toe. They just gave him a special boot to wear and now he is still here.

My options, I'm told, are going to be running a bomber, a fighter, a troop transport plane, or reconnaissance. I'm leaning toward the "recon" work, as it's called, because it seems safer and more likely to get me home to you without injury. They would give me a fancy plane outfitted with cameras, not guns, and I would be flying over big areas and taking pictures of them for the generals. It's a lot like what my father did in the last war, only I would be using a plane instead of a balloon.

Because I'm doing so well, I'm hoping they let me pick. I'll let you know as soon as I find out what I'll be doing. Write soon and tell me what you think!

How is everything in Kenmore? I got a letter from my mother telling me she and Dad are back from the hospital. She said everything is good again. Have you been over there? Is this true? Where is Grandma Barney?

I miss you so much; please give yourself a big hug and kiss for me.

All my love,
James

★

Dear James,

It was lovely to hear from you, though I do wish you wouldn't brag. I fear you will fall prey to friendly fire once the other men get tired of listening to you. I myself became somewhat queasy upon reading of all your self-proclaimed success. Proud, but queasy nevertheless.

I did hear a joke that made me think of you:

Q: How do you know if there is an Army pilot at your party?

A: Don't worry, he'll tell you.

Things here are fine. It's been raining, but I keep remembering how you told me the sky is blue above those dark clouds, and it makes me smile.

Your mother and dad are home and seem

to be fine. I stopped by once with some cookies and a vase of flowers from our garden; your mother was very kind and asked me to stay. She wanted to talk all about you and how much she misses you, had I heard anything, etc. etc. etc. She had not been drinking and it was a nice, if stilted, visit.

I don't know where your Grandma Barney went. She left Kenmore in an awful rush and I haven't heard from her at all. I'm quite worried, actually. I like her and want to keep in touch.

As far as your assignment is concerned, I don't think it is a big surprise that I like your "recon" idea the best. Whatever is safest makes me happy.

All is well here. I am volunteering for the Red Cross now and thinking about getting a job. More and more ladies are working and I don't have much else going on. Your mother says I absolutely should NOT go to work; that I am too good for that sort of thing, but I don't know. It would keep me busy and stop me from fretting too much about the war and you being anywhere near it.

Please stay safe—cookies are enclosed, along with hundreds of kisses for you!

Love,
Mary Jane

★

It was a peaceful Saturday morning in August. It was Aunt Norma's birthday and the entire Harris family had gathered at the house on Duck Lake to celebrate. There was fried chicken from Aunt Mary's coop—a rare treat during wartime.

After lunch, Les and Johnny went out swimming in the lake with Roger, Kitty, and Dee. The lake was mucky and weedy along the bottom, but the water felt cool. The kids splashed and played and hunted for rocks and minnows, contentedly ignoring all the grown-up talk they could hear coming from the house.

Les and Johnny had been eyeing Uncle Bob's rowboat, tethered at the end of the dock. Nobody had taken it out since Uncle Bob had left for the war, and Les told Johnny it needed a little cruise, just to make sure it was fit.

"You can't take that boat," Roger said. "You'll be in huge trouble if you do."

"Why?" Les asked.

"You have to have a grown-up with you; that's the rule," Roger said. "If you get caught, you're going to catch it."

"Nobody's paying attention," Les rejoined. "And it will only be for a minute."

"I don't know," Roger said dubiously.

"You just watch us," Les said. "If we have trouble, you go get help. Otherwise, we'll be back in a hot minute."

Johnny and Les clambered, dripping, into the vessel and untied the ropes. Les rowed while Johnny navigated and laughed gleefully about their "adventure on the high seas." Johnny was talking animatedly in a fake pirate voice and it was pretty funny.

They rowed far enough out that they could still see the house and the dock. Les was getting into the spirit of their pirate play, and occasionally snarled his own soft, "Argh, matey" into the conversation. Johnny was giggling and rolling all over the boat.

From the shore, Roger watched them. Kitty and Dee weren't paying any attention, and eventually they got cold and went back up to the house. Roger sat on the dock, his feet dangling, wishing he'd gone along for the boat ride.

Uncle Bob had filled an old coffee can with cement and attached it to a length of chain for an anchor. The boys dropped it into the water to hold their position. They called commands to each other and jumped around on the old rowboat, imitating pirate adventures and carrying out famous naval battles. Eventually their activity degenerated into a game of "let's see who can push the other off this boat."

Johnny won. Les hit the water with a huge splash—though with no shriek—and the boys laughed themselves silly. Johnny handed out an oar for Les to grab hold of, but Les refused. "No," he said, laughing. "I'm not getting back up now. The water's too nice. I've had it with you and am going for a swim." With that, Les began paddling out away from the boat, into the deeper waters at the center of the lake.

Les floated on his back, enjoying the way the summer sun sparkled on the water and warmed his skin. In contrast with the coolness of the water, the sensation was heavenly. He enjoyed it so much, in fact, that he forgot to notice how far he had come until he was much too tired and cramped to swim back to the boat.

He righted himself vertically, began treading water, then called to Johnny. Because of the distance, however, Johnny seemed not to hear him. So Les began to motion and splash with his hands, which did get Johnny's attention but also caused the younger boy to presume Les was drowning.

From the shore, Roger saw and assumed the same. He started hollering to Johnny, and went tearing up to the house for help.

"I'm coming, Les!" Johnny screamed. "I've got you!" He grabbed an oar and began to row as hard as he could. It took several minutes before Johnny remembered the anchor and realized it was the reason why he wasn't going anywhere at all. "Cripes," he swore, pulling on the chain desperately, and then—inexplicably—Johnny began to laugh.

It was a terrible hyena laugh, born of desperation and fear and hysteria. Les was all Johnny had in this world. If he lost Les, nobody would ever tell him what was going on and he'd never learn anything good. Just thinking back over the summer, Les had taught Johnny how to shave a card deck and tell when dice were loaded. He'd shown Johnny how to break into a locked car and hot-wire the engine, and how to solder five pennies together to save time in a poker game. If something happened to Les, Johnny would be not only bereft, but also ignorant of all this important knowledge.

So Johnny rowed, laughing feverishly and trying to figure out how he was going to explain to Nanny and Grandad that he'd let his brother drown. Criminy, couldn't this boat go any faster?

On the shore, all the aunts and uncles were hopping up and down, shouting instructions to Johnny. Grandad and Nanny stood anxiously waiting to see what would happen.

Finally Les was close enough to grab. Johnny let out an oar and Les pulled himself grumbling back on board. "Sheez, what's with all the laughing?" were the first words from his mouth.

"I don't know," Johnny admitted. "I was scared, I guess. And I forgot to pull up the anchor."

"Well, you are crazy as a bug and I am done with you," Les said, disgusted. "Row us back home. I'm tired. I can't believe you almost let me drown."

When they reached shore, there was more punishment waiting. Les and Johnny were sent to an upstairs bedroom for the rest of the day, and Roger was lectured for letting them take the boat.

★

In all the chaos of Les and Johnny's boat ride, nobody had noticed when Charlie slipped away and walked the three miles back to town. He was glad of the solitude, grateful for the time on his own, and single-mindedly focused on his project in Aunt Myrtelle's garage.

Walking also gave him time to think. He thought about his Aunt Myrtelle and how much she seemed to love him. Their conversations over the summer had been so good. She always took notice of what he was doing and working on, and she treated him with extra care. She and Uncle Fred never fought, not like his own Mother and Dad, and it settled Charlie to be in a home where there was peace. He felt his own temper so much less keenly; maybe that's what Aunt Myrtelle was trying to say the other night when they talked.

Of course, Charlie also thought about the old Model A. Remembering what he knew about cars, he knew they were symbols of progress—human progress, away from horses and buggies and wagons and hay, toward cities and factories and a future that was still too far away to see clearly. But Charlie also felt it was a symbol of his own progress. Progress away from that dark, stringy ball of surliness and anger that kept him caged up all the time. Progress away from constantly being compared to James and found lacking; progress toward being his own person with his own talents and interests and adventures.

Perhaps that's what drove Charlie to town now. He needed to finish that car, to make it run, in order to make himself believe again. He wanted to know that all this progress was going somewhere, that it wouldn't end with a half-fixed car that he might or might not get back to later. He needed the hope.

And so he walked.

★

The upstairs bedroom at Aunt Norma's was very interesting. Les found a book and Johnny was looking through an old photograph album. There were pictures of Nanny and Grandad, along with all the aunts and uncles and even Mother. She had been a beautiful girl, just as she said. Johnny touched her face with a finger and wondered how she was doing.

The door opened and Nanny came softly into the room. "I see you found the photographs," she said, coming to sit on the bed next to Johnny. She looked at the page and saw Mother's image gazing seriously back. "She was lovely, wasn't she?"

Johnny nodded and Les, setting his book down, came to look too. Nanny turned to face them both. "She's not lovely anymore, is she?"

"She's still pretty," Les said. "But she is upset a lot."

Nanny nodded. "Pretty is as pretty does, I always say," she began haltingly, then stopped. If Johnny didn't know better, he would think she seemed to be fighting tears. But Nanny never cried.

"We're sorry about the boat, Nanny," Johnny said.

"Oh, bless you," Nanny said. "That's fine. I'm just glad you're all right."

Nanny lifted the photograph album away from Johnny and turned a few of the thick pages. "A family is an interesting machine," she said, her voice thick. "It's a crazy contraption, made up of parts that are always moving, changing shape, or breaking down. We spend our lives trying to make that crazy contraption work just the way we want it to, when we know perfectly well it never will. All we can do is hope for a few smooth moments every now and then. A few good times to tide us over when life isn't so good."

She closed the book. "I have been worrying about you boys a great deal," she said. "I know your life in Kenmore has not been what it should be. I am having a very hard time imagining how I am going to send you back to it."

Johnny felt his eyes beginning to fill with tears.

"But go back you must," she said. "I am not your mother, and Springport is not your home."

"We can't stay?" Les whispered. "We want to stay."

Nanny shook her head. "You cannot stay," she said. "You and I each have our rightful places, and your place is with your mother and dad, in your own family."

"But *you* are our family too," Johnny protested.

"Yes, I am," Nanny said, her voice breaking slightly. "And I will always have a place for you when you need it. But look around you, boys. Life is not about taking the easier, gentler path. We all must give more than we think we can, if we are to improve life for ourselves, our families, and the world."

"You sound like President Roosevelt," Les said sarcastically.

"Maybe," Nanny smiled sadly. "But I think it is true that there is reward in the harder path. I want you to take that path, and know that I'm a phone call away whenever you need me."

"When do we have to leave?" Johnny asked, tears running down his face.

Nanny was spared having to answer the question by a mind-numbing roar from the road. Within seconds they could hear cheering and applause from downstairs, spilling out into the front lawn.

Nanny, Les, and Johnny leaped up and ran to the window to see what was going on. There, in the driveway, sat a fully functional Model A Ford with Charlie at the wheel.

Beaming.

chapter sixteen

★

Just as Nanny said, the day soon came when Les, Johnny, and Charlie had to make the train trip back to New York.

Mother and Dad were home from the hospital and, in keeping with their desire to make a fresh beginning for themselves, they had moved to a new house. It was a smaller place on Hazeltine Avenue, considerably north of where they had lived on St. James Place, and Les was heartsick to lose his secret laboratory and all his equipment. Yet another move, yet another house. At least now the boys would still be able to attend the same school.

Les was sure Mother and Dad hadn't bothered to check the attic bedroom for the boys' possessions before they left; they never troubled themselves about the children's belongings when they relocated. The map, the laboratory—it was all still there, just waiting for some lucky new family to discover it.

None of the boys wanted to leave Springport and, no matter how many times Nanny promised them they could come back and stay the following summer, they refused to be consoled. Charlie reluctantly put his Model A in storage at the lumberyard, and Johnny and Les helped Nanny clean their room and close it up for the winter.

There were almost too many good-byes for Les to handle. It seemed as though he spent all of his time pushing past the tightness in his throat, trying not to show how truly upset he was at the thought of going home. It felt to him like going backward.

Making matters worse, the whole Harris clan came to the house on Grand Street to say good-bye. All the aunts and uncles and even Roger, Kitty, and Dee were there to press hugs and kisses upon the boys. Even Charlie seemed to be clenching his jaw more than usual, overcome with the emotion of the farewell.

The front bell rang and Johnny ran to answer it. It was Madam, dressed in her customary way, with her large satchel thrown over one velvet-clad shoulder. "Hello, young man," she said. "I'm here to say good-bye."

Johnny stepped aside to let her pass. Nanny came out and greeted her friend with a kiss on the cheek. "I've brought something for the boys," Madam said by way of explanation. "It's on the porch."

Johnny scrambled out to the front porch and saw, there on the wooden planks, a rather large cardboard box with holes punched into the top. He walked slowly toward it and peeked down through the small openings. Inside were three baby ducks. They were covered with fuzz and cheeping contentedly.

Nanny was right behind him. "My stars, Madam!" she exclaimed. "Where on earth did you find baby ducks at this time of year?"

"I have my ways," Madam said cryptically.

Johnny laughed out loud. The ducks were a funny, wonderful gift. It was so like Madam—with the incongruous contents of her satchel, the crazy stories, and the eccentric ways—to give the boys something like this.

"For not understanding kids," he said, "you sure got this one right!" And he ran up, threw his arms around her neck, and hugged her tight.

★

Grandad drove them all to the station. The boys were somber and morose, especially when it came time for them to unload and go inside.

"Just a minute," Grandad said. "Charlie, I want you to know that we'll keep that car nice for you. When you come back next summer, you can drive it all you want. All I ask is that you call me every now and then and tell me what's going on at home."

Charlie agreed.

"All three of you boys will be back next summer to work for me," Grandad said. "Correct?"

"Yes, sir," Les said. Charlie and Johnny nodded.

"Well, I surely do thank you boys for all you did this summer," Grandad said. "The whole operation ran better with your help."

He stopped suddenly by the curb and reached into his pocket. He drew out three white envelopes, both embossed with "L.P. Harris Lumber Company, Springport, Michigan." The boys' names were written in Grandpa's square hand on the front of each.

The boys opened them and found they each had crisp new fifty-dollar bills. "Grandad—" Les began, but his grandfather cut him off. "You worked very hard, and you have it coming," Grandad said. "You have more than earned it. Nanny and I both think so."

Les was embarrassed but relieved. Now he could pay back the IOU he had written for James—in full—and his summer was complete. All would be well.

Grandad cleared his throat. "Next summer, when you come back, can you make sure to call first?"

★

In the train on the way home, Johnny sat thinking about summer in Springport. The ducks were sitting in their box, an overcoat concealing their presence, on the seat beside Johnny.

Charlie had not wanted to take the ducks with them on the train. "We'll get thrown off for sure," he said. "They don't allow animals on trains."

But Johnny had cried and insisted. "All right," Charlie finally said. "But the minute someone catches us with those ducks, they are going right out the window *and* you have to give me your fifty dollars."

So far, so good. The ducks had been quiet and the only damage done was to Charlie's nerves. He was so convinced they were going to get into trouble that he couldn't relax at all. He sat stiffly upright, waiting for the metaphorical ax to fall on them.

As the train inched closer and closer to home, Johnny's thoughts began to turn back to Mother and Dad and what they would find when they got there. He suddenly remembered Les's theory that they were adopted and finally decided to ask about it. He'd have to get at the truth before they got home anyway, and maybe the boys could use their money to hop a different train and go in search of their real family.

"So, I've been thinking about our real parents," Johnny began. "Do you guys ever think we might want to go in search of them?"

"What?" Charlie asked, stupefied.

"You know, our real parents," Johnny said. "The ones who had us before Mom and Dad adopted us."

"You think we're adopted?" Les said, incredulous.

"Don't you?"

"Of course not!"

"Then why did you make the list of reasons you know you are adopted?" Johnny felt like he had gone down the rabbit hole in *Alice in Wonderland*.

"What list?" Les asked, his eyes narrowing with suspicion.

"The one I found—" Johnny began, realizing too late that he was about to make a huge mistake.

"The one you found where?"

"Um, on your dresser?" Johnny said.

In the box next to Johnny, the ducks began to cheep. The conductor, walking past, heard the noise and paused. Johnny saw him stop and began to make cheeping sounds himself, to cover.

Charlie groaned and put his head in his hands.

Les turned away to look out the window, stifling laughter. This was indeed an interesting situation. He had an opportunity to really mess with Johnny on this whole adoption thing, but on the other hand, he really wanted to pound him for going into the secret laboratory without permission. Was there a way he could do both?

Finally he spoke. "So you were in my secret laboratory, right?"

"Yes; I'm sorry."

"And you found the truth about our parents."

Johnny nodded, and began cheeping again as a passenger approached. This was going to be a very long trip if he had to cheep the entire way.

"Are you interested in finding your real family?" Les pressed still further.

"I think I know," Johnny said. "I think Spencer Tracy is my real dad. I'm going out there to live with him in Hollywood."

Les tried to keep a straight face. "Hm," was all he could manage. He turned toward the window again to try and compose himself.

Johnny began cheeping wildly again as the conductor came back down the aisle, looking suspicious. Seeing nothing, the man passed on into the next car.

Just as Les was about to turn back and really cause some mischief, Charlie spoke. "Don't even think about it, Les," he said.

"What?" Les asked, all innocence.

Charlie raised his eyes and looked at Johnny. "Nobody is adopted," he said. "Lester is messing with you and you are falling for it hook, line, and sinker. I have to tell you the truth before you really embarrass yourself."

"How do *you* know?" Johnny asked. "Or are you in on the scheme, too?"

"What scheme?" Charlie asked.

"The ration stamp scheme," Johnny said, frustrated. "Mother and Dad got us so they could collect more ration stamps."

"Oh, for heaven's sake," Charlie said. "There is no ration stamp scheme. What's your first memory?"

"Um… " Johnny thought. "Playing on Nanny's front porch. I think I was three or four."

"Yeah, genius, three or four," Charlie said. "The war hadn't even started yet, let alone rationing. If you came first, then it's obvious you're not some strange human currency for Mother and Dad to use in wartime."

Light dawned. "Of course," Johnny said.

The door opened and the conductor entered once more. Johnny cheeped.

Part Three:

Hazeltine Avenue

chapter seventeen

★

Autumn that year in Kenmore was better than the boys could ever remember. Mother and Dad had made a comfortable home on Hazeltine Avenue, and they were fighting and drinking less. There were fewer empty glasses on end tables and kitchen counters, and Dad was home in the evenings more often.

The house was smaller and had a more modern design. There was a type of linoleum in the kitchen, and the fixtures were all new and shiny. There was no attic, so Les and Johnny shared a real bedroom on the second floor, just down the hall from Charlie and their parents. The cats, Adam and Jinx, were glad to see them (Adam was more or less relieved, Johnny thought, that he had less distance to fall when tossed from the bedroom window, anyway).

The ducks, sadly, didn't remain in the house for very long. Adam evidently located vast reserves of energy and ate the baby ducks the first week they were home. Johnny caught him sitting in the box where the baby ducks had been living, licking his paws amid a huge pile of yellow fuzz. Johnny was furious and actually felt glad about dropping the cat out of the window in the house on St. James Place.

Charlie had his own room, though he still had to make some room for James's possessions. But something still seemed not quite right. "Where is Grandma Barney?" Charlie asked as soon as they had unpacked.

Mother looked uncomfortable. "She had to leave," she said. "We simply didn't have room for her in our new house."

"But where did she go?" Charlie pressed.

"Back to Michigan," Mother said.

"I thought she sold her house."

"She did, but she found a little apartment and seems very happy there," Mother said. "I'm sure we'll hear from her very soon."

Something isn't right, Charlie thought, but he didn't ask any more questions.

At school, the boys found little that had changed. Their status as second-class citizens after last year's snowball fight debacle had not altered. But it didn't matter much to them. It seemed to Les and Johnny that they could put up with anything as long as they had Springport to go back to. They knew they were L.P. Harris's grandsons and that this counted for something even if stupid Red and his cohorts couldn't see it. In the long run, who they were was more important than what happened to them every day.

But Johnny had a new problem this fall and, for once, it was concentrated inside the classroom rather than outside it.

Johnny was in third grade now and his teacher, Mr. Palmer, was extremely strict. He was not a big man; his suspenders and bow tie framed small shoulders and he walked with a slight limp. He was balding and bespectacled, completely ordinary and unassuming until he spoke.

His was the sort of classroom where one didn't speak unless spoken to and where every instruction was to be followed immediately and without question. Although Johnny had developed good strategies for "blending in" and not calling attention to himself, he also had difficulty concentrating or focusing for sustained periods of time. He sometimes failed to act immediately or follow all instructions to the letter. He felt like Mr. Palmer was always catching him without the proper supplies on his desk for a given project. Johnny was also chastised frequently for "daydreaming" or not being careful in his schoolwork. There were 25 other children in the classroom, but only Johnny seemed to be having trouble in this way.

Things came to a head just before the Thanksgiving holiday. It was reading time in class, and all the students were silently perusing their books. Johnny finally finished the book he'd been working on all fall—a story by Horatio Alger called *Ragged Dick*—and went over to the shelf to pick out some new reading.

"What are you doing out of your seat, young man?" Mr. Palmer's voice rang out like a shot in the quiet classroom. Several people jumped, including Johnny.

"I'm getting a new—" Johnny began, but before he could finish, Mr. Palmer was shouting. "Sit down!" he said. "You know you are to be in your seat the entire time you are reading. I will not have such outright insubordination in my classroom."

"But—" Johnny started again, only to be interrupted again. "I WILL NOT TOLERATE YOUR INSOLENCE!!!!" Mr. Palmer shouted. "Take your seat at once!"

Just as Johnny headed for his seat, however, Mr. Palmer changed his mind. "No, Mr. MacGregor, I want you up here at the blackboard," he said. "Come here at once."

As Johnny made his way forward, angry but saying nothing, Mr. Palmer pulled a ring of keys from a desk drawer. He grasped Johnny by the shirt collar and marched him forward to the blackboard. "Lean forward," Mr. Palmer said, pushing Johnny's nose through the hole in the center of the key ring until his nose was touching the board. The keys hung between his face and the board, dangling heavily against the bridge of his nose.

"Mr. Palmer," Johnny began to speak again, but Mr. Palmer interrupted once more. "You WILL stand there, and you WILL hold those keys against the board for thirty minutes. The minute you move and those keys strike the floor, you will be sent to the principal's office immediately. If you can't discipline yourself, then you will be disciplined by me."

"Okay," Johnny said, a note of indignation in his voice. He felt tears welling in his eyes and battled them back viciously. It was so unfair; all he was doing was what he was supposed to do—specifically, get a book during reading time. What a rip-off. He wanted to scream and throw Mr. Palmer's keys at his head but he couldn't do anything. Mr. Palmer was a dictator—worse than Hitler or Mussolini or anyone else Johnny could think of.

Johnny stood there, battling tears of frustration, anger, and rage. The weight of the keys on his nose, the humiliation in front of his classmates—it was all too much. He had half a mind to let the keys drop so he could go tell the principal what Mr. Palmer was really like.

But he didn't. He kept his nose to the blackboard the entire time. Finally Mr. Palmer came over and reached for the keys. "You are done, MacGregor," he said in a gruff, low voice. "I hope we will not have such troubles in the future. You are too smart to behave so stupidly on a continual basis. I would very much like to know why you do. Can you answer that for me?"

It was astonishing, Johnny thought, for a teacher to speak to him in this way. It was all he could do not to either fall apart crying or turn around and throw the biggest punch he could muster. His chest felt tight and anxious, as though he were standing on the ledge of a tall building and about to leap off. He struggled for air.

Johnny did not answer his teacher. There *was* no answer to that question. He simply turned and walked back to his desk, head held high, trying to figure out what actually *did* make him so stupid that he couldn't figure out how to put matters right.

At home that night, Johnny tried to talk to Mother about what had happened.

"I don't understand," Mother said again. "You must have done something very wrong for your teacher to say such a thing to you."

"But I didn't," Johnny protested. "I was just getting a book."

"Well, were you not supposed to be out of your seat?" Mother asked. "If that was the rule, you should have known it and not gone to the bookshelf."

No, Mother was going to be no help at all. Dad wasn't home, so Johnny ended up going to Les instead. Les knew Mr. Palmer; maybe he had an answer that could help.

Although Les was actually somewhat sympathetic, his answer was simple. "Sometimes the world just isn't fair," he said. "Maybe it's something you're doing or maybe it's not. But either way, you've just got to live with it until it's over."

"But I don't want to," Johnny insisted. "Won't somebody do something?"

"Why should they?" Les asked. "Eventually we've all got

to figure out how to deal with problems on our own anyway; you might as well get used to it."

Johnny huffed out the door and went back to his own room down the hall. He spent the remainder of his evening trying to figure out the answer to Mr. Palmer's question: What was it, indeed, that made him so stupid?

Perhaps when he knew the answer he would not be stupid any more. Perhaps then he would not mind so much that there was so much unfairness in the world. Perhaps he would know how to deal with it when it happened.

Part of Mother and Dad's fresh beginning was attendance at church. They went to the Church of the Advent in Kenmore, where people seemed friendly enough and the services were interesting. The building was a pretty stone structure, old-fashioned and lovely with stained glass and heavy wooden doors.

The boys quickly got used to the service. Everything was written down in the Book of Common Prayer, so it was easy to follow along and the music was nice.

They went to church every Sunday, with make up services available on Wednesday mornings. Every person had a nametag to wear; when services ended the boys had to put their nametags into a basket at the exit. If they didn't, the rector would know they hadn't been there and they would be required to attend the make-up service the following Wednesday.

Mother and Dad took their new religious responsibilities seriously. They brought the boys every Sunday without fail and prayed fervently for James, so far away from them in the military. Mother became involved in some of the ladies' auxiliary activities, which largely centered around knitting clothing for the war effort. She brought Mary Jane with her sometimes, and they knitted socks, sweaters, scarves, mittens, and even bandages for the soldiers overseas.

The boys went to Sunday school, and Les was glad to find that his old friend Pete Webster attended too. Without Red Bartlett around to see, Pete was glad to spend time with Les and their friendship could continue, even if it was only secretly. Pete was still very much afraid of Red, who had grown bigger over the summer and whose voice had changed. Red continued to bully and harass the other kids, sometimes beating them up or taking their things.

Pete and Les tried to think up ways to get around Red, but it was impossible. The other boy was simply too big, too scary, and too… everywhere.

★

James came home three days before Christmas. He looked big, strong, and important in his uniform, and the younger boys weren't sure how to talk to him anymore. Even Mary Jane blushed shyly when she saw him again.

Mother and Dad were so proud of James; they were fairly bursting with their enthusiasm for everything he had done and seen and become. They asked him a million questions about his training, adventures, and plans.

"Do you know yet where you're going?" Mother wondered. "What will you be doing?"

"They're shipping me over to England, to a place called the Midlands," James said. "I'll be flying reconnaissance, which means that I'll take out an unarmed plane and make photographs of battlefields."

"So you'll be safe," Mother said, visibly relieved. "You won't be fighting."

"That's right," James answered.

"Smart boy," Dad said, winking at James. "Just like his old man."

James cringed and looked over at Mary Jane, who was sitting innocently next to Mother.

Les and Johnny were disappointed, however, that James wouldn't be shooting any weapons from his plane. "What if someone shoots at you?" Les asked. "You won't have any guns to shoot back?"

"No," James said. "Every place on the plane where other guys have weapons, I'll have cameras instead. If someone shoots at me, I'll just have to fly faster and try to get away. I've been trained in maneuvers, not in gunfighting or bombing."

"What a rip-off," Johnny muttered.

"Oh, no it's not!" James exclaimed. "I have the best situation of all. I won't be flying during battles, taking flak or getting shot at. I'll show up long before a battle starts, to map battlefields out for the generals. It's the safest place I can possibly be."

"Still sounds less fun than a gunfight," said Johnny.

"Well, I don't mind, anyway," James returned.

"When do you leave for overseas?" Charlie asked. He wanted to know when he'd have his own room again. He had gotten used to James being away, and he liked living outside his brother's enormous shadow.

"The day after Christmas," James said. "I have to go down to Florida, where there's a ship waiting to take us all over. Planes, too."

"What'll you fly?" Les asked.

"A P-51D Mustang," James said. "I've been training on one for months; when I get to Miami they'll give me my own to use."

The boys were intrigued, but Mother told them they had to stop talking about James going to England. She said she didn't want to spoil her holiday thinking about the war. James's departure would come too soon as it was.

★

As if matters with his teacher and his friends were not enough, Johnny was experiencing a Santa Claus crisis that December. He had overheard Red Bartlett telling Davey Parker that there was no Santa Claus.

This was indeed an upsetting report.

Johnny had questioned a great deal over the past year or so of his life, but this was perhaps the most serious of all. No Santa meant that he'd been seriously duped for years, that the status of all future gifts and stockings was in jeopardy, and that he probably looked like an idiot to his brothers and other boys who actually knew the truth.

But the real problem was that he couldn't ask. If his folks were, in fact, posing as Santa and buying him gifts every year, his knowledge of the truth would make them less likely to keep buying those extra Santa presents. It was to his practical and financial advantage to keep mum and see what shook out.

It was an extremely disconcerting problem, and Johnny had spent most of the month of December chewing on it.

He started to ask Les once, but figured he'd run into the same problem with his brother. Les could say something to Mother and Dad, and that would have the same effect of limiting his gift intake. Plus, he wasn't sure he wanted the truth if the news was bad.

So he said nothing, but wondered.

All day Christmas Eve, Johnny thought about it. He wandered through the rooms in the house, gingerly lifting bed skirts and opening closet doors to see if he could spy anything.

Nothing.

Finally Johnny realized how he could figure out the answer for himself. He would stay up late and watch for Santa. There was a perfect hiding spot behind the sofa, where it angled up against the wall, and whether it was his parents or the Man in the Red Suit placing the gifts, Johnny would be sure to see all the action.

All during the Christmas Eve service at church, while they lit candles and prayed for an end to the war, Johnny plotted. He would pretend to go to bed at his appointed time, and then sneak downstairs and hide. Nobody would see him, and he could get back upstairs and go to sleep after it was all over. Perfect!

Johnny carried out his plan to the letter. He sneaked back down to the front room undetected, slipped into his hiding place, and watched for what seemed like hours as his parents sat with James and Mary Jane, sipping hot cocoa and talking. He sat, and sat, and waited… and then fell asleep.

It was the one flaw in his operation.

He awakened the next morning in his own bed, where someone had undoubtedly placed him long before the real action had started. Rats!

Johnny didn't mourn for long, however. It was Christmas morning, after all—the pinnacle of the year! At that moment he didn't care how the presents got there, just that they *were* there, waiting to be opened. He shouted for Les and took off running for the Christmas tree.

Johnny half-ran, half-fell down the stairs. Charlie, James, and the others followed more slowly, rubbing their eyes and cinching bathrobes around their waists.

It was a rich Christmas for everyone, especially with James home. Mother and Dad were peaceful, exchanging their gifts and smiling as they watched the children. The younger boys enjoyed their presents—model airplanes, books, and discounted field gear from the Army surplus store—and the older boys were grateful for a family that felt, for the first time in many years, like it wasn't disintegrating.

When they finally sat down for breakfast, Les had an announcement that finally set Johnny's mind at ease on the Santa Claus issue. He told everyone at the table he had seen Santa the night before and that he had obtained proof of his existence in the process. Johnny's spoon clattered to the table and he exclaimed aloud. "You saw him?" he nearly shouted. "You have proof? How?!"

Les finished chewing, then explained. "I positioned myself by the front window after midnight," he said. "I knew if I waited long enough—and stayed awake—that I would be sure to see something. And I did. It was just like the story, with the sleigh and the reindeer on the front lawn and everything. Santa wore a red suit trimmed in white, and had black boots and a pipe."

"Oh, stop," Johnny said. "That's not proof. That's storytelling."

"Oh, really," Les answered. "You want proof? Here's your proof. Follow me." Les got up and walked out to the front room again. Johnny leaped up and walked behind.

Les marched straight toward the fireplace, where the stockings hung limply. There, caught on the folding edge of the fire screen, was a torn shred of red cloth. It was stained black with accumulated soot and looked fairly worn.

"See?" Les said. "It's his suit. It looked just like that when I saw him. He must have torn it when he was leaving, and didn't notice with all his rushing around."

Johnny let out a long breath. "So it's true," he said. "It's all true."

Les put an arm around his brother. "Of course it's true," he said.

James went over to Mary Jane's after breakfast. He had a large poinsettia plant for her mother and a bottle of nice wine for her dad. The elder Soderquists thanked him for their gifts, then tactfully left the room so Mary Jane and James could be alone. They sat together on the sofa, holding hands and looking at each other.

"I'll bet you're wondering what I brought for you," James said with a grin.

"Not half as much as you're wondering what I have for *you*," Mary Jane replied, lifting her chin.

"Well, would you like to go first, or shall I?" James asked.

"Let me give you my gift first," Mary Jane said. "I've been so excited about it for such a long time; I honestly can't wait another minute!"

She walked over to the Christmas tree and pulled a thin, narrow box from its branches. It was wrapped in white tissue, which she had decorated with a sketch of an airplane. "We didn't have any bows this year," she explained. He opened the box and found an engraved pen inside. It read, *More than kisses, letters mingle souls*, followed by his initials, then hers.

"That is a quotation by an English poet, John Donne," Mary Jane said. "It is a promise from me to you that our letters will hold us together until you come home to me again."

James kissed her gently, and said, "I'll treasure it. And I'll use it often, I promise, to write to you."

He sat for a long moment, gazing at her. "You are so beautiful, Mary Jane," he said finally. "I love you so much; I am afraid to stop looking at you. I have to memorize everything as much as I can, so I can carry you with me overseas."

She let her eyes fill with tears. "I can't wait for you to come home again," she said. "I can't wait for the rest of our lives to begin."

"Me neither," said James. "Which brings me to my gift."

He handed her a small square box. "I get a military salary now," he said. "And I've been saving it for this."

She opened the box and saw, for the first time, her engagement ring. It was a small diamond set in garnets. The band was gold, and it fitted her hand perfectly. "Oh, James," she breathed. "It's beautiful."

"As are you," James said, kissing her again. "But I will admit I'll miss your other ring. I had to eat an awful lot of Cracker Jack boxes to find that."

"I have it in a very safe place," Mary Jane said. "And I'll keep it always."

They sat together on the sofa for a long while, making plans for their future together. They felt safe now, knowing that James would be doing reconnaissance and staying out of harm's way, to begin talking of homes and children and life beyond the war.

It could not come soon enough for them.

chapter eighteen

★

James left for Florida on the 26th as planned. Once again the entire family went to the station to see him off, including Mary Jane. This time, however, Mother held Les's hand firmly in her own the entire time, just in case he should take it into his head to run off again.

The good-byes were fast, out of necessity. They were late getting to the station, and James's train was already boarding when they arrived. The boys all shook James's hand seriously, and Dad gave James a quick hug. Mother and Mary Jane were both crying, and James was happy that the good-bye was short, lest he begin crying too. He didn't want to leave them so soon, and for so long.

"Good-bye," James said, hugging Mother tight. "I promise to come home to you soon."

"You'd better," Mother said, then stood back, wiping her eyes.

"Use your pen," Mary Jane said as they embraced. "I love you, and will wait for as long as it takes."

James held her closer. "A talented guy like me will have this whole mess in Europe sorted out in about six weeks," he said, and he felt her laugh. "Don't worry."

"What a swelled head you have," she said softly, then let him go.

The train chugged out of the station and with each rotation

of its giant metal wheels the war became that much more real for James. Soon he would be in Europe for real, not just in his fevered imagination. He was frightened, which made him even more eager to be with the other troops in his unit. Once he was with them he knew he would feel insulated and protected again. The good thing about working in the Army was that you never felt too close to anything. There were always a hundred people between a man and any perceived danger.

He just hoped it stayed that way.

When he got to Miami, he took a bus to the Miami Army Airfield. The airfield was large and busy, with men and airplanes everywhere. The place was buzzing with soldiers organizing themselves; the very sameness of this military place made him feel better almost immediately. He dropped his bag in the barracks and went out to meet the rest of his unit by the hangar.

He found the men standing next to a row of planes. They had all been painted with the dull khaki-and-green colors of camouflage, and looked new.

The commanding officer showed him which plane would be his. It was a P-51D Mustang armed with the latest in reconnaissance equipment. James looked at it carefully. This craft would be his partner, his lifeline, until the war ended. He walked slowly around the plane, touching its surfaces and thinking about what kinds of action he would see from its cockpit. He felt the faint stirrings of fear, then shoved them back down. Recon was different; he had nothing to worry about.

The entire unit was summoned with a loud shout from the commanding officer. They hustled into a straight line, chins out, shoulders thrust back. The officer put them at parade rest and they relaxed to listen to his instructions.

"You will spend the next thirty-six hours testing your planes here," he said. "You will train with them, make sure everything is fit and in good working order, and provide your reports to me. Then, once you and your craft have been cleared, you will travel on board ship to England.

"Now for the bad news," the CO continued. "As you see, these planes have been painted with camouflage colors. They were painted that way because they were slated for different use. Now that they are going to Europe and being deployed for recon, they need to be scraped down and repainted silver. Your time on board ship will be approximately five days; during that time you will be expected to ready your plane for service."

Not one man groaned, but inside they were all disgusted with the work that lay ahead.

In the end, however, the task of scraping and painting his plane ended up keeping James occupied on the long and tedious trip overseas. It also made James feel better to know that he was intimately familiar with each and every inch of his craft.

The journey was slow and tedious. James thought it felt like a dream most of the time.

It was only when they docked and moved into the Midlands that he realized exactly what he'd gotten himself into.

★

At church the following Sunday Les got to horsing around with Pete to such an extent that he created a real problem for himself.

Mother allowed Les and Pete to sit together during the

service, and the boys began to pass notes back and forth. The sermon was very boring that day, so the boys were making observations about various ladies' hats. Two pews up, Mrs. Monroe was wearing a broad-brimmed orange hat with a fake bird on one side, which Les and Pete thought was hilarious. *Maybe it's not fake,* Pete wrote. *Maybe it will take off any second and scare the heck out of everyone.*

I'd just settle for a single chirp, Les wrote back.

At that Pete stifled a giggle then looked straight ahead as if something in the sermon had completely captured his attention. Les shrugged and looked forward too, to find out what was so interesting all of a sudden.

Les was startled when he heard a soft *peep.* He thought perhaps he'd imagined it, and when he heard it again, he looked around. The bird on the lady's hat was motionless, but the peeping noise sounded again a third time.

He looked at Pete, who was having a hard time controlling himself, and nearly shouted with laughter. He worked to keep his face serious, but the harder he tried the more impossible it seemed. He was going to explode.

Les leaned forward, placing his head against his hands on the pew in front of him, as if deep in prayer. He bit down on his lips and tried to think of anything else—like train wrecks, bank robberies, or math problems. But his best efforts were stymied when he again heard Pete make a soft chirping sound next to him. Les let out a great puff of air and a helpless snicker, then stretched back his foot and kicked Pete in the shin.

The two boys became so disruptive that a man two rows ahead of them turned and gave them a look. This made them laugh even harder behind their hands, and finally Les had to get up and leave. He stood on the back step of the church holding his sides until he could finally get control of himself.

Mother was furious with him after the service ended. She gave him a stern look and made a face that let him know a lecture would be forthcoming when they returned home. Les was ashamed of himself (though he was still able to chuckle when Pete winked broadly at him) and felt so terrible that he completely forgot to take off his nametag when he left.

Les knew the punishment for not leaving your nametag at church was attending the Wednesday morning service before school. He was mad at himself but decided it was probably appropriate-enough punishment for him to have to go to church on Wednesday morning too. He had behaved badly enough during today's service that God probably expected a do-over.

Charlie found life in Kenmore very different than he had left it. Or, more accurately, he found *himself* very different. The progress and hope he had gained in Springport did not leave him, and he felt the iron bands of anger that used to tighten around his insides lighter and easier to bear.

He even got himself a job. He worked after school at a local garage, tinkering with cars and engines and learning all he could. They seemed to like him there and he was glad of a good place to be after school.

Best of all, Charlie had a friend. Larry Phelps was not the kind of guy who was easily shaken off and, once Charlie had helped save his little brother from the likes of Red Bartlett, Larry was loyal to the bitter end. Larry and Charlie ate lunch together at school and, on the Saturdays when Charlie didn't have to work, they would catch a matinee together and scope out girls in the malt shop.

Charlie enjoyed Larry's company, but there were times when he felt something wasn't quite right with his friend. Larry was given to strange moods; sometimes he would be so gloomy and depressed that it seemed like nothing could pull him out. Charlie would see Larry disappear inside of himself somehow; his eyes would be at once empty and desperate, and he would act like he couldn't hear what was happening around him. If Charlie invited him to do something fun, Larry would shrug and say, "One thing's as good as another, I guess." On those days Larry was no fun at all and Charlie felt irritated with himself for trying.

At other times, however, Larry would become brighter and more engaging than ever. Charlie had a hard time keeping up with Larry when that happened; he was quick and hilarious and energetic and he seemed to want to do everything he could all at the same time. One day, for instance, Larry and Charlie went to the malt shop and Larry suddenly stood up and loudly promised to treat every girl there to a free milkshake in exchange for a kiss. Larry ended up kissing more than a dozen girls and owing the shop owner fifteen dollars. Charlie was horrified; where would Larry get fifteen dollars? But Larry just laughed it off and danced across the street to the movie theater.

In these moods, Larry would make Charlie's sides split with laughter. But Charlie worried, too, about what kinds of trouble Larry would get himself into when he got this way.

Whether Larry was up or down, Charlie did his best to take care of his friend. For a time everything seemed fine, but it was not long before Charlie's relationship with Larry took its first bad turn. They were walking downtown after school, and Larry was glum. "What's wrong?" Charlie asked, already knowing the answer. Larry usually responded with a shrug of the shoulders, or a wistful "Nothing."

This time, however, Larry sat down on a bench and said, "Do you ever feel like it's just not worthwhile? All this grinding away at life?"

"What do you mean?"

"I look at my dad, working so hard all the time, and I wonder if that's what ahead for me. I wonder it that's really what it's all about. I think about math tests and war and trying to fit in and all the rest, and it just doesn't seem like it matters."

"I understand that," Charlie said. "I've felt that way before."

"Have you ever thought about doing anything about it?" Larry asked.

"Like what?"

"Like, I don't know—like just ending it all for yourself."

"No, I haven't thought that," Charlie said, his brow furrowed. "Have you?"

"Yeah, sometimes," Larry answered. "I'm not sure why I don't."

Charlie was worried. He had no idea what to say to his friend; this was really bad and he felt that he should do something about it, but he didn't know what. As angry and sullen as he'd ever felt, he couldn't imagine being so sad that he'd want to end his own life.

He decided to try to lighten the mood. "Aw, Larry," he said. "Everyone has bad days—even a bad year or two. Did I ever tell you about how I got held back a grade in school? Sometimes—"

"Shut up, Charlie," Larry said. "I'm not joking here. You are my friend; it is your job to listen to me and help me figure this out."

"Of course," Charlie said, swallowing hard.

"How do you think I should do it?" Larry asked. "Jump in front of a train? Take poison?"

"I don't have an answer for you," Charlie said. "Because I don't think you should do it."

"You are not being helpful," Larry said.

"This isn't something I think you should do," Charlie said. "So of course I'm not going to help you figure out how. You are a good guy, Larry; you shouldn't be thinking about this stuff."

"Who are you to tell me what to think?" Larry exclaimed suddenly, rising to his feet. "You don't know anything. Anything at all."

Turning on his heel, Larry stalked away. Charlie called after him, but didn't follow. The truth was he didn't know what to do.

Charlie became alarmed when Larry was not in school the next day, or the next one after that. He went down to the office to ask, but they didn't know anything.

By the third day, Charlie was worried enough to leave school in the morning and go to Larry's house directly. All the blinds were drawn; when he rang the bell he could hear it echo, but there was no accompanying sound of footsteps approaching the door.

Charlie rang again.

Finally he saw the shadow of Larry's mother in the hallway. She was untying her apron as she opened the door, and she apologized. "I was up to my elbows in dishwater," she said. "I couldn't make it right away. How are you, Charlie? What are you doing here?"

"I was worried about Larry," Charlie said. "He hasn't been in school."

Mrs. Phelps ushered Charlie inside. "He should be," she said. "He's been leaving here every morning with his books, and he comes back every afternoon at the end of the school day."

"He's not there," Charlie insisted.

"What is that boy doing?" Mrs. Phelps muttered. "I'm going to have to talk to his father and straighten this all out." She stood and walked over to the phone.

"Mrs. Phelps," Charlie began, just as she was about to lift the receiver. "I think there's more."

Charlie told Mrs. Phelps everything he could about Larry. He sat with her as she cried, then offered to wait with Larry's little brother while Mrs. Phelps went to the police.

The cops found Larry sitting in an alley behind the malt shop. He was curled up on the ground, crying, with a knife in his hand. He let himself be taken to the hospital, where he remained for a very long time.

As far as Charlie knew, Larry would never forgive him for telling the truth. But secretly Charlie felt it was the right thing to do. The world would be a less interesting place without Larry Phelps in it.

★

Les found church on Wednesday morning to be a fascinating experience. He arrived at 7 a.m. on the dot. Les held up his nametag and made his way down the church aisle to the front row. He was the only person there.

The church was silent as the rector entered. Les turned around, but nobody else appeared to be coming. Well, it was 7 on Wednesday morning; perhaps that wasn't a surprise.

The rector went up to the front of the church and looked out over the pews. Les expected him to address Les directly, or perhaps invite him up to the front for a discussion rather than for a full church service.

However, the rector went on as if the pews were full. He gave the sermon, complete with oratory flourishes, just as if it were Sunday morning. Les gave him the courtesy of his full attention this time, especially since he was the only person to appreciate it.

A half hour later, after the service ended, Les shook the rector's hand and went to school.

Les became a regular at the Wednesday morning service after that. He wasn't particularly religious, but it seemed to him that the rector deserved an audience.

★

Mother and Dad had an ongoing, though good-natured, debate all that spring. Dad had been playing cards at the bar most nights, and he hadn't been winning. They were still working hard to be kind to each other, but Mother was clearly unhappy with Dad.

"You never win," she said one night, trying to keep it light but clearly irked. "I might be better able to withstand this if you won at least occasionally."

"Oh, I'm tired of hearing you with your raft of crap," Dad teased. "My luck is going to change soon. Then we'll see who's able to withstand what."

"Oh, for heaven's sake," Mother said.

"Stick with me, baby," Dad said. "You'll be farting through silk."

Johnny squirted milk through his nose, which made Les laugh too.

Mother groaned. "I shudder to think what these boys are repeating at school."

Dinnertime was fun and the MacGregor family felt whole, despite James's absence.

chapter nineteen

★

It was April 1944. James had flown four reconnaissance missions so far, including two missions in Germany. When he thought about it, going to Germany was still a frightening concept in theory. It was tantamount to walking up and knocking on the door of Hitler's bunker and asking to be invited in for tea. But in practice it wasn't so bad. James had taken hundreds of photographs of military installations and terrain all along the German coast and deep into the Ardennes mountain region of Belgium.

In order to take good reconnaissance photographs, he had to fly over enemy territory several times, capturing lots of different angles. It was tedious, potentially dangerous work but his photographs were vital to the formulation of future war plans. The generals needed to use the pictures to determine the enemy's fortifications, the topography of the land, and other critical details needed to plan battles and win the war.

He'd been assigned his fifth mission already. On the afternoon of April 6th, he would fly from his base in the Midlands to the beaches of Normandy in northern France. He was to traverse the length and depth of those beaches and the surrounding areas, photographing German positions and making maps for Allied leaders back in England. Then it was back up and across the French coast to Calais, to throw the Nazis off his tail and make them think the Allies were hoping to attack there instead.

James was relieved to be flying in France. There were fewer threats to him there, he thought, than there had been in Germany. He wouldn't always be listening for gunfire to interrupt the droning hum of his engine or anticipating the sudden lurch of his stomach as the plane dropped out of the sky. He would just take his photos, look around, and then come home.

A quick trip.

He took off in the late afternoon just as the sun was beginning to dip. He always enjoyed his first few moments up in the air when he felt himself climbing and saw the light reflecting off the painted silver of his wings. That feeling had never gone away, not since the earliest days of his training in Kansas. He was man and machine again, trusty and reliable. All would be well, at least until he got over the Channel and into the occupied areas of France.

While he flew, he thought of his brothers at home. It was strange; he hardly ever thought of them at all anymore, so occupied was he with daily life in the Army and with thoughts of his precious Mary Jane. But he stopped that day to think how much Les would have enjoyed seeing what he saw, how Johnny would have exclaimed over the thrill of being up so high. He wondered about Charlie.

Flying, James thought, was the ultimate form of running away. Pulling the yoke of the airplane, feeling the wheels lift off the ground, and seeing the whole world literally behind you as your nose climbed into the clouds. It was like no other sensation James had ever known. He hoped that when the war was over he could continue to fly; it was so liberating and wonderful to push away from the dull forces of gravity and feel himself rising into something airy and powerful.

He thought about Nanny and Grandad all the way back in Springport. They would probably never know this sensation. He wondered what they were doing now and what they would think if they could see him. He thought of his whole family, aunts and uncles and cousins; their world seemed so far away from him now. James was supposed to be defending their way of life back home, he knew, but all he could think was that their way of life seemed so much smaller when he was up here.

James took his pictures and circled up to Calais. Dusk was beginning to fall; the twinkling lights of the city were beginning to shimmer on the ground beneath him. He swung around and headed out over the Channel. Almost home now.

He wished Mary Jane could be with him. He pictured her face in his mind, imagined her talking to him while they flew together. What would she think of Europe? Maybe he would bring her for a visit once the war was over.

He would fly her here, so she could feel the same delight he did at flying above the clouds.

Suddenly James realized he had a problem.

A dirty fog had swelled up over the English Channel that evening. It was thick and soupy and James couldn't see a thing. His earlier feelings of elation were almost instantly transformed into a sense of paralyzing vertigo. He couldn't tell from looking which way was up and which was down. All he had were his altimeter, which told him how high up he was, and a little gauge that showed him whether his wings were straight.

Looking down at these gauges, James glanced over at his fuel level and realized he was getting very low. All those passes over the French coast had taken their toll, and he had very little gas left to get home.

He eased up on the yoke and descended a little bit, trying to get a clear view of something, anything. If he could spot the horizon, he might be able to see where the coastline began.

Suddenly the engine sputtered. James felt absolute panic surge through his body; adrenaline flowed through his muscles and his heart began to race. A sick feeling grew in his stomach.

His training kicked in and he looked at the instrument panel. *Trust your instruments,* he remembered. *When you can't see, trust your instruments.* He looked at the gauges to see what he'd missed. Had he lost altitude? Was there an engine issue?

The needle on the fuel gauge was resting squarely on "E." He was out of gas. No fuel, no visibility. James's panic grew. The only real option he had left was to go into a controlled descent and land in the water. He thought back to that day in Denver when he lost his engines; he asserted control of the craft and began to descend.

This was just the same, right?

If only he could see. He had no idea where he was or what might be waiting on the ground below. He grew nauseous and began to sweat.

Trust your instruments, he told himself. *It's okay. Ignore the fog. Trust your instruments.*

This was very different from the lucky escape in Denver. Back then, he'd been able to see. Now he was not only flying blind, but also in wartime conditions. Someone on the ground with radar could see James's plane better than James could see him.

"It's okay," he said, out loud this time. "It's okay."

He was at 1,200 feet over the English Channel and descending. Still nothing—just the blasted fog, gray and heavy and thick. He kept dropping.

It was going to be okay. James promised himself that. He remembered back to his brother's last birthday, when he'd taken him out for ice cream and Les had said he wanted to prove himself someplace. Well, that's just what James was doing right now: proving himself. "I sure wish I didn't have to, though," he muttered, deepening his descent as the engine went silent.

It's okay, it's okay, it's okay, he thought, his chest tight with panic. But it wasn't; not really.

The plane dropped to 800 feet. There was no going back now. He could see nothing; whatever was in the water below, he would be hitting it.

"Mary Jane," he said aloud. It was more than a prayer, more than a plea. It was an insistence.

He was at 500 feet… then 350… then 250. He should be able to see something soon, he knew. But, "I see nothing," he muttered, feeling helpless. *I see nothing.*

And then, right out of the mists, something materialized.

It was a great white cliff, and James was headed right toward it.

"Oh, no," he breathed. "Oh, no."

★

The knock at the door came during breakfast. It was still early, before school, and Dad was just getting ready to leave for work. Les peeked out the window to see who could possibly be visiting them so early on a weekday, but all he could see was a bicycle propped against the railing of the porch. Mother went to the door, and then all motion stopped.

★

James was gone; there was nothing to be done. He would never bolt in and out of the door, always on his way to do something big and important. He would not take Les out for ice cream or tease Johnny or cast a shadow too big for Charlie to escape. He would not give kisses to Mary Jane, talk to Mother, or play a game with Dad.

Kenmore mourned James. The local newspaper wrote an article saying that he had "lived more helpfully inside of twenty years than many people do in an entire lifetime." There was a service at the Church of the Advent. Mr. Kraus came over with roses and tears in his eyes. Mrs. Soderquist brought a casserole and spent a long afternoon weeping with Mother.

Springport mourned him. Nanny and Grandad had a black ribbon on their door, and the family drew together in a silent, painful grief. The lumberyard slowed to a standstill. There was a small memorial service that the whole MacGregor family attended. Mother and Dad came on the train with the boys, Mother looking pale and drawn and barely speaking to anyone.

At home, a gold star hung in the window.

The Army seemed to mourn James too. They got letters from several of James's superiors, all saying how they missed James. And, of course, there were endless letters from the War Department, returning James's personal effects, settling the life insurance and Army pay, and getting affairs back in order for the government.

Les was having a hard time believing it was true. It seemed like James would come flying through the door at any moment, just like always. He'd been buried in England so there was no coffin, no body to help make it real. There was just the gold star in the window and the endlessness of a future without James.

★

Mary Jane was by turns inconsolable and angry. First her brother and now James. Was no young man to be left standing after this war was over?

She could not hear—or chose to ignore—the words of those older and wiser who told her that life would go on, that she would find love again, that she was still very young. All she knew was that her beloved James was gone; her best friend had left her behind.

The worst part, Mary Jane thought, was wondering about what happened. Did James suffer? Had he, at the last moment, thought of her? What was it like to die?

She hoped he was a ghost, that he would haunt her forever. She found herself talking to him often during the day, as if he were watching her go about her daily routine of church work, lunch, housework, and dinner.

"Did you hear how they talked about you today? I imagine that, wherever you are, you're probably pretty insufferable by now," Mary Jane said, washing dishes by herself one afternoon. "Even if you are, I wish you would talk to me. I would give anything to hear you, even if all you were doing was bragging. Isn't that sad? What will we do together from now on? It is hard to imagine."

She pulled a plate from the water and absently set it into the rack to dry. It felt better to talk to James, to imagine him as a ghost beside her.

"I don't think I ever told you the rest of the quotation I

had put on your pen. The one by John Donne? The whole passage says, 'Sir, more than kisses, letters mingle souls; for thus friends absent speak.' I am so glad to have your letters, so that you can continue to speak with me forever."

Mary Jane lifted another dish to the rack. "I'm only sorry you are absent now," she said. "I enjoyed your presence so very, very much."

Her voice broke on this last, and she raised her hands to her face and wept.

★

But there was nobody who mourned more significantly than Mother, who simply went to bed and stayed there.

She didn't come out for several days at first. Grandma Barney had come home for the funeral and stayed, so the house still ran and meals were still on the table. She took dinners up on plates and kept clean handkerchiefs by the bedside, but even this was not enough to take care of Mother.

Eventually, Grandma Barney pressed Charlie into service. "Your mother's a mess up there," she said. "I can't do anything anymore. Maybe if she spends time with you, she'll realize she still has three boys at home and get out of bed."

Charlie knew it was bad, because Grandma Barney actually fixed a whiskey and water for Mother. He carried the drink upstairs and set it by the bed. "Mother?" he said. She looked up at him and held up her arms. He sat down and gave her a big hug, then laid down over the covers alongside her. "You okay?"

She wasn't.

Over the next two weeks, Mother cried, slept, talked, and

moaned in her bed. She would drift off to sleep, then wake up, screaming, only to settle into soft sobs: "James, James; where are you? Can you hear me? Come home, my baby, come home to me… "

When she was awake she would talk to Charlie, telling him stories about what a wonderful boy James had been and how proud she was of him. "He never crawled when he was a baby; did you know? He just stood up one day and was off and running. He did everything that way—faster, better, bigger. None of you other boys were that way."

There were other times where she would ask after Dad. "Where is he? Why hasn't he come to apologize to me for killing my son? It was his idea to have the Army in our lives, to send James to his death. Go get your father. Tell him I want to see him now." Then when Charlie would stand up, ready to go looking for Dad, Mother would cling to him. "No, no… don't go. I need you. Don't leave me; I can't have another son leaving me. Stay here."

And so Charlie stayed with Mother, patiently listening to her the entire time. He patted her hair, brought her handkerchiefs and water, and tried to make up for the loss she must be feeling. He listened to her stories about James and how wonderful he was and how the world would never be the same without him. He lay on the big bed next to her, crying and holding her hand and trying to help her get through the worst of the grief.

Days passed in this way, but still nothing changed. Charlie began to think that Mother needed something to move her out of this bed and back into real life. He remembered Nanny describing an Irish wake, where the family of the deceased would make high-pitched wailing noises and cry out to God.

They called it "keening;" that was what Mother needed. A little keening would reflect the grief she was feeling and give her a way to vent her anguish. It was, in a way, the only outlet that would work. It was definitely better than this long silence punctuated with moans.

After a while Charlie told Mother about the keening, and they actually tried it. Charlie went first, even though he didn't know what keening was supposed to sound like. He tightened his vocal cords and made a long, high "eeeeeeeeeeee" sound in his throat.

It was a completely incongruous sound coming from an adolescent male, and Mother laughed. She actually laughed!

"Well, you try it!" Charlie said, smiling.

"All right," Mother said. She cleared her throat. "Geeeeeeaaaaiiiiiieeeeeeee!" she cried out, and then promptly started coughing and hacking. She giggled again and said, "Well, so much for that."

Charlie thought it felt good, after two weeks of sitting here in the dark, feeling sorry, to have something to laugh at. The lines erased themselves from Mother's face and she seemed better, if only for a moment.

Charlie wished he could feel better too. But he felt strange instead. He was a selfish boy, he thought, to be so happy to be here with Mother. He'd never had her all to himself before. She always loved James so much better than anyone else: always proud, always talking of him and his accomplishments, always comparing her children and finding only James worthy of praise. But now James was gone, and Charlie was there instead. It felt good to him, like maybe he would get to take James's place in the family.

But wasn't that wrong?

Charlie had felt only animosity toward James for such a long time that he wasn't sure what he should do now. All he'd wanted for years was to get out of James's shadow. Now that the shadow was gone forever, Charlie felt guilty for wishing it away. It was all wrong, and Charlie felt it in a way he'd never felt anything before. He must be a horrible person.

He bent his head and began to cry. "I'm sorry, Mother," he sobbed. "I'm sorry he's gone. I'm so sorry."

Mother got up from her bed and came over to where Charlie sat in his chair. She put her arms around him and kissed his forehead. "Me too," she said. "Oh, me too. Nothing will ever be the same again for us, will it?"

She didn't understand why Charlie was sorry, but he didn't correct her. He let her go on thinking he was a better person than he truly was.

★

Grandma Barney was doing her best to keep the rest of the household functioning while Mother recuperated from her loss. Dad was quiet and distant, and only the growing pile of whiskey bottles on the back porch gave any testimony to his anguish. He slept on the couch every night, when he was home, and went to work looking worn and haggard.

Les and Johnny continued to go to school and tried to stay out of everybody's way. The only person they had to talk with anymore was Grandma Barney; she tried to help but she was clearly out of her depth when it came to handling grief. She was accustomed to maintaining order and keeping house, not talking about sadness or sharing feelings.

Every day she asked the boys, "How are you feeling? Are

you okay?" When they shrugged or nodded, she would act a little relieved and go back to the little household tasks with which she was most comfortable.

It was not as if they were the only family in America losing a son, Les thought. Every day hundreds, possibly thousands, of men were killed in the war. But this was their boy and, if Mother was right, James was the most special of them all. For the first time, it occurred to Les that this war was going to take the best and brightest of all the young men in his country and that soon there would be nobody left.

Les wondered what it had been like for James. Did dying hurt? Was he proud to be giving his life for his country, or was he scared? Did he wish he'd stayed home and worked at Mr. Kraus's store forever?

And what's more, what would Les choose to do when and if his time came to serve?

But most of all Les wondered how bad life would get for his family. They had not just lost a son; they seemed to have lost one another too.

chapter twenty

★

It was the time when the worst of their grief was wrenched from them.

Charlie stayed in Mother's room with her for a grand total of three weeks, leaving only to shower and fetch food and whiskey. He didn't go to school; he just stayed with Mother, listening and holding her hand. She would not leave her bedroom or come downstairs. She just lay there with the blinds drawn in the hot, dark room, crying and talking to Charlie.

The depth and extent of Mother's grief was sometimes frightening for Charlie. "I don't think I can go on living in a world without James," she told him at one point. "What is going to become of me? I just want to fade away and die."

Charlie wept when she said this. He needed Mother; he couldn't lose her on top of everything else. Somehow he had to find a way to restore her to herself and to her family.

He thought about getting Dad to come up, but he wasn't sure that would help at all. Mother told him how she blamed and hated Charlie's father for sending James into the Army. She said she wished Dad had died, not James, and that she had half a mind to kill Dad herself, out of vengeance.

That frightened Charlie too, and made him feel more helpless than ever.

Even the pleasure of having her undivided attention and company began to wane for Charlie. She began to ask for more and more whiskey, and Charlie started to wonder if she would have a problem again. At one point he even went downstairs to ask his father, but he found Dad lying asleep on the couch, an empty bottle and glass next to him on the floor.

Les and Johnny seemed to have disappeared. Charlie went into the kitchen and found Grandma Barney with her head down on the table, crying. "Grandma?" Charlie asked. She looked up, her eyes rid-rimmed and sad. "What are we going to do?" he asked her.

"I don't know, Charlie," Grandma Barney said. "We've just got to get them through this somehow. I've been trying to think of ways, but I'm out of ideas."

"Me too." Charlie sat down next to her. She pushed over a plate of cookies and rested her chin in her hands. He began to eat, slowly, but the cookies tasted like sawdust in his mouth.

Grandma Barney reached over and put her hand over his. "Do you remember when I told you that you needed to channel your temper? That if you took all your energy and put it toward something positive, it could work for you?"

Charlie nodded. That was right before he got into the fight over Larry Phelps's little brother.

"The chip on your shoulder is gone now," she continued. "Life has knocked it off for you. But—thank God—your spirit is still strong. You are using every inch of it in caring for your mother. You are the only one in this house who has the strength to do it. I am grateful for you every day."

Charlie felt a lump in his throat. "Thank you, Grandma," he said.

"Yep," she said. "It's us bad-tempered people who often

get along best when the chips are down." He looked sharply at her, but her eyes were twinkling, and he smiled too.

The next day, the truant officer came from school looking for Charlie. Grandma Barney apologized, explained the situation, and told him Charlie would be in school the next day. Charlie shook his head, trying to communicate silently that it was still too soon to go back to school, but Grandma insisted. After the truant officer left, Grandma Barney explained that this was just the "kick in the pants" Mother needed.

"Stay here," Grandma Barney instructed, and she marched up the stairs to Mother's room. Charlie could hear raised voices and the shattering of something glass before Grandma came back downstairs. "She's getting up now," Grandma Barney said. "Stand firm; you ARE going to school tomorrow."

Mother came downstairs blinking and rubbing her eyes as if she hadn't seen the sun in a while. She was obviously angry and upset, and she glared daggers at Grandma Barney. Charlie mumbled something and went upstairs to his room; he'd let the grown-ups fight this one out.

And fight it out they did. All that night, Charlie and his brothers could hear raised voices and shouting, punctuated with the sounds of objects being thrown or slammed. Dad came home and Mother accused him of all sorts of terrible acts. She said he'd sent James to his death in the Army and that he'd never cared about her or anybody else other than himself. Mother started bringing up choices that had been made years and years ago, before even James had been born, and she wouldn't stop.

Grandma Barney gave up and came upstairs to go to bed.

But still Mother and Dad fought and fought, keeping the boys awake long after they should have been asleep.

"You killed him, just as sure as if you'd held a gun to his head yourself and pulled the trigger," Mother sobbed. "He never would have gone into the Army if it hadn't been for you!"

"*He* was the one who wanted to go into the service; he came to me!" Dad shouted back. "Do you think this would have happened if he hadn't wanted it? When did James do anything he didn't want to do?"

"He was always doing things he didn't want to," Mother hissed. "Those hours of work, giving us money to help the household, just because *you* couldn't bring home enough to take care of our family, or because you went out every night to gamble it away. You *ruined* his life, short as it was! And then you helped send him to his death."

"Why, you… " Dad said, his voice low, menacing.

"Get away from me. I hate you!" There was a smashing sound, a thud, and then the shouting started again, with fresh accusations and more tears.

It was a long night.

When Les came downstairs the next morning before school he found Dad asleep on the couch. The entire front room was in shambles; shards of glass were all over the floor and even some of the pictures on the wall hung askew. Mother and Dad had fought many times before but their talk had been getting better. Now that James was gone, all promise for a brighter future seemed gone. This was the worst Les had ever seen.

Dad had his arm up over his eyes and was snoring. His sleeve had a rip in it and there was an empty glass on the floor next to him. It was the only glass in the room that appeared not to be broken.

Mother was nowhere in sight, so Les went into the kitchen and got himself something to eat. He put out something for Johnny too and then went to school.

He wondered who would be there when he got home.

★

Johnny fell asleep in class that day. He was ashamed when he woke up and found himself having dozed through math and science; half the morning was gone. Mr. Palmer didn't say anything to him, which Johnny thought was surprising. Sleeping was not good, disciplined behavior, that was for sure.

But when Johnny caught Mr. Palmer's eye, the teacher only gave a small nod. He motioned Johnny to his desk and told him that he wanted him to spend an extra few minutes after school so he could get his assignments. Johnny was sure he'd be getting a talking-to then.

The rest of the day passed quickly. When the bell rang, Johnny went up to Mr. Palmer's desk prepared for a stern lecture. He braced himself when Mr. Palmer came around and leaned against the front of the desk next to him and was surprised when his teacher's voice sounded soft and kind.

"How are you doing, son?" Mr. Palmer asked. "I heard about your brother. Is your family okay?"

"I guess so," Johnny answered, still waiting for the lecture to start.

"You seemed tired today."

"I haven't been sleeping very well."

"I don't usually make allowances in my classroom for

sleeping, you know," Mr. Palmer said. "I like my students to come to school rested and prepared."

"Yes, sir."

"Look, Johnny, I know we've had our share of disagreements this year," Mr. Palmer began. "You are obviously not the boy your older brothers are."

"Yes, sir."

"Because of your obvious limitations, I am going to ask that you allot some extra time after school," Mr. Palmer continued, as if Johnny hadn't spoken. He cleared his throat gruffly, then went on. "I have some jobs that need doing, and you need some extra time to do your schoolwork. You don't seem capable of doing it at home, so you'll do it here. I haven't seen any of your homework in weeks, and that's completely unacceptable."

Johnny nodded.

"Now, please sit down and pull out your books," said Mr. Palmer, rising briskly from his chair. "I'll go down to the office and have them telephone your house."

Returning to his desk, Johnny sat down and put his chin into his hands. His eyes slipped closed; he wanted nothing more than a nap, and now he had to sit here for who knows how long. Stupid Mr. Palmer.

Johnny laid his head down on the desk. His world could not get any worse. Between home and here, life was thoroughly rotten. He felt tears behind his eyes and blinked to keep them away. His eyes closed, held. He was asleep.

When he awoke—either half a minute or half an hour later, he never knew—Mr. Palmer was working quietly at his desk, grading papers. The teacher looked at him sternly and motioned to his books. "Get busy," he said, his tone sharp.

Over the coming weeks, Mr. Palmer and Johnny developed a working relationship of sorts. Johnny stayed after school for an hour each day, finishing his assignments and helping with various jobs around the classroom. He cleaned the chalkboard, clapped erasers, and swept the floor. Mr. Palmer did not appear to care to talk with Johnny and Johnny certainly had no desire to talk with him. They would simply remain in near silence for the duration of the hour and then Johnny would finish his work and leave.

Then one day there was a pile of junk on the back table in the classroom. Some copper wire, an old oatmeal container, and a few other odds and ends lay strewn about. "Do you want me to do something with this?" Johnny asked.

"Yes, I do," Mr. Palmer said. "I want you to build a crystal radio."

"What?" Johnny exclaimed. "How?"

"That's your job," Mr. Palmer said. "Figure it out."

"Why?"

"Because it needs doing. Get busy."

Johnny stared at the pile. What was he supposed to do? *Les would know,* he thought. *But Les isn't here.*

Johnny walked over to the blackboard and picked up an eraser. He wiped the entire chalkboard clean, then clapped the erasers and tidied the desks. He swept the floor and emptied the wastebasket. But still no ideas came to him.

He walked over and stood before Mr. Palmer's desk. "Can I go home now?" he asked.

"*May* I," Mr. Palmer began.

"May I go home now?"

"No. You still haven't done anything about that radio."

"But I need to ask my brother what to do," Johnny said.

He was embarrassed that his voice sounded plaintive, almost whiny.

"You are not allowed to ask your brother," Mr. Palmer said. "Your brother isn't going to be there to take care of you your whole life long. You need to learn to do things on your own, to take care of yourself."

Johnny considered this. "But I don't know where to begin."

Mr. Palmer sighed heavily. "Think about it," he said. "Where do you go when you need to learn something—*besides* to your brother?"

"I don't know," Johnny said again.

Mr. Palmer rose and kicked his chair backward. He rounded the corner of the desk and stood directly above Johnny. The boy was cowering, terrified. Was the teacher going to hit him?

"*Think* about it," Mr. Palmer almost hissed, his hands fisted at his sides. "Think! Think! Think!"

Johnny's chin began to wobble. "I can't think!" he exclaimed. "I don't know what you want!"

Mr. Palmer ran his hand through his thinning hair and pointed at the door. "Pull yourself together and go to the library," he said. "Don't come back here until you've found a book that tells you how to build a crystal radio."

Johnny turned and ran. He didn't stop until he'd reached the library door and nearly fell across the threshold, panting and red-faced. The librarian looked worriedly at him, helped him up, and showed him how to find what he needed.

During the next few weeks, Johnny managed to put the radio together all by himself. Using a library book as a guide, he wound the copper coil, placed the crystal diode, and even marked the radio signals he was able to receive. When it was finished, he carried up to Mr. Palmer's desk and set it gently down in front of the teacher.

Mr. Palmer looked it over, turning it carefully. He adjusted his glasses and looked up at Johnny. "Well done," Mr. Palmer said, and allowed himself a half smile. "You'll share it with the rest of your class tomorrow."

Johnny felt as if he had conquered the world. He picked up the radio and walked it back to his desk.

"Mr. Palmer?" he asked. "Why is it again that you wanted me to build this?"

"I'm a teacher," Mr. Palmer said. "I teach."

"I don't understand," Johnny said.

"No, you probably don't," Mr. Palmer said. "You lack mental discipline. All I can say is that it needed doing, and you needed to do it. Now go on; get busy. You've got work to do."

★

Things had gotten no better at home in the weeks since Mother had gotten out of bed. She and Dad were still drinking and fighting every night, keeping the boys awake and making them worry.

Grandma Barney kept the house relatively tidy, cleaning up after the fights and making sure meals stayed on the table. But she went to bed after dinner, leaving the boys to do their homework and listen to the angry accusations of their parents. She told Charlie she was furious and didn't trust herself to be in the room when the arguing started; it was too hard not to add to the misery.

The boys did their work quickly and generally went to

bed as soon as they could. But they still had to lie in their beds and hear the angry back-and-forth from the rooms downstairs.

Les felt very strongly that the war had cost them much more than James. Their whole family was slowly destroying itself, day by day. How was it that losing just one person could bring about such chaos for everyone else? Was that one person so vitally important that normal life couldn't continue without him?

Perhaps it was only a matter of time until Mother turned her anger on Grandma Barney. Their relationship was already difficult, and Mother's unhappiness couldn't help but make a bad situation worse.

When it happened, however, it was nevertheless astonishing in its intensity.

Mother was in the kitchen pouring herself a drink in the late afternoon. Grandma Barney passed through the room and, though she said nothing, she spoke volumes with her glance. Mother saw the raised eyebrow, the setting of the teeth, and exploded.

"You're not in a position to judge me this time," Mother said. "You don't have the slightest idea what I'm going through, the kind of loss I've experienced. And it's not going to stop; every day the whole rest of my life I will have to wake up and face it all over again."

"You think I don't understand, but I do," Grandma Barney said. "My heart aches for you, for my son, for the boys. I'm not here to judge; I'm here to help."

"Help, my eye!" Mother spat.

"Yes, help!" Grandma Barney insisted. "It's probably not that evident to you, but you actually have three surviving sons who need care. Oh, and—even more unbelievably—you have a husband. My son is suffering alone because you can't seem to think beyond your own feelings. If I weren't here, I can't begin to imagine what would happen to this family. You are obviously incapable of caring for anyone, even yourself."

Mother gasped. "How dare you?"

"Somebody has to," Grandma Barney said coolly. "Oh, go ahead, pour yourself a drink. But don't be surprised when I'm still here in the morning, trying to pick up the duties you have selfishly abandoned."

"Get out!" Mother cried. "You get out, you hateful old woman. You have exactly one hour to pack up and leave my house. Get moving!"

★

"Perhaps it's for the best," Grandma Barney told Charlie later, as she was packing her suitcase. "When I'm not here to make dinner and keep the house in order, your mother will be forced to come to her senses."

"I'm not sure," Charlie worried.

Grandma Barney sat down on the edge of the bed next to him. She set her hand on his knee. "Then you will have to do your best to make the difference," she said. "You are old enough and strong enough. I am leaving you in charge."

"Me?" Charlie gulped.

Grandma chuckled. "It is sad when I tell a sixteen-year-old boy that he's the closest thing to a real adult functioning in this household," she said. "But it's true. You are going to have to grow up even faster now so you can take care of your brothers and your folks."

Charlie did his best after Grandma Barney left to do as she asked. He cooked meals, talked to Mother, and kept the home running as best he could. He got the mail, sorted the bills for Dad, and even did laundry. With school and work and everything else, it was not easy for him but he slowly felt himself rising to the occasion.

It was funny, he thought, but he almost felt like he was turning into James.

It was in the course of sorting the mail one day that he found the letter that could have changed everything. It came from the War Department, and it notified the MacGregors that the official cause of James's death had been determined. Although information about James's mission was classified, the letter disclosed that he had been coming across the English Channel. He was low on fuel and flying at a low altitude, looking for a suitable place to land. He had crashed into the cliffs at Dover.

The letter used the phrase "controlled flight into terrain," and indicated the cause of the accident as pilot error.

"Pilot error," Charlie repeated. It seemed impossible to believe that his talented, hardworking older brother would have done something so stupid as to fly his plane into a cliff.

It wasn't even as though James had died a hero, having been shot down in action by German guns. He hadn't lost a dogfight or been hit by flak or even had engine trouble. He'd done it to himself.

So, Charlie thought, the great and perfect James MacGregor wasn't so great and perfect after all. When it really counted, James had goofed up. Colossally.

But even as this thought flitted through Charlie's mind, he recognized it as a fragment left over from his old way of thinking. The surly, resentful, chip-on-his-shoulder Charlie would have seen this letter as vindication, and would have told everyone in town that his brother was just as big a loser as everyone else.

The new Charlie, however, the one who made progress and built a Model A, the one Grandma Barney called "the only functioning adult in the household," the one who was taking care of everyone else and doing a good job, knew better.

It would make a bad situation even worse if Mother and Dad knew about James's mistake. There was nothing to be gained with this new truth, and everything to lose.

It wasn't like telling Mrs. Phelps about Larry. The truth would help Larry in the end. Who would be helped with this truth?

The only person with anything to gain—anything at all—was Charlie. And he was becoming wise enough to know that any gain he would have would be temporary, fleeting, and not really worth all the loss it would cause for everyone else.

I wish Grandma Barney were here so I could talk to her about it, Charlie thought. *She would have good advice, I know.* He tried to imagine what she would say, but all he could come up with was that she seemed to trust him to make the right choices.

So Charlie decided to trust himself, too. He tore the letter into a million tiny pieces and burned it in Dad's ashtray.

Nobody would ever know of James's mistake. Everyone would think he died a hero's death.

That was the way it should be, Charlie knew, and he felt glad. He had done the heroic thing.

★

The situation with Mother and Dad was fast becoming unendurable for Les. If he'd thought about running away before, now it was nearly a compulsion. He had to get away from the sadness, the grief, the fighting.

Les had decided on Springport. Nanny and Grandad would help him, he knew, and maybe they would send for Johnny and Charlie too once they learned how bad their lives were. Les would go on his own first, though; it would be easier for him to travel alone.

He loaded his rucksack quietly and shoved it under his bed. He would leave after he'd taken care of a few loose ends.

First Les needed to call Nanny and Grandad to let them know he was coming. Nanny had said she was only a phone call away; Les found her number in the kitchen and went to dial.

"Hello?" Nanny's voice sounded very far away.

"Nanny?" Les said. "It's Les."

"Les! How are you?"

"Not so good, Nanny," Les said. His throat felt tight, like he might cry. Her voice touched his very soul. "Things are bad here again, and I want to come to your house."

"What's happening there?" Nanny sounded worried.

"Mother and Dad are fighting all the time," Les said. "They keep us up at night, and it's scary."

"Is your mother there now?" Nanny asked.

"Yes, but I don't want you to tell her I called you," Les said. "I just want you to let me come. Can you wire money?"

Nanny was quiet. "Les, I need a little time to think," she said. "I need to talk to Grandad. I promise, I will be calling back later. Can you let me do that?"

"Yes," Les said. "I'll wait for you to call. I love you, Nanny."

A few hours passed, during which Les sat on his bed, anxiously waiting for the phone to ring. When it finally did Les was disappointed to hear Mother pick it up before he could get downstairs.

About twenty minutes later—the longest twenty minutes he could remember—he heard Mother's tread on the stairs. She came up and sat down on the bed next to him. Her eyes were red, as if she'd been crying.

"I just talked to your Nanny," Mother said. "She told me you'd like to go to Springport."

Les nodded.

"I see. Have you packed?"

He nodded again.

Mother looked down at her hands. "Nanny and I talked for a while," she said. "I understand I have been letting my feelings get the best of me lately. I'm sorry about that."

"It's okay," Les said. "Are you mad at me for calling Nanny?"

"I don't think so," Mother said. "I was, at first, but I understand why you did it. I wish you didn't feel you had to."

"I'm sorry," Les said.

They sat quietly for a minute. Mother cleared her throat. "I was wondering if I could have another chance," Mother said. "Dad too."

"A chance to do what?" Les asked.

"Well, before you decide to leave, I was wondering if you would let us make an effort to be better," Mother said. "Dad and me."

Les didn't say anything.

"We have lost one son," Mother said. "We're hoping not to lose any more. Nanny made it plain to me that we need to 'clean up our act,' as they say, if we are going to keep you with us. I'd like to try."

Les felt a lump in his throat. He nodded.

"Nanny said we all have responsibility to do our part for our family," Mother said. "I have not been doing mine. If I start doing it, will you keep doing yours?"

"Yes," Les said.

Mother reached out her hand and Les shook it.

"Deal."

chapter twenty-one

★

Nearly two months had passed since James's death. The weather was warm and school was nearly finished for the year.

One bright afternoon Charlie came home and saw Mary Jane sitting in the kitchen, talking to Mother. Mary Jane's hand, with James's diamond-and-garnet engagement ring still on it, was covering Mother's on the table.

They had both been crying, he could see, and he stiffened. But Mary Jane looked up and saw him and reached out her other hand. "Come and sit with us, Charlie," she said, her smile soft and serene. "I was just giving your mother a message for you."

Charlie slid into the kitchen chair next to Mother. Mary Jane lifted a knuckle to push up her glasses in that girlish way of hers. She looked pale and drawn, but better than the last time Charlie had seen her, at James's funeral.

"I got a letter from your Grandma Barney the other day," Mary Jane told Charlie. "She wanted me to tell you hello." When Charlie nodded, Mary Jane went on. "She's back in her apartment and doing well. She asked me to tell you not to worry about her, Charlie. She was very specific about that."

"Thank you," Charlie said.

"I have some news," Mary Jane said. "I'm going to college in the fall. I think it's something James would have liked me to do, and it will be good for me to move on and begin thinking about the future again. My parents are very supportive; in fact, they're kind of insisting on it."

Mother began to cry again, very softly. Looking worriedly at her, Charlie congratulated Mary Jane. "I'm sure you will do very well," he said, and he meant it.

"It's important for all of us to keep going, I think," Mary Jane said, her voice wobbly. "But it is very hard. Part of me feels like when I leave I'll be saying good-bye to James forever. I'm not sure how that's going to be. But James lived so fully; he would be upset with me for living half a life."

Charlie couldn't speak.

"You know, James wrote to me once and told me what it was like when his plane came up through the clouds," Mary Jane continued. Her tears fell freely now. "He said no matter how cloudy or rainy it is down here, the sky is always bright and blue when you make it above the clouds. That's what I'm trying to do, you know; I am trying to make it past all these shadows and clouds, so I can see the sun for myself."

"Why did he go? Oh, why did he have to go?" Mother sobbed. Her head fell into her arms, and she sat with her face down on the kitchen table, sobbing.

"Oh, Mrs. MacGregor, he *wanted* to go," Mary Jane said. "It was so important to him. Of course he was afraid, but he made the best choices he could. I am proud of him for going; should he have stayed home to please a couple of women, or gone out to fight and protect the way of life we enjoy? He was very set on doing the right thing and I can't help but honor his commitment."

"He wanted to go?" Mother asked. In all these months she had never allowed herself to hear or believe these words. Now she was saying them aloud.

"Yes," Mary Jane said quietly.

Mother got up and went into the living room. She came back with a small wooden box that she opened slowly. She began pulling the contents out and laying them on the table. Papers, a broken watch, a pocket Bible.

James's personal effects.

"I think this is yours," Mother said, giving Mary Jane a gold pen with engraving on it. "There's also a letter in here, which he'd started for you."

Mother passed Mary Jane a slip of paper with James's familiar handwriting.

★

My dearest Mary Jane,

I have to go out again tomorrow; more photographs to take. It's quiet here tonight and I can't help but think of you. I remember swinging with you on the porch, watching your face as you opened your Christmas gift, the notes we passed in history class. Every moment is there for me, and I am sustained on long nights like this one.

Other guys here are not as lucky as I am, to have known someone like you. I am so glad you are part of my life.

Here's the night watch... lights out. More tomorrow when I get back.

★

Charlie heard Mary Jane say, "Friends absent speak." Then she stood up, her eyes filled with tears, hugged them both, and was gone.

Mother looked for a very long time at Charlie. She seemed to have aged twenty years in an instant. She slowly rose from her seat, walked out into the hallway, and went up the stairs. Charlie heard her bedroom door close with a *click.*

That night, Dad and Mother sat up talking for a long time. There was no shouting, no breaking of glass, just the weary tones of two people tired of fighting.

"How are we going to move past this?" Les heard Mother say.

"I don't know," Dad answered.

"I know you weren't responsible for James joining the Army," Mother said. "I think I knew that right from the very beginning. But it was better to blame you than to blame James."

"I know," Dad said. "But I'm sorry anyway. I should have discouraged him somehow. I can't believe it's come to this."

"How will we get through?" Mother asked. *Good question,* Les thought.

"We'll figure it out," Dad said. "Somehow, we'll figure it out. We always do."

School was coming to an end. Desks were being cleaned, books returned, and windows opened to the warming air.

For the first time in his life, Johnny was sad to see the

first day of summer vacation. He had come to rely on Mr. Palmer's steady presence every day, and Johnny would miss him. After the bell rang, Johnny went up to the teacher's desk to see if he could stay after and help for a while, as usual, and his offer was met with stern nod. "Of course," Mr. Palmer said.

For a time they worked in silence, stacking chairs and cleaning the chalkboard. Finally Mr. Palmer asked Johnny what he was doing for the summer.

"We leave next week for my grandparents' in Michigan," Johnny said. "My Grandad owns a lumberyard, and we'll probably help out there this summer."

"Do you like it there?"

"More than anyplace in the world," Johnny answered.

Mr. Palmer handed Johnny the erasers. "Why don't you clap these out," he said. Johnny finished, then went over to lay them on the teacher's desk. He looked around the familiar classroom; everything seemed to be done. There was no more reason to stay.

"I guess it's time to go," Johnny said. "I hope you have a good summer."

"You too, Johnny."

Johnny walked over and held out his hand. He'd never shook a man's hand before, and it felt very strange and grown-up. "Good-bye," he said.

"Good-bye," Mr. Palmer replied.

Johnny picked up his brown rucksack and walked over to the door. Suddenly he turned. "Mr. Palmer?" he asked. "Why did you make me build that crystal radio? And why did you ask me to be here every day after school? I know you don't like me." Part of Johnny was fishing, hoping Mr.

Palmer would contradict him and say he thought Johnny was a good kid after all.

But Johnny was disappointed.

"It needed doing," Mr. Palmer said simply. "I'm a teacher, so I teach. Now, get going. I've got work to do."

★

Les walked home slowly, counting the cracks in the sidewalk as he went. He was definitely not in any hurry to get home, where Mother was likely already drinking and upset.

He was so lost in his own thoughts that he barely heard his name being called. "MacGregor!" he finally heard. "Holy cow, are you deaf AND stupid?"

Les looked up to see Pete Webster walking toward him. Pete was grinning, and Les wondered what was up. It was broad daylight and someone was speaking to him. Where was Red Bartlett? What would the consequences be?

"A bunch of us are going over to Bernie's to play war," Pete said. "I'm bringing you with me."

"Won't Red be there?"

"Nope," Pete said. "Red left for a reformatory this morning."

"What?"

"You know, a reformatory," Pete said. "One of those places where bad kids go to get turned around. He got caught stealing and his parents decided they'd had enough. They sent him away for a few months to get straightened out."

"Will he be back?" Les asked.

"Maybe; who knows?" Pete shrugged. "Anyway, now that he's gone we can play all we want."

"What happens when he comes back?"

"Can't say," Pete said. "Guess we'll sort it out later. I don't know much, but I know that it's not worth worrying about something that ain't happened yet."

Les nodded slowly, his grin spreading. "That's for sure."

★

The guns were made of pieces of wood and old inner tube that had been cut into six- or eight-inch bands. One end of the band was caught on the front end of the wood and held in place on the back end by half a clothespin and a rubber band. When a boy saw his enemy, he would aim and squeeze the clothespin and it would release the inner tube band—POW! It was quite painful for boys that got hit.

A mini grenade was created by stuffing two gun caps into a hex nut and twisting bolts into both ends. When it was thrown, it made a huge popping sound and was instantly destroyed.

The boys played all afternoon, laughing and injuring one another until they forgot all their past troubles.

It felt good to have friends again, even if it was only temporary. It had been too long.

★

Les and Johnny came home before dinnertime tired and sunburned. Mother was sitting at the kitchen table looking sad but not drunk. She called after them as they passed through the room, letting them know that they were going out for dinner.

The boys looked at each other, unsure what to expect.

The family went to Dinty Moore's that night. It was the

bar Dad most liked to frequent when he played cards; it was at the end of the street where they lived and was very dark and mysterious inside. They specialized in seafood there, and the smell greeted patrons long before they reached the door. Johnny always thought the restaurant belonged in a gangster movie; the people there were tough-looking and the only detail missing was a tinny piano. There were red-and-white checked tablecloths, drippy candles, and even a long bar with big bottles stacked against a mirrored wall.

The family went to sit in one of the booths along the backside of the restaurant. Les noticed there was a great big stuffed swordfish hanging on the wall at the end of the room. A thin man came and brought their menus and Mother commented that if you didn't want to order anything you could eat the food stuck to the menu and not go hungry.

The family ordered. Les and Charlie both had steak, and after a protracted discussion Johnny agreed to try the frog legs. Mother and Dad ordered whiskey drinks and some lobster.

"It's about time we were back in society. Right, boys?" Dad said.

Mother smiled and lit a cigarette.

"How was work today?" she asked Dad.

"Oh, fine," Dad said. "I heard a new chemistry joke."

The boys groaned. Dad's chemistry jokes were terrible.

"So these two atoms were walking down the street," Dad said. "One atom said to the other atom, 'I think I lost an electron!' The other atom says, 'Are you sure?' and the first atom says, 'Yes! I'm positive.'"

Dad laughed at his own joke; he was the only one.

Mother said, "Do your work friends laugh at those jokes?" But she went no further. She didn't say anything hurtful to

Dad or try to spoil his good time. Les saw Dad give her a tense smile and realized both his parents were trying hard to be on their best behavior.

Les felt himself beginning to relax when their food came and still nobody was arguing.

Five minutes into the meal a large shadow was cast over the table. Everyone looked up to see Leo, the proprietor, standing over the table. Leo was a massive Austrian Jew who looked like he didn't care what anyone thought and never had anything to say. Johnny thought he must be the person who actually killed everything they ate. He wore a full-length apron that looked like it hadn't been washed in a year; there were colors on it that the boys had not seen before and might never see again.

Leo greeted Dad and nodded at Mother. He reached into his right front pocket by pushing the apron aside and withdrew a roll of paper money at least five inches thick. Using one thick, greasy hand, Leo removed a rubber band from around the roll and slipped it onto his wrist. He found the edges of the first bills and began to peel them off, one at a time, and lay them onto the table in front of Dad.

They were hundred-dollar bills. Johnny and Les had never seen one before but they sure knew what they were.

Leo continued to lay the money down, one bill at a time. With each bill, his thumb hesitated as if he were performing a solemn duty. He clearly didn't want to part with the money.

Once all the bills were down, Leo stood up to his full height, shook Dad's hand, and then left. He disappeared around the end of the booth and back to the bar area.

Dad was looking at Mother with his head tilted back and a twinkle in his eyes. Finally he spoke. "What do you think of that?" he said. "You going to stop giving me grief about playing cards?"

Mother burst into laughter.

The boys relaxed, and the rest of the meal was fun. They enjoyed one another's company for the first time in years. The only thing missing was James, and somehow it felt like he was there too.

It was the first time any of them had felt hope in months.

That hope continued into the following week. That Tuesday, June 6th, the Allies invaded Normandy. The tide of the war was turning. There was a feeling of buoyancy across the country, and renewed optimism in the face of incredible adversity and sacrifice.

Four days later the MacGregor boys stood on the station platform in Buffalo waiting to board the train to Springport.

"You'll be good?" Mother was saying. "You'll do just as Nanny and Grandad say?"

"Yes," Charlie said. Les and Johnny just nodded.

"All right," Mother said, raising an eyebrow. "We'll be up for the Fourth of July; you know we'll hear of any bad behavior then."

There were kisses and hugs all around and the boys boarded the train. Johnny looked back to see his parents standing on the station platform. They were actually holding hands.

As the train rolled down the track Charlie thought of his Model A, waiting in Aunt Myrtelle's shed, and of Grandma Barney, who wrote that she'd be coming to see him as soon as he got to Springport.

Charlie had high hopes for a very good summer. Impulsively, he reached over and put his arm around Johnny, who was seated next to him.

Les saw Johnny's look of surprise and turned his face toward the window. Johnny began talking to Charlie about what they would do when they got to Springport, about what the aunts had to talk about this summer, and whether or not Charlie could drive him in the Model A.

Les watched his brothers. He observed the smile on Charlie's face and the excitement in Johnny's expression.

How was it Nanny had described a family? *Oh, yes—she said it was a crazy contraption,* Les remembered. She had said a family was made of parts that are always moving and changing, and that all we can do is hope for a few smooth moments every now and then.

It made sense. Looking at Johnny and Charlie, Les felt that one of those smooth moments was upon him. He tried to memorize it, to hold it tight.

Mother and Dad might never stop drinking and fighting, not completely. It would always be part of their history as a family. James would certainly never come back to them, but he was part of their shared history too. And there might be other, more difficult problems the likes of which Les couldn't even imagine right now. But there would be good times too. It was Les's job to watch and learn and do his best with whatever came his way. Like Pete had said, it wasn't worth worrying about events that hadn't happened yet. Les would have to take things as they came.

No more running away. If the "crazy contraption" of his family was to function well, Lester MacGregor was going to have to stay at home and do his part.

The End

Victory on the Home Front
Discussion Questions

1. The MacGregor family would today be called "dysfunctional." What abuses and misbehaviors are obvious? How does each individual cope? What defense mechanisms become family staples?

2. How did Mother and Dad become the way they are? Is it possible to understand or sympathize with them?

3. Why did Les and Johnny challenge Red Bartlett, the undisputed leader? Was Johnny justified in reinforcing his snowball with a rock? How does this snowball fight mirror the actual war?

4. Why does Father send for Grandma Barney? What is he hoping she will be able to accomplish? Why does he ignore his wife's opposition?

5. What does Springport offer to the boys? Metaphorically, what does Springport symbolize?

6. Each of the boys witnesses poverty and sacrifice. What shortages are evident, and how are they handled? Is one type of deprivation worse than another?

7. How will James's death continue to affect the family? Does James's accidental death negate his image as a hero?

8. Technology advanced considerably during the 1940s. In what ways do the boys take part? How does human progress emerge as a theme in this story?

9. Charlie describes doing "good things for bad reasons, and bad things for good reasons." Does the reason behind an action matter as much as the action itself? How do intentions stack up against consequences?

10. Is it possible to have a "family" version of the truth that differs from each individual's version of events? What is the MacGregor family's truth? How does it change from the beginning to the end of the story?

Acknowledgments

The author wishes to acknowledge the contributions of the beloved family members and friends who provided support and assistance during the life of this project. ***Victory on the Home Front*** began as a series of family reminiscences, and the wisdom of the real-life brothers who were part of these stories has been priceless. The life-giving love of the "crazy contraption" of the Van Koeverings, Griers, Hoags, Hinckleys, and Randalls makes all things possible.

Many thanks are due to Erika Berry, who reviewed the manuscript and subsequently provided bold, no-nonsense direction about how to take the next step. Leigha Landry also deserves a great deal of credit for moving the project forward, as do Lise Marinelli, Ruth Beach, and the entire team at Windy City Publishers.

The author also wishes to acknowledge the support of Jackie Goodman Merritt, the librarian and champion of the small town of Springport, Michigan. Jill Wineland and the entire staff and student population of Herbison Woods Elementary School in DeWitt, Michigan, also are commended for their input related to the title and cover design.

LITERACY CHICAGO

Windy City Publishers works closely with Literacy Chicago, a nonprofit organization that empowers individuals to achieve greater self-sufficiency through language and literacy instruction.

For more than four decades, thousands of area adults have participated in the broad range of programs Literacy Chicago has developed, including basic literacy, GED preparation, and English as a Second Language. Literacy Chicago continues its learner-focused programming by relying heavily on the efforts of volunteer tutors, and frequently offers ancillary classes such as health literacy, computer literacy, and financial literacy to support the language/literacy options.

We applaud their efforts and encourage any of our readers to support this wonderful organization as well.

LITERACY CHICAGO
17 N. STATE STREET, STE 1010
CHICAGO, IL 60602

312/870-1100 X 105 (P)
312/870-4488 (F)

WWW.LITERACYCHICAGO.ORG
INFO@LITERACYCHICAGO.ORG

About the Author

D. S. Grier is an explorer, detective, and philosopher with an insatiable appetite for good stories. Bolstered by obsessive curiosity (and a patient family), Grier takes no prisoners when it comes to tracking down an exciting tale. Fortunately, the family adventures included in ***Victory on the Home Front*** were available very close to home.

Grier lives in DeWitt, Michigan, and is currently researching a second novel.

CPSIA information can be obtained at www.ICGtesting.com
Printed in the USA
BVOW071657030612

291631BV00002B/1/P